Everyone is talking
about Kari Lynn Dell

LAST *Chance* RODEO

KARI LYNN DELL

sourcebooks
casablanca

To Greg, who never once told me to give it up, even when any sane person should have. Every writer should marry someone as crazy as they are.

Sourcebooks © 2017, 2019 by Kari Lynn Dell
Cover and internal design © 2019 by Sourcebooks
Cover art by Judy York
Blackfeet Nation logo art © Sammy Jo Bird/Palamino Paintings

Published by Sourcebooks Casablanca, an imprint of Sourcebooks
P.O. Box 4410, Naperville, Illinois 60567-4410
(630) 961-3900
sourcebooks.com

Printed and bound in the United States of America.
OPM 10 9 8 7 6 5 4 3 2 1

Also by Kari Lynn Dell

Chapter 1

WHEN DAVID PARSONS RODE INTO THE ARENA IN CODY, Wyoming, he knew in his gut he'd ride out a winner. He was on that kind of roll. He'd drawn the right calf and, Lord knew, he was riding the right horse. And in case that wasn't enough, he was wearing the never-fail lucky blue shirt he'd saved just for the Fourth of July.

Muddy rooted his nose, pushing into the bit as David turned him around in the roping box. When David tugged on the reins, Muddy kicked up his hind feet, revving his engine like a drag racer burning his tires, a quirk he'd developed as a colt and never outgrown. Then he jammed his butt into the corner of the box, ears forward, every molecule of his body cocked and ready.

David kept a tight hold on the reins, his attention zeroing in on the calf. *Head's turned. Wait. Wait. Make sure he's standing square. Let him take the first step.*

The instant the calf looked forward, David nodded. The gate banged open. David's rein hand barely twitched and Muddy exploded from the box, the start perfectly timed. The loop sliced through the night air. *One, two, three swings, and throw.* Zap! Clean around the calf's neck. David felt the sizzle of the rope dragging through the hondo as he pulled his slack.

Muddy's stop was like slamming into a brick wall on a motorcycle. Wham! Sixty to zero in a single stride. David swung out in the right stirrup and let the momentum launch him down the rope, so fast he was standing at the calf's head as it spun around, still on its feet.

Muddy scrambled backward, pulling the calf into David's lap. He flipped it onto its side, had the loop of his piggin' string snugged tight around the front leg before the calf hit the ground. He scooped up the back legs, crossed them over the front, took one, two wraps and a half hitch and threw up his hands to signal for time.

David hustled back to his horse, vaulted into the saddle and rode Muddy forward a few steps to put slack in the rope, adrenaline pounding through his veins as applause washed over them. Muddy bobbed his head, acknowledging the ovation.

"Seven point three seconds!" the rodeo announcer shouted. "Ladies and gentlemen, there is your tie-down roping champion!"

David grabbed his hat by the brim and sailed it into the clear night air, laughing from the sheer joy of the moment. A committee member retrieved the hat from where it landed in the arena and handed it to David at the gate as he rode out. "We need you behind the bucking chutes for the television interview."

"Give me a minute to tie my horse up." He swung off and wove through a gauntlet of backslaps and congratulations to the spot along the fence behind the roping boxes where he'd left his rope can. Muddy flattened his ears at the next horse in line.

"You're not big enough to win that fight," David said. He reached up to give Muddy a scratch for a job well done.

Muddy jerked his head away, pinning his ears again.

David laughed. "Cranky little bastard. Good thing we don't get paid for your personality. Or your looks."

Muddy shot him a look that was the equine equivalent of a middle finger. David laughed again, flipped the reins around the fence rail, and patted Muddy on the butt as he left, just to annoy him.

The committeeman led the way, hustling along the inside of the fence as a brand-new pickup circled the arena, setting out the barrels for the barrel racing. David's escort ducked through a narrow pass gate into the chaos behind the bucking chutes. This was foreign territory for David, bulls snorting and banging in the chutes, cowboys crawling all over like ants as the bull riders settled their ropes into place and the chute boss yelled at everybody to get their asses moving. The television crew had commandeered a space back in the corner. David stepped in front of the camera, self-conscious despite the number of times in the past six months he'd had to stand in the spotlight.

The blond interviewer tipped her head back and smiled, holding the microphone almost over her head to make up the difference between his six-four and her five-and-a-half feet. "Congratulations on winning the tie-down roping here at the Buffalo Bill Cody Stampede. This is the last stop on the big Fourth of July rodeo run. How's it been going up until now?"

"Couldn't get much better," David said, the grin coming easily. "I've been drawing some great calves, and Muddy gives me a chance at the money every time I nod my head."

"You trained him yourself. How did you happen to choose this particular horse? To look at him...he doesn't exactly catch your eye."

David laughed. "Nah, he ain't real purty. I sure wouldn't have picked him out of a herd. It was just meant to be, I guess. A neighbor bought him for his son 'cause he's small, but Muddy...well, he's no kid horse." David shook his head, amazed all over again at the stroke of divine intervention that had brought Muddy into his life. "They traded him to me in exchange for my old pony, and I knew he was something special the first time I roped a calf on him. He suits me better than any horse I've ever ridden."

"You've made a huge move in the world rankings compared to last season," she said. "How do you account for your improvement?"

"It's all Muddy. He was still a little green at the beginning of last year, but he just kept getting better and better, and the past few months he's really come into his own."

"He's not the only one," she said, and the gleam of interest in her eyes wasn't entirely professional.

David shuffled his feet, wishing they'd hurry up and cut to a commercial. "I owe most everything to my family and my fiancée, Emily, for always being there to support me, and the good Lord for letting me compete in the greatest sport in the world."

"And Muddy?" the blond added.

"Definitely. Without him, I'm just another guy with a rope."

She laid a hand on his arm. "Well, after your win here at Cody, it looks like you're also a guy who's headed to his first National Finals Rodeo. Congratulations, David, and best of luck down the road."

"Thank you." He smiled awkwardly into the camera as she signed off.

When he tried to move away, her grip on his arm tightened. "Are you leaving tonight?"

"No. This is our last stop." The end of ten straight days of roping hard and driving harder. He should be exhausted, but he was pumped so full of adrenaline he felt like he could go on forever.

Her voice went husky. "I'll be down at Cassie's later. I'd love to buy the champ a beer."

David blinked. Had she not just heard him mention Emily? "I'm not much for bars," he said stiffly, feeling the heat rise under his collar as he eased out of her grasp. "I'll be hitting the sack soon as I get my horse put up."

Which wasn't the whole truth. He intended to call his parents to share the good news, sip a cold one, and wind down with a few of the boys, then crawl into his trailer, prop his phone on his pillow, and talk to his best girl until one of them fell asleep. He didn't have to work at being faithful. From the day he'd met Emily, he'd been incapable of looking at another girl.

The blond backed off a step, and her smile turned mean. "Don't drink, don't smoke, don't fool around… You're just a regular Dudley Do-Right."

Was he supposed to be insulted? He shrugged. "Yeah, I guess I am."

She huffed, turned on her heel, and flounced away. David made his escape into the milling crowd, not slowing until he reached the concession area. His stomach rumbled at the smell of grilled beef, a reminder that his last meal had been before he roped in Red Lodge eight hours earlier. He detoured to a hamburger stand. Muddy would be fine for a few more minutes.

Behind him, music blasted out of the loudspeakers as

each of the barrel racers thundered into the arena. David could guess when they rounded the third barrel by the swelling roar of the crowd pushing them down the home stretch. He listened to the names and times with half an ear while he ordered.

"Excuse me?" a female voice said behind him. "David?"

He tensed, afraid to glance over his shoulder, but instead of the blond, he saw a pink-faced woman in a rumpled sundress, one hand on a stroller and the other clutching a wide-eyed little boy dressed to the hilt in boots, hat, and a shiny belt buckle. Just guessing, this lady probably wasn't looking for a date.

She thrust out an eight-by-ten sheet of glossy paper. "Could you please sign this for my son? He's a big fan."

David took the photo, wincing when he saw his smiling mug. After his win at Houston, he'd picked up a small sponsorship from a rope company, but the picture in their ads didn't even look like him. They'd primped and starched, airbrushed and photoshopped until they'd turned him into a Clark Kent look-alike, all square-jawed and laser-eyed.

"What's your name?" he asked the boy.

"Matthew." The kid gazed up at him, head tilted back so far his hat almost fell off. "Wow. You're really tall. And you look kinda mean."

"Matthew!" his mother exclaimed.

"It's okay." David rubbed a hand over his two-day stubble with an apologetic smile. "I've been runnin' down the road pretty hard the past couple of days. Haven't had much time to clean up."

Not that it made much difference. His beard was so

heavy and so black that even when he shaved in the morning, he looked like a hobo by that night's rodeo. He took the pen the woman offered and scribbled on the picture.

To Matthew. Ride hard and rope fast. David Parsons.

"Thanks," the kid said, clutching the photo to his chest. "I'm gonna rope just like you when I'm big. And I'm gonna have a horse just like Muddy."

"I bet you will," David said, even though he was thinking, *Only if you're really lucky.*

The baby in the stroller started to fuss, and the woman thanked him and herded her little clan away. David paid for his food, then doused the burgers with enough ketchup to float a canoe. The first bite was absolute heaven. What was it about rodeo burgers? They never tasted the same anywhere else. Probably because he was never as famished as after he roped. Plus, everything tasted good when you were winning.

The announcer introduced the first of the bull riders as David polished off the first burger, tossed the crumpled wrapper in a trash can, and started toward the roping chutes, peeling the foil off the second burger as he walked.

"Hey, hotshot!" a voice called. "You too cool to hang with us losers now?"

He looked over to see a trio of cowboys lounging against the fence and sipping beers. *Losers. Hah.* Between the three of them, they owned enough gold buckles to pave the road to Oz, including the one given out at the previous year's National Finals.

The one who'd yelled waved an empty cup. "You've been takin' my money all year, least you could do is buy an old man a brew."

Old man was stretching it, but legend wasn't. David hesitated, glancing toward where he'd left Muddy, then angled over to join them. He'd grown up idolizing these guys, dreaming of someday hanging out with them, shooting the bull. He fetched four fresh beers and passed the others around before taking a deep draw off his own. Ahh, yeah. Something else that never tasted quite the same anywhere but at the end of a long, hot rodeo day.

"So is it true that after you won Tucson, some rich guy walked up and offered you a hundred grand for Muddy?" the reigning world champ asked.

"Yeah." David shook his head, indignant. "His kid decided he wants to be a roper, and the old man figured he oughta have the best horse money can buy."

"As of right now, that would be Muddy," the old guy said. "I'd take him, hands down, over anything else going down the road, including that stick I'm hauling."

"Did you tell the stupid prick to go screw himself?" the third member of the gold buckle club asked. "I mean, shit. As if you're gonna sell a horse like that."

They all nodded in agreement at the nerve of some people.

"You shoulda got him to put it in writing for your insurance company," one of them said. "You could up your coverage."

David grimaced. "I gotta do something about that soon as I get a chance. A hundred grand might be stretching it, but he's worth four times what he was when I took out the policy."

"And you couldn't replace him even at that. Where you headed next?"

"Calgary."

"Ever been?"

"Nope." The Calgary Stampede was by invitation only, and until this year, David hadn't even been a blip on their radar. "How do you like that quick setup and roping without a six-second rule?"

The three of them launched into a spirited discussion of the pros and cons of waiving the requirement that the calf had to remain tied for six seconds after the roper remounted his horse. Faster times, one said. Guys taking more chances, a wrap and a hooey instead of two wraps made it more exciting for the fans. Sloppier, another said, and besides, it was called tie-down roping. Wasn't the integrity of the tie supposed to be at least half of the game? David listened, basking in the knowledge that he'd been accepted by this most exclusive club as, if not their equal, at least a worthy contender.

He was halfway through his beer when the arena lights went out and one of his companions drawled, "Oh goody. Fireworks."

Oh shit. David whipped around, tossing his beer into the nearest trash can. "I gotta go."

He moved as fast as the dim lights and the crowd allowed, his heart hammering in his throat. Dammit. It was the Fourth of July. How could he have forgotten the fireworks? He should've busted ass right after the interview to get his horse back to the trailer. Muddy might've settled down in most ways, but he still went ballistic at the first sign of a bottle rocket, let alone the big overhead boomers.

The grandstand had started to clear, and people strolled toward their cars, clogging David's path. He dodged and ducked, hip-checked one big drunk guy out of the way, but the first rocket burst overhead before he fought his way clear. He broke into a jog, rounded the last turn, and ran straight into chaos. Bodies flying, shouts, and the thud of hooves as men tried to capture escaped horses.

At the epicenter of the melee, the spot where Muddy had been tied was empty, a broken rein dangling from the fence. A cowboy grabbed David by the arm.

"Muddy went that way." He waved toward the parking lot. "Pulled back and busted his reins at the first big *boom* and then blew down through here and scared the hell out of everything else."

David launched in the direction he'd pointed. The exit-gate attendant came running to meet him, sobbing in panic. "I tried to stop him. He almost ran me down!"

"Which way?" David called over his shoulder as he skidded around the corner.

"Out there," she said.

When he saw where she pointed, his guts twisted into a knot of barbed wire. Even as he pushed into a sprint, he knew he'd never get there in time.

He couldn't beat Muddy to the highway.

Eighteen hours later, David slumped onto the fender of his horse trailer, exhausted and sick to his soul. The sheriff's deputy who'd been his companion and search partner for most of the night scrubbed a hand over bloodshot eyes.

"Well, the good news is we haven't had a report of a horse being hit on any of the highways," the deputy said.

David nodded. He'd started out terrified Muddy

would run through a fence or in front of a car, or step in a hole in the dark and break a leg. But that was hours ago. There hadn't been so much as a glimpse of a stray horse since Muddy cleared the parking lot. David swallowed hard, choking on dread and guilt. How could he have let this happen?

"Damnedest thing," the deputy said, shaking his head. "It's like he just dropped off the face of the earth."

David slumped, burying his face in his hands, exhaustion crashing down on him as he faced the awful truth. Muddy was gone, and he had no one to blame but himself.

Chapter 2

Sisters, Oregon. Four years later.

DAVID UNHOOKED THE STRAP OF HIS HARD FIBERGLASS rope can from his saddle horn and heaved the can as hard as he could at the nearest tire of his horse trailer. It missed, skidding like an oversize hockey puck and landing under the trailer instead.

Shit. He couldn't even throw a decent tantrum.

"Trashy little bastard," a cowboy at the next horse trailer said, referring to the calf David had just roped and tied in two seconds too long to win a check.

"Yeah." But not that bad. If his horse had stopped a little quicker, got back a little faster to take out the slack, the calf wouldn't have had time to come up the rope and get his head past David's thigh. He gave the horse in question a disgusted glare, then immediately kicked himself when Frosty gazed back, his eyes soft and uncomprehending.

Frosty was doing his best. He couldn't change the tendency to pedal his front feet and slide a little extra when he stopped. Considering David's uncle had loaned him the horse and refused to accept more than half of the usual twenty-five percent of his winnings for mount money, Frosty was a steal.

He just wasn't Muddy. No horse was...or ever would be. After all this time, David could still feel the slam-bang power of Muddy's stop. Still caught himself looking for that ugly little bastard around every corner, in every roadside pasture.

The official search had been called off after two days, when the sheriff's department had concluded someone had picked him up and hauled him off. It was the only logical explanation, supported by testimony from a woman living a couple miles from the rodeo grounds in the direction Muddy was last seen running. She'd noticed a horse trailer stopped on the road for a few minutes while she was watching the fireworks in the distance. She'd thought nothing of it until she'd seen one of the missing-horse posters David had distributed around town.

Mystery solved. Muddy hadn't vaporized. Some jerk had caught him out of the road ditch, jumped him in his horse trailer, and driven away.

Three months later, a friend had recognized David's saddle at a pawnshop in Billings, Montana. The owner vaguely recalled a Native American woman bringing it in with a story about how her boyfriend had left it to her when he died, which David assumed was a line of bull. The jerk had probably been waiting out in the pickup.

David had papered every sale barn, feed store, and gas station in five states with posters offering a reward for Muddy's safe return. He'd posted messages on Facebook, taken out ads in every horse-related newspaper and magazine in the country. Trouble was, Muddy was a plain brown horse with no distinguishing marks, not even a decent brand, thanks to a wire cut when he was six years old that had mangled the Circle P on his shoulder.

The offer of five grand for information leading to

Muddy's return had netted David dozens of calls, but none of the horses had turned out to be the right ugly brown gelding.

David uncinched that same saddle with hard, quick jerks. *Stop moping, dammit.* He'd vowed to look forward, make the best of what he had now. Let go of the fantasy that Muddy would reappear and all would be right with the world, the way it hadn't been since that night in Cody.

"You've sure had shit for luck the past few weeks," the cowboy at the next trailer said as he coiled his ropes and stowed them away. "Starts to make a guy wonder if he oughta go to church more or something."

"Yeah. Or something."

The lanky cowboy grinned over at David. "Come on home to Louisiana with me. I'll take you out in the bayou, introduce you to an old lady who knows all kinds of somethin'."

David huffed out a laugh. "If I keep going like this, I might have to take you up on that."

He wasn't sure even voodoo could lift this hex. After all, he'd broken the cardinal rule of roping. Take care of your horse first, then yourself. Christian or not, every cowboy knew the rodeo gods could be harsh bastards, and they would have their payback.

In his more fanciful moments, David imagined them somewhere up above, grizzled buckaroos kicked back on a sagging wooden porch, spitting tobacco between what was left of their teeth and boring each other with old rodeo stories while they rendered judgment. Shaking their heads in disgust at his foolishness.

"We gave you a great gift, a horse above all horses,

and that's how you took care of him? Five years of bad luck for you, sonny. And if we hear you bitchin' about it, we'll make it ten."

They'd taken everything that mattered. His confidence. His girl. He might've even blamed them for torturing the land he loved, the ranch his family had worked for four generations, but all the neighbors were suffering just as bad, and even David wasn't superstitious enough to think it was his fault.

Year by year, the rains had become more scarce, until the lush grass of the Colorado plains withered away and the earth cracked into a mosaic of despair. With every passing cloudless day, the chances of keeping their herd intact withered, too.

His cell rang, snapping him out of his pity party. He glanced at the number before answering. "Hey, Dad. What's up?"

"Just wondering how it went out there."

David swallowed a sigh, wishing he had better news. Anything to lift some of the weight from his dad's shoulders, if only for a few minutes. "No good. Drew a pig, couldn't get him flanked clean."

"Ah. Well. That's how it goes."

"Yeah." But it had been going like that for close to a month. David had run through his entire collection of lucky shirts without a trip to the pay window. Even the one his grandma had given him for Christmas hadn't done the trick, and it used to be damn near foolproof.

"Anything new down there?" he asked. *Like a couple inches of rain?* Except he knew better, because he checked his hometown weather every morning.

"There's showers in the forecast later in the week.

Doesn't look like it'll amount to much. But I found a place in South Dakota to get some hay for a decent price."

Feeding cattle in June. Geezus. David pushed his hat back on his head and wiped away sweat with a shirtsleeve as he stared over Frosty's back at the trio of snowcapped volcanic peaks that gave the town of Sisters its name. If he could only scoop up all that moisture and take it home with him.

His dad cleared his throat. "Your mother thought you should know… Emily has been home visiting. She's expecting a baby in November."

The news was a sucker punch to the gut, even though David had known it was only a matter of time. She'd been married for over two years, and she'd always wanted kids. Preferably with a man she could count on to keep them in diapers from one year to the next, like the doctor she'd met while doing her nursing practicum a few months after Muddy went missing.

"Deceitful, gold-digging bitch," his sister had said of her former close friend. His mother had been kinder, saying not every woman was cut out to be a professional cowboy's wife, and wasn't it better they'd found out before they were married?

David would rather not have found out at all.

"I bet her parents are thrilled," he choked out.

"Over the moon," his dad said, and changed the subject. "Are you heading to Hermiston tonight?"

"Yeah. I'm not up at Reno until Friday afternoon." Which gave him five days to hunker at a friend's place near Hermiston, Oregon, tuning himself and Frosty up in the practice pen and shoeing a few horses to pad his very thin wallet.

He rotated his shoulders, wincing at the twinge in his back. The longer this dry spell went on, the more he had to count on his skill as a farrier to keep him going. The bending and lifting took a toll on his body, but he'd squirreled away enough cash to get through until the middle of July, assuming nothing unexpected jumped up and bit him in the wallet.

Lord, he was tired of skating this razor-thin edge. He couldn't remember the last time he'd had more than a lungful of breathing room in his budget. When he'd been able to ride in the arena and rope without the added pressure of knowing he really, really needed the money.

The wad of cash he'd accumulated in the months before he'd lost Muddy had disappeared almost as fast as the horse. He'd spent hundreds on ads and flyers, then he'd had to lease a mount to finish out the season. They'd never really clicked, but David had pushed on, sure his luck would turn—if not during the regular season, at least at the National Finals.

Wrong. His debut at the big show had been a disaster. In ten rounds, running at over twenty thousand dollars every time he nodded his head, he'd won zilch. Nada. Skunked.

His parents patted his back and said, "Don't worry, you'll get 'em next time."

His sister said he'd never be competitive again if he couldn't get over believing in his so-called curse. David said nothing.

But he didn't quit. He kept pushing, even when he didn't have a dollar left in his checking account. Sooner or later, he'd break loose. Hit it right at a couple of big rodeos, be back in the green. He kept entering, like a gambler shoving one more dollar into the slot machine until he'd maxed out every credit card and gas card he owned.

When the collection agencies started pestering his parents, he'd had to admit he was in completely over his head. The local banker in his hometown had helped him work out a debt repayment plan, but they wanted to see proof of a steady income, so he took a job at the feed store. Two years of peddling cattle mineral and feed supplements, shoeing and training horses on the side, earning his keep at home by helping out when they needed an extra hand, and he'd dug himself out of the hole.

Financially, anyway. Emotionally, he couldn't pull out of the tailspin. The days stacked up, one on top of the other, the sameness and the drudgery weighing down his soul, pushing him farther under until his dreams were nothing but a distant speck of light. He took to stopping at the bar after work, sipping a beer or two, sometimes more, so it would be late enough when he got home that he could go straight to the bunkhouse and avoid his mother's concerned gaze.

Sometimes, if the right woman made the right offer, he didn't make it home at all.

As the drought worsened, so did the market for his skills. Everyone was cutting back. There were fewer horses to shoe and ride, fewer ranchers able to afford the goods he was peddling. The night the feed-store manager laid him off, he hit bottom, and he led with his face. He woke up the next morning with a black eye, a killer hangover, and no real recollection of why he'd taken a swing at a former high-school classmate, other than an overwhelming urge to punch something. Anything.

Two days later, his uncle offered him Frosty. When David tried to decline, his mother sat him down and set him straight. "It's time, David. Roping is your heart and soul, and you've put it aside long enough. Being here, moping around…it isn't good for you."

His face was still throbbing like an exposed nerve, so he couldn't exactly argue. He did as he was told. Got back in shape. Got back on the road. Managed to win enough to keep himself and Frosty fed. Last season, he'd clawed his way into the top twenty-five in the standings, but not the magical top fifteen and another trip to the National Finals.

So far this year, he'd been scraping along, picking up checks on a steady basis, but no major paydays. He made good runs when he got the chance, but for every decent calf he drew, there were two running, ducking, kicking pieces of crap, and he didn't have the horse power to level the playing field. Still, he was within striking distance. He could close the gap in a hurry if he got on a hot streak during the run of big rodeos around the Fourth of July, known as Cowboy Christmas because there was so much prize money being handed out.

With a little luck…

"Well," his dad said again into a silence that had stretched too long. "I'd better let you go. Call us when you get to Hermiston."

"I will. Give Mom a hug."

They hung up, ending another in a string of pained conversations. David knew they worried, and he wished he had the words to convince them he was better now, if nowhere near his best. His dad knew David worried about the ranch, the drought, but he didn't believe in complaining. Between the two, it didn't leave a whole lot to talk about.

Even David's sister didn't have the nerve to suggest he should try to get on with his love life. They all understood that Emily had broken more than his heart. She'd shattered his most closely held convictions about the meaning of love and commitment, left him without the will to gather up the pieces and cobble them together again. Why bother? So someone else could come along and destroy him all over again?

He stowed his gear in the tack compartment at the rear of the trailer and filled a bucket of water from the built-in tank. While Frosty drank, David sat on the fender of the trailer and gazed out at the mountains. He had to focus on the positive. Frosty had some flaws, but he was still a better horse than what eighty percent of the guys were riding.

Late at night, when the road was long and the paychecks hard to come by, David couldn't help but wonder if the horse was really the problem. What if it was true, what he'd said to that little blond gal in Cody? That without Muddy, he was just one more guy with a rope. A guy who didn't quite have what it took when push came to shove.

His phone rang again, an unfamiliar number. "'Lo?"

"David? Hey, it's Shane Colston. Where are you?"

"Sisters. Why?"

"Listen, you're not going to believe this…"

His heart sank. Not again. How many times had he gotten this call from a well-meaning friend? Every single one had been a false alarm, but his pulse still jumped and that wiggle of hope squirmed in his gut.

"I'm at the Montana State High School Rodeo Finals in Kalispell. My brother's girl is competing," Shane was saying. "And I swear to God, David, I'm standing here looking at Muddy."

David made a noise that was supposed to pass for an answer, but it didn't matter because Shane kept going.

"There's an Indian kid from Browning, name's Kylan Runningbird. When he rode in the arena, I thought, 'Damn, that horse is almost as ugly as old Muddy.' Then the kid threw his rope, and holy hell, David. Nothin' can stop like that."

David felt his heartbeat pick up and was disgusted by his response. Why was he doing this to himself again? It'd been four years. Muddy wasn't going to pop up out of nowhere.

"You can see for yourself," Shane insisted. "I videoed the kid's next run on my phone. I'm sending it right now."

When the message came through, David hesitated, his finger poised over the button. This was stupid. It would be another brown horse with a hammer head and a better-than-average stop, and all he'd get out of it was a chill when one more tiny flare of hope died.

He pushed the button. Shane had managed to get close enough for a decent shot, but on the puny, scratched screen of David's not-so-smart phone, he could only see that the horse was the right size and color. He watched the kid ride into the box, turn, and start to back into the corner.

The horse shoved hard into the bit and kicked up both hind feet.

David dropped the phone. It bounced off his boot and

under the trailer, and by the time he fell to his knees and fished it out, the video was over. He played it again, squinting so close to the screen his nose touched the keys. There was the kick in the box. And that stop. *Wham!* Numbness swept over him, starting at his feet and crawling upward like he was having a stroke. The phone fell on the ground again.

Holy hell was right. It really was Muddy.

Chapter 3

THE SUNDAY AFTERNOON PERFORMANCE WAS WELL UNDER way when David pulled into the Kalispell fairgrounds. He'd left Sisters as quick as he could get his rig rolling, but it had been an eleven-hour drive, and he'd had to stop a couple times to give Frosty a break.

His hands fumbled with latches and ropes as he unloaded the horse, hung a bucket of water and a hay bag on the side of the trailer, and then took off for the arena. His instinct was to rush straight to the roping box and find the horse that almost had to be Muddy, but he forced himself to steer clear. The middle of a high school rodeo was not the time or place to make a scene.

He worked his way through the warm-up area, the mob of kids trotting circles, double-and triple-checking ropes and cinches, but there was no sight of Muddy. Around the infield side of the arena, he found a spot to lean in the shade of the bleachers. Just in time. The calf roping had started.

He watched half a dozen ropers compete, barely noticing whether they were good, bad, or otherwise. Then Kylan Runningbird rode into the arena, and all the air in the Rocky Mountains wasn't enough to keep David's head from spinning. He knew that dirt-brown horse as well as his own face in the mirror.

Muddy, in the flesh, looking exactly as David had last seen him. Fit, glossy, and cocky as all get out.

David tore his gaze off the horse long enough to
check out the rider as the announcer prattled on about
Kylan Runningbird. A high school junior, state finals
rookie, and here he was in fifth place so far with a solid
shot at qualifying for nationals. The kid looked soft,
slouchy, the brim of his beat-up hat crooked in the front,
the tail of his shirt slopping out of his jeans on one side.

He also looked too nervous to spit.

Muddy, on the other hand, was all business, whipping
around in the box and slamming his butt into the corner
without waiting for the kid to steer him. The kid's head
jerked, enough of a nod for the gate to open. Muddy
exploded out of the corner and arrowed in behind the calf.

Man, what a pup. The little potbellied Hereford loped
out, head up, practically screaming *Rope me*. Kylan took
two swings and threw. The loop bounced on the top of
the calf's head and, by some miracle, fell over his nose.

Muddy stopped, as quick and hard as the slam of
door. The sight of it made David's heart skip. Kylan
flew off his side, more of an ejection than a dismount.
His legs buckled and he went to his knees, but he got
his left arm hooked over the rope. Muddy hustled backward, pulling the calf so when the kid stood up, it was
right there under his nose. Kylan fumbled it onto its side,
strung his piggin' string on the top front leg, gathered up
the hinds, applied three deliberate, two-fisted wraps and
a hooey, and then threw up his arms.

The crowd went wild. One section of it anyway, a
cluster of at least fifty people seated on the end of the
grandstand. From the way they cheered and pounded
each other on the back, David guessed they hadn't
expected Kylan to come through in the clutch. He could

see why. The kid wasn't much of a roper. Lucky for him, he was riding the best horse on the planet.

David's horse.

Fury exploded in his head, as white-hot as those damn fireworks in Cody. David spun on his heel and strode around to the back of the arena, drawing startled looks from the people he shouldered past. By the time he got there, Kylan was surrounded by a huddle of friends, all slapping palms and bumping fists with him like he'd won the state championship instead of barely edging into fourth place. And there was Muddy, tugging at the reins, impatient as always to get back to the trailer now that his job was done.

The kid spotted someone in the mob of people streaming down from the grandstand and started in that direction. David stepped into his path. Kylan squinted up at him, confused.

"I need to talk to you," David said, voice hard, muscles knotted as he fought the urge to yank the reins out of the kid's hand.

Kylan looked past him, as if for help. David glanced over his shoulder to find two girls with their arms around each other, their smiles fading as they saw his expression. The smaller one pulled off her sunglasses. Her face was freckled under the brim of her baseball cap, but there was nothing childish about those eyes.

Not a girl. A woman. "What do you want with Kylan?" she demanded.

The tiny part of his brain still capable of logic could see she wasn't old enough, but David asked anyway. "Are you his mother?"

"Close enough."

"Good," David said. "Maybe you can explain why your kid is riding my horse."

She flinched. Surprise? Or guilt? "Who are you?" she asked, recovering fast.

"My name is David Parsons. That horse was stolen from me four years ago in Cody, Wyoming."

"Nu-uh." Kylan stepped back, arms extended as if he could hide the horse behind them. "He's mine."

The younger girl edged around David and grabbed the kid's hand. "Don't worry, Ky. He's got the wrong horse."

"No, I don't." David stared down at the woman, daring her to argue. "I'm betting you don't have any papers on him."

A crowd had begun to gather, the inner circle mostly dark-haired and dark-skinned, Kylan's friends from the Blackfeet reservation and their parents.

"Do you?" the woman asked.

"Not with me," David admitted. "I wanted to be sure it was him. Now that I am, I'll have his papers faxed up to the sheriff's office."

At the word *sheriff*, a murmur went through the crowd, which had grown as bystanders realized something serious was happening.

"He's *mine*!" Kylan was breathing hard, almost sobbing. "We bought him fair and square."

The woman gave David a stony-eyed stare and spoke to the kid. "Take your horse back to the trailer, Kylan."

"But—"

"Just do it. Go with him, Starr."

Kylan hesitated, but the girl hooked his elbow, wheeled him around, and dragged him away toward the contestant parking area, darting worried glances over

her shoulder. Muddy trailed along, supremely uncon-
cerned with the whole drama.

The wall of people closed off behind Kylan, and
several of the men looked more than willing to take
David on if he followed. He seriously considered trying
it anyway.

"I'm Mary Steele," the woman said, pulling his attention back to her. "And, yes, I do have a bill of sale for
that horse, so you'll have to excuse me if I'm skeptical.
You get your papers and whatever other proof you have,
and then we'll see what's what."

"Fine," David said. "I will."

She gave a slight nod. "In the meantime, stay away
from my nephew."

She angled past David. The crowd parted to let her
through and then closed ranks again. Over their heads,
David watched her leave, her stride confident, her shoulders square. He continued to watch until she disappeared
into the maze of pickups and trailers in the infield. Then
he faced the angry mob. "You got no right accusin' that
boy," a woman declared.

"I've got every right," David said. "Give me an hour,
and I'll prove it."

Chapter 4

SO MUCH FOR NOT MAKING A SCENE. DAVID COULD FEEL the angry stares boring into his back as he strode away, could see the gossip rippling across the rodeo grounds, expanding in rings from the humongous splash he'd made. But the more he thought about it, the more it twisted him up. Four years of Muddy's prime wasted with a kid who roped like he'd never seen the inside of a practice pen.

David stumbled and ran square into the side of his own pickup. He braced both hands on the fender, dizzy with pent-up emotion. Exhaustion. Shock. He hadn't really believed it. Not until he'd seen Muddy in the flesh, still ugly as a mud fence, untouched by the years that had aged David a decade.

Dear sweet God. He was alive.

David needed to touch him. Lay his hands on Muddy's neck, feel the hard quiver of muscle, the warm pulse of blood. David had honestly believed he was dead. Otherwise, why hadn't he surfaced? If the person who'd taken Muddy had had any idea of his true worth, he would've tried to sell him at some point. A horse that good would attract attention. Someone would recognize him.

But what if the guy who took Muddy didn't know what he had? He could've stolen him just for the tack. David's saddle and bridle were worth a couple thousand dollars, even at pawnshop prices. As for what he'd done with the horse—the thief might've figured he was disposable. Or realized how much he really was worth and panicked.

Either way, it would have ended badly for Muddy, a thought that had made David sick every time it had weaseled into his head over the past four years.

Well, Muddy was definitely not dead. David straightened, wiping the sheen of sweat from his face with a shirtsleeve and getting a whiff of body odor in the process. Yikes. He could use a shower. First, though, he had to round up the proof needed to repossess his horse. He started to dial his parents' number and then stopped, remembering they were out of town. He dropped down to the next number in his speed-dial list.

"Hey, baby bro," his sister said. "To what do I owe the honor?"

"I can't just call to say hello?" he asked, his announcement so huge he couldn't push it off his tongue.

"Not that I've noticed. What do you want?"

"I need your help."

"With?"

"I found Muddy." He held the phone away from his ear while she shrieked, and then he tried to get a word in edgewise while she peppered him with questions, for which he was short on answers. He intended to have those, too, by the end of the day.

"You think they knew?" his sister asked.

"I'm not sure," David said. "But that's not my problem."

"Tough deal for the kid, though."

No tougher than the last four years had been for David.

Computer keys clicked as his sister searched the internet for information on Kalispell, Montana. "Guess I have to take back what I said about how you were an idiot for not cashing in your insurance policy."

"Guess so." And thank God. The temptation had been huge when David had found himself buried under that mountain of debt, but he'd hung tough.

"That would've seriously sucked," his sister said, echoing his thoughts. "Finding Muddy and having to turn him over to the insurance company."

As far as David was concerned, the decision had been a no-brainer. Accepting payment meant if Muddy was found, the insurance company took possession and could sell him to the highest bidder, like any other piece of stolen property. He wouldn't have taken that deal even if he hadn't had his horse so ridiculously underinsured.

He'd canceled the policy without filing a claim, gambling a $20,000 insurance check that Muddy might show up some day. Damned if he hadn't won.

"Got it," his sister said. "Flathead County Sheriff. I'll call them, get an email address, and send a copy of Muddy's registration papers and a couple of pictures of you roping on him. That ought to do the trick."

"Thanks, Sis."

"You're welcome. Are you gonna call Mom and Dad?"

"Not until I've got Muddy tied to my trailer."

"Probably best that way." She hesitated the way she always did when she had something to say that he wouldn't want to hear.

"What?" he asked.

"What if he's not the same? You don't know where

he's been, if he was hurt. Plus, it's been four years…"
And she was afraid David might get his hopes too high,
fall off another emotional cliff.

"I'll be fine," he promised. "Believe me, I know it'll
be a miracle if he's the same horse he was when he
disappeared. I'm just thrilled I found him and he looks
okay. As for the rest…we'll see when I get my hands
on him."

And the sooner, the better. He hung up and unhooked
his horse trailer. Fifteen minutes later, he walked into the
sheriff's office. The woman behind the desk eyed him
warily, standing back from the counter as he explained
his situation, her expression skeptical. "Do you have any
identification?"

"Uh, sure." David pulled his wallet out and slid his
Colorado driver's license across the desk. She took her
time studying it, then him. "Well, this may be a first.
'Cause I gotta say, you look a lot better in your picture."

She tilted her head toward a mirror on the far wall.
David turned and did a double take. Geez. No wonder
she was acting like he was an escaped convict. He
looked it, his eyes more red than gray, his hair standing
on end from all the times he'd run his hands through it
during the endless night behind the wheel, and his beard
a day and half past a five-o'clock shadow.

"It was a rough trip," he said.

"Looks like it." Then she smiled. "But I bet you clean
up pretty good. Let me go see if that email has come
through."

When he walked out, he had Muddy's registration
papers and crisp color copies of the photos from his
sister, plus a promise that a deputy would be dispatched

to assist him as soon as one was available, but the whole process had taken longer than David had expected. Back at the fairgrounds, he found the rodeo was over and the stage in front of the grandstand was set up for the awards, which appeared to be in progress. He made a beeline in that direction. When he reached the gate, he paused to search the crowd.

He spotted Kylan among a cluster of his friends. The kid shot David a murderous glance, then slouched to stare down at his hands. Kylan's girlfriend was snuggled up beside him, petting him like an agitated dog, but David didn't see the aunt. Mary. Such a soft name for a very prickly woman. He found a spot to lean against the fence while the awards ceremony wound up and the crowd began to shuffle out.

Obviously, word had spread. A large percentage of the people stared at David as they passed, openly curious. He avoided eye contact for fear of encouraging any of them to strike up a conversation. Kylan and crew remained seated until most of the others had left. Then the girlfriend got up and made her way down to where David was standing.

She was shaped like Humpty Dumpty—narrow shoulders, widening to her waist, then rounding off again—all perched on stick-skinny legs. David couldn't fathom what kept her low-cut jeans from sliding off the bottom end of the egg. She marched straight up to him, dark eyes flicking side to side.

"No sheriff?" she asked.

"They were tied up with an accident out on Highway 2. They'll send someone quick as they can."

"Oh." She bit her lip and then dug her fingers into

the back pocket of her jeans to fish out a piece of paper and offer it to David, who unfolded it to find a roughly sketched map.

"What's this?" he asked.

The girl lifted her chin and did a fair job of staring him down, her gaze sharp in an otherwise soft face. "Mary said to bring your papers and stuff. She'll meet you at her attorney's office in Browning in the morning. That's the phone number and directions how to get there. You can put your horse up at the rodeo grounds."

"Browning?" Panic spurted adrenaline into David's system. "She doesn't expect me to let her haul Muddy out of here?"

"She already did," the girl said, then turned and fled.

David's heart dropped like a stone to the pit of his stomach. This couldn't be happening. He'd lost Muddy...again.

Chapter 5

BY THE TIME HE TOPPED THE CONTINENTAL DIVIDE AND rolled down the east slope of the Rockies, David's fists were sore from pounding the steering wheel in frustration. At the town of East Glacier, Highway 2 spit him out of the mountains and onto the prairie without warning. He arrived in Browning twenty minutes later, low on fuel, so he drove on through town to find a station that could accommodate his extra-long rig.

The four-lane main drag was cluttered with out-of-state RVs, campers, boats, and other tourist paraphernalia heading into Glacier National Park. The locals drove rattletrap Buicks with mismatched doors and beefy four-wheel drives caked with enough mud to make David squirm with envy. Obviously, the drought hadn't dug its bony fingers into this part of the plains.

He stopped at a red light and waited for a greasy, bearded man to shuffle across the street, followed by a mangy dog. They joined a pair of equally grungy women lounging against the boarded-up front window of what had once been a gas station. One of them passed a paper bag to the newcomer.

Street people? In a little town like this?

The light turned and David went on, past more boarded-up buildings interspersed with businesses making a visible effort to attract the tourist trade—a mercantile with Indian patterns stenciled around the top of the walls and a row of miniature metal tipis along the front sidewalk, a motel that had some age on it but no trash along the curbs, a brightly painted burger joint with one whole wall sided in shiny chrome and colorful flags snapping in the breeze out front.

The road made a ninety-degree turn in front of a massive tipi built of concrete. The sign out front advertised espressos. Then another stretch of derelict buildings before David spotted a large gas station and convenience store called the Town Pump. Traffic whizzed by in both directions as he maneuvered into the jam-packed lot, around an SUV towing a pair of Jet Skis and a dually pickup covered in decals that declared the owner the champion of a team roping held three years earlier. The process was complicated by several stray dogs wandering aimlessly through the chaos.

Both diesel pumps were occupied, as were most of the gas pumps. As David waited his turn, a constant stream of people trickled in and out of the store carrying snacks, sodas, and beer by the case or the extra-large bottle.

Just past the Town Pump was a cluster of pristine, newer buildings that a sign declared to be Blackfeet Community College. Beyond that, the town ended and the hills rolled away. There wasn't a tree in sight, but the green of the grass was still fresh as spring, which he supposed it was this far north. Where the Blackfeet reservation ended, Canada began.

When his turn came, he filled his tank, wincing at the hit on his gas card. Not only was Browning eight hours out of his way, but he'd lost all the income he would've made from the horses he'd lined up to shoe in Hermiston. He pulled around the back, locked his rig, and went inside for a soda and something cheap to eat. The deli served damn near anything that could be made in a deep fryer, plus individual pizzas and pre-cooked burgers and such. David shelled out five bucks for chicken strips with ranch dressing and half a dozen potato wedges.

He accepted his change—yes, even the penny, because they added up—and stuffed it in his pocket. "I was told there's a rodeo arena in town?"

"Yah." The big guy at the register had a glossy black ponytail that hung to the middle of his back. "The Stampede Grounds. Right past the casino."

David had seen the casino as he came into town. A blocky building dressed up at the front with a covered entry and painted pillars and what looked to be a brand-new hotel next door. He retraced his route and discovered the Charging Horse Stampede Grounds, bigger and cleaner than he'd expected from the size and look of the town.

The last rays of the sun were just spearing over the mountaintops as he rumbled to a stop beside the stock pens. The clock on the dashboard said 9:46 p.m. If a man worked daylight to dark this time of year, he could wear himself to the bone. David eyed a metal water spigot. With any luck, he could hook up the hose and have decent pressure for the shower he needed even more after cussing and sweating all the way across the mountains from Kalispell. The water pump was one on a long list of repairs his aging trailer needed, but keeping tires under it was all the maintenance he could afford.

He should've filled the propane bottles, though. The wind had a bitter edge, like it had rolled straight down off the mountain snowcaps. David grabbed a jacket from the pickup, checked out the stock pens, picked out the largest, and made sure it was free of weeds, trash, or moldy hay. Then he tested the water spigot. Nothing. Figured.

He was backing Frosty out of the trailer when he heard the crunch of tires on gravel. A car rolled to a stop behind his rig. *Blackfeet Tribal Police*. The officer was probably thirty years old, thick-bodied, with ebony hair clipped into a bristly square top.

He rolled down his window and braced a beefy forearm on the frame. "This facility ain't for public use."

But Kylan's girlfriend had said—

And she most likely didn't have David's best interests at heart. Might've even set him up just to get even. David swallowed a curse. If he couldn't stay here, he'd have to go on to the next town, another twenty-five miles. More gas money down the drain, and that much farther from wherever they'd taken Muddy. "I just need a place to camp for the night. I have business in town—"

"I know what your business is," the cop said, and his tone made it clear he wasn't the welcoming committee.

So. That's how it was gonna be. Did they think they could scare him off? Not hardly. Before David could figure out the best way to tell the cop so without ending up in the local slammer, a faded black pickup rumbled in and parked next to the police car, stirring up a cloud of dust that drew a curse from the cop when it rolled in his open window.

David cast an envious glance at the pickup's flatbed, loaded with half a dozen bales of hay. Nice-looking stuff, worth at least ten bucks a square in Colorado these days. The man who climbed out looked as road-tested as his pickup with his battered black hat, wire-rim glasses, a sprinkling of silver in his brushy black mustache, and a rolling hitch in his gait as he ambled over to join them.

"Hey, Galen," the cop said. "I was just tellin' this guy we ain't runnin' a campground here."

The newcomer frowned, but at the cop, not David. "Don't be a dick, JoJo. Ain't gonna hurt nothin' by lettin' him stay here." Galen turned to David with an apologetic shrug. "Kylan's his cousin."

David nodded, thinking this would be a good time to shut up and see what happened next.

The cop's face set into mulish lines, but Galen waved him off. "I got this. Go be a real cop and get a doughnut or something."

JoJo grumbled and shot David another glare, but wheeled his car around and left.

"Sorry. JoJo's got a soft spot for Kylan, but that ain't the way to go about helping." Galen stuck out his hand. "Galen Dutray."

"David Parsons." Which Galen obviously already knew. They exchanged a quick, hard handshake.

"Are you in charge of the fairgrounds?" David asked.

"Nah. I work for the Blackfeet livestock department."

Livestock department? Would Galen demand to see Frosty's brand inspection, health certificate, Coggins test? Not that it would be a problem. With the number of state lines David crossed in any given week, all of his papers were in pristine order.

"Nice-looking horse," Galen said, eyeing Frosty. "I like grays."

"Thanks."

Frosty turned a lot of heads with his near-white coat,

flowing mane and tail, and classic Quarter Horse head. Definitely easy on the eyes…and hard to lose in the dark. Always a plus.

"Mary asked me to come down and see if there's anything you need." Galen dangled a set of keys. "I'll turn on the water on the way out, and I brought hay in case you're short."

David blinked, stunned. "Mary sent you?"

Galen shrugged. "We got a mess on our hands, for sure. No sense being assholes while we're sorting it out. You got your papers and stuff for the brown horse with you?"

"Yes. You wanna check 'em?"

"Nah. Tomorrow mornin's soon enough. I'll swing by, bring you to her lawyer's office at nine."

Crap. She was serious about the attorney. David had hoped it was a bluff. He couldn't afford even a few hours of a lawyer's time. But why should he have to? Muddy belonged to him. He could prove it. Case closed.

Galen gave him a sympathetic look. "He's a hell of a horse. Must have been tough to lose him."

"Yeah. It was." Then David realized what Galen was saying. "You already know he's mine. How?"

"Even out here on the rez, we got Google. We found pictures."

"Then why—"

"We'll talk tomorrow. I'll be here a little before nine." Galen strolled back to his pickup, dragged two hay bales off the side and stacked them on the ground, then left David alone with his jangled thoughts.

He hunched his shoulders against the wind, watching it whip Galen's dust up and away. Mary knew she'd have to turn the horse over. So why force David to chase her back to Browning? Then again, David still had no idea how Kylan had ended up with Muddy. And it had been a woman who'd hocked his saddle in Billings.

Maybe the visit with the attorney wasn't about trying to keep Muddy. Maybe Mary was trying to keep herself out of jail.

Chapter 6

HE DEFINITELY SHOULD'VE FILLED THE PROPANE BOTTLES. David had used the last of the fuel to heat water for his shower, so there wasn't enough left to even kick on the furnace when the wind picked up during the night, whistling around the nose of the trailer with an occasional gust that made the whole rig shudder.

David layered on a sweatshirt and sweatpants, tossed an extra sleeping bag over the top of his bed, but he still couldn't stay warm. When he did sleep, he dreamed the old dreams. Muddy appearing, then disappearing again into the darkness, always out of reach. Or worse, maimed, bleeding, a broken leg dangling, his eyes wild with pain.

Awake, David fought the urge to toss and turn. Every movement disturbed the blankets, letting cold air leak into his cocoon. His body ached from curling into a ball to conserve body heat, his brain from trying to fathom how Muddy had ended up in Browning, and what Mary thought she could accomplish by running home. All she'd done was delay the inevitable.

It *was* inevitable. He would not leave without Muddy.

His mind bounced to the possibilities. A future that had suddenly opened up wide. Even if Muddy was no more than eighty percent of his old self, David's chances of scoring that big win were much, much better.

This had to be a sign, right? His luck had finally turned. If he had an exceptional Fourth of July run, he could crack the top fifteen in the world standings. Even a halfway decent streak would put him within spitting distance.

By six o'clock, the ache and the cold had penetrated clear to his bone marrow. The sun was well above the horizon, so he crawled out of bed, laced up his running shoes, forced his body through a few painful stretches, and then jogged west out of town. The mountains gleamed pink and gold in the morning sunlight, and he drank in long gulps of air, sweet as cold spring water. His muscles warmed, the kinks unwinding step by step.

After twenty minutes, he dropped to a walk. As his pulse slowed, he opened up his senses to let the sheer lushness of the countryside permeate his ragged soul. At its best, eastern Colorado wasn't this vibrantly green. So many shades, from the yellow tinge of the baby poplar leaves to the near-black of pine needles in the distance.

He'd followed a narrow local highway that hugged the curve at the base of a ridge to the beginning of what passed for foothills, nothing more than a couple of bumps at the base of the mountains. To his right, the ground flattened into grassland scattered with clumps of brush, cut by a winding creek, knee-deep with grass.

Horse heaven. No wonder Muddy looked so full of spit and vinegar.

David drew in a deep lungful of air and held it, sorting out the myriad aromas. Damp, rich earth, hints of sweetness from the star-shaped purple wildflowers blooming in the road ditch, a tantalizing whiff of peppermint, all sharpened by the cool edge of mountain air.

A house sat off to his right at the end of a narrow dirt driveway. David paused to admire the tipi in the front yard, banded top and bottom with black, with a herd of crudely painted buffalo racing around the broad white stripe in the middle. As lawn ornaments went, it beat the hell out of his mother's concrete garden gnomes. There was a neat pole barn and a securely fenced pasture, but no animals in sight. Hobby farmers, no doubt. Worked in town, had a dog, a couple of cats, maybe a horse that functioned mostly as yard art. There were a million just like this in Colorado.

Behind it all, the mountains reared up, a fortress of solid rock, jagged and impenetrable. A threat to frail human endeavors even in the golden morning light.

When David turned and started back toward town, he could see nothing but prairie rolling over hills and bluffs clear to the eastern horizon. If he didn't glance over his shoulder, he could almost imagine the Rockies weren't looming over him. Mountains or plains. No middle ground here on Blackfeet Reservation.

Back at the fairgrounds, he dug a set of barbells out of his trailer and pushed his sluggish body through lunges, squats, presses, and curls, then finished off with the stretches and abdominal exercises that kept his back in working order despite the time he spent hunched underneath the horses he shod.

Panting from the last set of crunches, he toweled sweat from his face, enjoying the ache of fatigued muscle. Of all the things he regretted during his two lost years, the way he'd let his body go was near the top of the list. Beer and self-pity...not exactly the diet of champions. In the past few months he'd slowly regained his stamina and strength and trimmed off the last of the belly that had crept out over his belt.

He stripped to the waist and scrubbed off sweat, his

nipples contracting to pinpoints at the cold insult of the washcloth. He definitely needed to fill those propane bottles and fire up the hot-water heater. That extra layer of fat he'd been packing would've come in handy right about now, but he was much happier with what he saw in the mirror these days.

He splashed water over his hair and mashed it into submission. A haircut was high on his agenda the next time he got home, but it still didn't seem right to wear a dusty cowboy hat to a lawyer's office. He was dressed and pacing his cramped living quarters when Galen's pickup rattled into the fairgrounds at ten minutes to nine.

As David stepped out of the trailer, Galen rolled down his window to extend a large foam cup of coffee.

"I got sugar and stuff, case you need it."

"Black's fine, thanks." Darn fine, in fact, David realized at the first sip. From the espresso stand at the concrete tipi, maybe?

"Climb in," Galen said.

David shoved a bag of cattle ear tags and a binder overflowing with papers out of the way to make space in the dusty cab. A generous coating of dog hair on the seat suggested the usual passenger was of the four-legged variety. Galen had dressed up for the meeting in a blue plaid shirt and a denim jacket with a multicolored medicine wheel embroidered on the front, although he wore the same battered black hat.

David had dug out one of his winter shirts, a heavy brushed-cotton in dark navy that his sister had bought him because she said it made his eyes look blue. Whatever. He usually didn't wear it after the first of

May, which accounted for why it wasn't in the laundry hamper with all the rest of his decent clothes. His jeans were clean, at least, but nearly worn through at the knees.

Maybe they'd think it was a fashion statement.

Galen didn't comment on David's clothes or anything else as he drove into town, weaving through the same bustle of cars, pickups, and RVs. The street guy and his dog were huddled alone on the cracked concrete in front of the boarded-up gas station, soaking up the intermittent sunshine.

The attorney's office was in a long, nondescript building a few blocks off Main Street. Galen parked on the street out front, and they walked inside to an office that was equally tired and dull. No plush carpets or gleaming wood here, just steel government-issue desks and scratched filing cabinets.

A woman popped out of her chair as they entered. David had to look twice and still might not have recognized Mary if it weren't for the freckles. Yesterday, his vision had been too blurred by anger to register much of anything in the few moments they'd squared off. His memory had painted her as wiry and hard-faced, not petite and...well, pretty damn cute, though he had a feeling she wouldn't like that word much.

She stared at him, blinked once, then again, as if she didn't quite recognize him, either. "Something wrong?" he asked.

"Uh, no. You're just a lot...um...cleaner."

"I tend to be that way when I've had time to take a shower," he said, scowling.

Her face flushed. Her gaze slid down to his chest and

away, her blush deepening. Nervous? Or scared? She should be both after taking off with his horse like that, but she was so petite he felt like a goon looming over her. She'd tried to look all serious and grown up in a tailored black jacket over a white shirt, with black jeans and dressy boots that added a couple of inches to her height, but she was still a little bitty thing.

Without the baseball cap, he could see her hair was cut short, sort of feathery on the sides and spiky on the top. It was lighter than he'd expected, with gold streaks that matched the flecks in her eyes, which were the kind of brown that could veer toward green in the right light. The freckles scattered across her face nearly blended with her tawny skin, as if her color came from a tan, not her heritage.

She didn't look Native. Not like Galen, Kylan, and the girlfriend, with their dusky skin and inky-black hair. Mary looked more like a golden-eyed pixie. She lifted her pointed chin and their eyes locked. Held.

A part of David's brain that had been dormant for a very long time perked up and drawled, *Well, hello. What's this?*

Oh, hell no. He hadn't looked twice at a girl in months, and now his man parts decided to pay attention? *No. Nope. Uh-uh. Not this woman.* That was plain stupid. So why couldn't he look away?

She blinked again and then gave a slight shake of her head as if she'd felt the same jolt. Turning on her heel, she marched to the interior office door. "Yolanda is waiting for us."

Nice butt, that rogue voice muttered in his head.

Not much wider than the span of his fingers. And

dammit, there he went again, but he couldn't help sneaking another look before Mary plopped into a chair and he was forced to redirect his attention.

The woman behind the desk was not small, in height or girth. She offered a brisk smile that matched her handshake. "Yolanda Pipestone, attorney at law. And you're David, of course."

Three chairs were lined up in front of her desk. Mary had taken the far one. Galen settled into the middle, a protective buffer between Mary and David, who wedged his big frame into the third.

"Well, this is a fine mess," Yolanda said, folding her hands on the desk in front of her ample bosom, which might cause a man to miss the sharp intelligence in her eyes. "I suppose we should start by explaining how we believe your horse came to be in Kylan's possession."

"That would be nice," David said, impatience layering sarcasm into his voice. Yeah, he wanted to know the whole story, but he was more concerned about where Muddy was right now.

Yolanda gave him a long, measuring look and then transferred it to Galen. "Go ahead. You know it better than me."

"Ah-right." Galen pulled a piece of yellow notebook paper from his shirt pocket and squinted down at it, as if to be sure he got the facts just right. "Mary bought the horse two years ago from a friend of mine named Otis Yellowhawk. Lives down in Lodge Grass just north of the Wyoming border. Otis got 'im when his granddad passed away. Old man had a whole herd running on a tribal lease down by the Pryor

Mountains. Otis remembers his granddad saying his cousin Jinks left one of the horses there right before he got killed."

"Killed?" David echoed, remembering the pawnshop in Billings, the story the woman had told about her boyfriend leaving her the saddle.

"Car wreck. Drunk. 'Bout a week after you lost your horse." Galen fished in his pocket again, pulled out a copy of a newspaper clipping printed on white paper, and handed it to David. "He went to a team roping in Meeteetse the day Muddy disappeared, woulda been driving home through Cody about the right time with a half-empty trailer."

"And he just happened to be the one who found Muddy?" David asked, squinting at the blurred face attached to the obituary in his hand.

"Guess so." Galen hitched a shoulder. "He wasn't a real upstanding citizen. The neighbors' cattle had a habit of going missing when Jinks was short on meat, that sort of thing. Guy like him finds a horse running loose with an expensive saddle and bridle, he counts it as easy money. Far as we can guess, he hightailed it home, stashed the saddle at his girlfriend's house, and dumped the horse out with his granddad's herd."

"And just left him there?" David asked.

Galen's mustache twitched in disgust. "Knowing Jinks, he had a plan. Find a horse running loose right down the road from a big rodeo and packing a fancy trophy saddle, sure bet he's worth a lot and somebody's gonna be willing to pay to get him back. Too bad for everybody he ran his pickup into a bridge before he could figure out how to collect."

David stared down at the clipping. All this time, he'd been raging at a dead man. It felt...weird. An uncomfortable stew of guilt and disappointment. "I put up posters in Lodge Grass and Crow Agency."

Galen nodded. "Otis remembers seein' 'em, but Jinks traded horses all the time, and you gotta admit, Muddy don't look like much. Sure as hell if their granddad had known, he'da hit you up for the reward. No reason not to, with Jinks dead."

And now the old man was dead, too. Nobody left to blame or to answer questions. Convenient. David looked over and caught Mary watching him. Her eyes jerked back down to her hands. His gaze got hung up on the delicate curve of her cheekbone, the pattern of freckles sprinkled across her tipped-up nose, and he scowled at his reaction. "A woman sold my saddle at a pawnshop in Billings that fall," he said curtly. "The owner described her as young and skinny."

Mary stiffened, snapping her head up, anger sparking in her eyes. "You're accusing me?"

"Just saying."

"I was nowhere near Billings at that time."

David raised his eyebrows. "I didn't say exactly when it was sold. Do you have an alibi for the entire year?"

"Yeah, I do." That pointed little chin lifted another notch. "I was riding shotgun on convoys from Kandahar airport into the Helmand province. That's in Afghanistan, in case you're not familiar."

David felt his jaw drop. "You were in the army?"

"The Montana National Guard. I was deployed two months before your horse disappeared, didn't come home for ten months after. Is that a sufficient *alibi*?"

David couldn't muster an intelligent response, so he shut up.

Yolanda smiled ever so slightly and then nodded at Galen to go on.

"Two years ago in April, Otis gathered up his granddad's herd," Galen said. "Anything that rode decent he kept, the rest he hauled to the sale barn in Billings."

Where they were most likely sold for slaughter. David's skin went cold at the thought of Muddy being loaded on that particular trailer.

Galen checked his notes and continued. "When he saw how Muddy took to handlin' cattle, Otis assumed Jinks had roped on him. He knew we were looking for somethin' for Kylan, so he called me, and Mary bought the horse. He seemed to be a natural."

A natural. Yeah, after about a thousand runs beginning when David got him as a four-year-old.

"I have the original bill of sale here, signed by Otis Yellowhawk," Yolanda said, tapping a file folder with her finger. "Jinks did tell his girlfriend about picking up the horse. She's willing to testify if she's promised immunity from prosecution for selling the stolen saddle. We're hoping that won't be necessary."

David took a deep breath, let it out. What did it matter? He didn't want a fight. He just wanted Muddy. "No. I'm good. So now what?"

"That's what we're here to negotiate." Yolanda took a deliberate pause, let her words sink in.

"*Negotiate?*" David repeated. "He belongs to me."

"My client has invested a considerable sum of money in this horse, David. A purchase price of two thousand dollars plus two years of boarding, shoeing, and veterinary expenses."

David felt his lip curl. "That's a pretty small price to pay for the use of a horse like Muddy."

"Probably true," Yolanda said. "But for Kylan, the horse is irreplaceable at any price."

David clenched his fists on the narrow wooden armrests of his chair. "What are you trying to say?"

Yolanda pulled a piece of paper from her folder and held it up. David recognized it instantly and grunted like he'd been punched in the gut.

"You expect me to pay the reward money in order to get Muddy back?" he sputtered, so furious he could barely speak. "That poster is four years old!"

Yolanda glanced at the missing-horse poster she held, then at him. "There is no expiration date on the offer, and I wasn't able to find any public record of a retraction on your part."

David swallowed, sucked in air, swallowed again. Five grand had seemed like nothing when he hadn't even cashed the check from winning Cody. But now…

"Your *client* has had use of my horse without my permission for two full years," he said, leaning forward to bounce a glare from Galen to Mary. "Soon as Kylan started roping on him, you had to know he was a whole lot more than some stray, but you never wondered where he really came from?"

They both stared straight ahead, stone-faced as the concrete tipi.

Yolanda pulled out another sheet of paper. "This is a transcript of your 911 call, the night your horse disappeared. You told the dispatcher, and I quote directly,

'It's my own fault. I got distracted, forgot about the fireworks. I never should have left him tied there.'"

Shame heated David's face. "What's that got to do—"

"By your own admission, you are at least partially culpable for the loss of your animal," Yolanda cut in. "Given the circumstances and the time that passed between when your horse was stolen and when Mary bought him, even if she had tried, the chances that she would have been able to identify him were minimal. She purchased him in good faith and took excellent care of him. I can't think of any reason she shouldn't be paid the full reward…but she is willing to consider another option."

"And that is?" David managed through clenched teeth.

"She'll settle for half if you'll agree to leave him with Kylan until after the National High School Rodeo."

"That's almost the end of July!"

Yolanda inclined her head. "If that isn't acceptable, she's willing to take the reward in full and turn the horse over to you immediately."

David swiveled in his chair to glare at Mary, who still refused to glance in his direction. He met Galen's implacable gaze instead and found no sign of the previous sympathy. Fury shot David straight up out of his chair. "You want to hold Muddy ransom? Fine. I'm more than willing to call in the state cops."

Yolanda leaned back with a pitying smile. "This isn't the State of Montana, Mr. Parsons. This is the Blackfeet Nation. A dispute of this kind will have to be settled in tribal court. Unfortunately, that court has a large backlog and takes a recess for the first week of July, so I wouldn't expect your case to be heard by the judge until at least August."

Wham! There it was. The reason Mary had run home to the reservation.

David stared at Yolanda, mind flailing. This couldn't be right. They didn't just get to opt out of the law of the land. But from the red haze inside his skull, he fished a memory from history class. Wounded Knee. The Pine Ridge Reservation. A standoff with the FBI because they were the only outside law enforcement with jurisdiction on an Indian reservation.

The feds wouldn't come blazing to David's rescue. He was just some cowboy, and Muddy was just a horse. They were on their own.

He whirled around, kicked his chair aside, and slammed out of the office.

Chapter 7

DAVID SLAPPED THE FLAT OF HIS HAND DOWN HARD ON THE flatbed of Galen's pickup, then cursed when a sliver from the wooden deck speared into his palm. He wanted to yell, kick something, but he was already drawing enough curious stares from the pair of old ladies hunkered on a bench outside the entry of the building.

He took off down the sidewalk, needing to work off some steam before he exploded. A plastic grocery bag rolled in front of him, pushed by the wind. He stomped it flat, ground his heel for good measure, then relented and picked it up, though it didn't make a whole lot of difference considering the drift of trash against the chain-link fence down the block.

He wadded the plastic into a tight ball, jammed his fists into the bottom of his coat pockets, and kicked an empty soda bottle down the sidewalk and into the street where the wind sent it skittering across the crumbling pavement.

It wasn't fair, dammit. Finding Muddy was supposed to be the happiest day of his life. The answer to his prayers. After all the months, all the heartache...now this?

His phone rang and he fished it out, fully intending to let it go to voicemail if it was his dad. He couldn't begin to pretend to be normal right now. He didn't recognize the number. A 406 prefix. Somewhere in Montana, and he couldn't think of a soul in the state who knew his number. But when he answered, the voice was vaguely familiar.

"Hey, David. It's Rusty Chapman."

"Rusty." David had to roust the memory from a back corner of his brain. "Hi. Been a while."

Almost four years. David's first trip to the National Finals had been Rusty's last. He'd retired from the road to concentrate on his growing family and their ranch. David knew Rusty the way he knew a lot of the other ropers...as members of the same fraternity. The road warriors—a relatively small group of cowboys who lived on and for the pro tour, following the rodeos to every corner of the country. They went head-to-head in the arena but looked out for each other, too. Rodeo competition was tough, but the travel was flat-out brutal. Everybody needed a hand somewhere along the way, whether it be a spare tire, an encouraging pat on the back, a ride to the next big show.

Or in this case, a friendly voice on the end of the line when a man was feeling badly outnumbered.

"I heard you were in the area," Rusty said.

"You live around Browning?"

"Not too far off. I'm north of Cut Bank. Is the rumor I'm hearing about Muddy true?"

"What, did they send out smoke signals?" David asked, kicking at a flattened beer can.

"Nah. Facebook. You're all over my wife's timeline."

Oh, great. Enough people knew Muddy's story for it to spread like wildfire across the Internet. And that scene he'd made in Kalispell... "Are there pictures?"

Rusty laughed. "Not your best look, buddy."

David groaned. His mother would tan his hide when she saw those.

"I can't believe he's been right here under my nose," Rusty said.

David angled across the street to a park where he could lean on the railing of a wooden bridge. "You ever see Kylan rope on him?"

"Not that I remember. Kylan doesn't rope well enough to attract attention outside the high school rodeos. My wife teaches fourth grade over in Browning, though. She works with Mary."

Whoa. Back up. "Mary's a teacher?"

"Special education. She's amazing. The rest of the staff thinks the world of her."

Great. A soldier. A teacher. Practically a damn saint. What next? Was he gonna find out she knit blankets for orphans in her spare time?

"She's trying to force me to leave Muddy here until after the high school finals," David said, the anger spurting again.

"How?"

David explained.

Rusty cursed softly. "I'm not surprised. Qualifying for nationals, that's huge for a kid like Kylan. Damn sure more than anyone ever expected. I imagine Mary would do about anything to keep it from being ruined for him."

Too late.

Guilt curdled in David's gut, kicking his anger up another notch. "So I'm the bad guy here? Muddy is *my* horse."

"I wasn't saying…" Rusty stopped, gave a pained sigh. "This whole thing just sucks. Mary and Galen and them—they're good people. I guarantee they had no idea Muddy was stolen."

"They had to wonder when they saw how good he was."

"Not necessarily. Jinks Yellowhawk could really rope. Went to the Montana circuit finals a few times, might've had a shot at the NFR if he could've kept his shit together, stayed off the drugs and all. I would've believed he'd have a decent horse."

Muddy was a hell of a lot more than decent. And Mary and Galen might normally be great people, but as far as David was concerned, this was nothing but pure extortion. If they thought he'd walk away and leave Muddy here for another month, they were insane.

Or desperate.

"Can they do this?" he asked. "Force me to pay to get him back just because they're on the reservation?"

"I don't know." Rusty huffed out a breath. "You could probably fight them, and you might win, but I'm guessing it would take more time and money than paying the reward."

"Which is what they're betting on."

"Yeah," Rusty agreed. "I wish I could be more help, but I don't know anybody who has much influence with the tribe. Hilary's got a friend who's a lawyer, though. Practices in Cut Bank. We could ask her opinion. Off the books," Rusty added.

Meaning free of charge. Just what David could afford. "Thanks. I appreciate it." His temper eased, his head clearing enough to make way for curiosity. "If Mary's a teacher and she's been in the army, she's gotta be older than she looks."

"Close to thirty, I'd say. She went to college at Montana State, then basic training and stuff. Then she was deployed for a year. This is her sixth year teaching."

At least two years older than David. "How come Kylan lives with her?"

"His mother's in prison for selling meth."

Oh. Geez. "Tough, having your mom arrested."

"Better than living with that woman. She's bad news, coming and going. Best thing that could've happened to Kylan, having Mary named his guardian. Hasn't been easy, though. Kylan is… Well, he's got some challenges."

David looked up and saw Galen shuffling out of the office building, swiveling his head as he searched for his missing passenger. "Listen, Rusty, I gotta run."

"No problem. I'll call you after I get a chance to talk to our lawyer friend. If you need anything else while you're here—a place to stay or a practice pen to run some calves—don't hesitate to call."

"Thanks. I'll keep it in mind." David tucked the phone away but stayed put, bracing his elbows on the railing to stare down into the murky creek. He had to settle down, use his head. Slamming around kicking things and antagonizing everyone in sight wouldn't help. Much as he'd like to paint Mary and Galen as the villains, they were getting the shaft here, too. And so was Kylan.

His conscience reared up and gave him a sharp jab. Hell. Why did it have to be a kid? Why couldn't Muddy have been with some thirtysomething rodeo stud who had four other horses in the pasture?

David contemplated his limited options as he walked the two blocks back to Galen's pickup. Leaving without

Muddy was not a possibility, but even if he could conjure up five grand out of thin air, that still left the kid without a horse, at least in the short term. And with nationals just over a month away, the short term was pretty important to Kylan Runningbird.

David stopped a few yards short of where Galen was leaning on the pickup's flatbed, seeming content to wait as long as necessary. The man must be a great poker player. That face gave away nothing.

"Who are you anyway?" David asked, irritated enough he didn't care that he sounded rude. Galen didn't flinch.

"How do ya mean?"

"What are you to Mary? An uncle or something?"

Galen gave a single deliberate nod. "Mary's brothers were my wife's nephews."

David blinked, not sure which part of that statement to try to comprehend first. "Mary's not your niece?"

"Not by blood. Her mom left my wife's brother and hooked up with some white man down in Great Falls for a while, came home pregnant. None of us ever laid eyes on him."

That would explain why she wasn't as dark as the rest of them. "What about Mary? Has she... Does she..."

"She went to see him once, when she was in high school." Galen shrugged. "Never went back, so we assume he ain't much."

David shook his head, baffled. He couldn't imagine growing up that way. Then he remembered Galen had referred to her brothers in the past tense. "What happened to your nephews?"

"Car wreck. Killed the two of them and a couple others."

"Oh."

They stood, taking a moment of respectful silence until a gust of wind peppered them with road grit.

Galen tugged the collar of his jacket up another inch. "Guess you got some thinking to do."

"Yeah."

Galen nodded, then circled the pickup to the driver's door. "Might as well see some of the country while you're at it. Hop in. I got a job down Heart Butte way."

David hesitated. He needed to get on the phone, figure out how to put together either the reward money or enough cash to hire a lawyer of his own, but he got the distinct impression Galen wanted to talk, so David got in the pickup.

If Mary's sort-of uncle had any bright ideas of how they could work this out, David was all ears, because he didn't have a clue.

Chapter 8

HEART BUTTE WAS SOUTH AND WEST OF BROWNING, nestled in the flanks of the mountains, or so Galen said. Their destination was a few miles shy of town. David wasn't sure why he'd been dragged along, and he didn't ask. He was pretty much on his own, fighting a battle on enemy turf. Wouldn't hurt to learn as much as possible about his opponent.

Besides, the scenery was a whole lot better than the inside of his trailer.

The day had turned off gorgeous, the sky an endless stretch of blue, the sun warm enough he could finally shed his jacket. The highway dipped and swerved through miles of spring-fresh range, past rainwater ponds and across a river frothing with snowmelt. A song came to mind that David had heard at a rodeo in Alberta. Something about heaven in the foothills of the Northern Rocky range and it not getting much better for a cow.

No kidding.

"What are we doing out here?" David asked.

"Gotta write brand papers for some bucking horses. They're takin' 'em to a rodeo in Choteau this weekend."

"You're a brand inspector?"

"Yah." Galen made a disgusted noise. "Damn poor one, considerin' I bought a stolen horse. Never could figure out what Muddy's brand was s'posed to be under that scar."

"Circle P," David said, stifling the urge to rub it in. "What does Kylan call him?"

"My wife, Cissy, named him Muttley, like the old cartoon."

David gave him a blank look.

Galen sighed. "Guess you're too young to remember. Damn near everybody is these days."

"It sounds a lot like Muddy."

"I s'pose that's why he seemed to take to it."

They lapsed into a silence more comfortable than it should have been, given the circumstances. Galen turned onto a gravel road that meandered along a rocky creek bed. Quaking aspens crowded the banks, white-barked trunks stunted and twisted by the wind, which had dropped to a stiff breeze that set the leaves quivering. Around one bend, a pair of mule deer peered at them from the tall grass in the ditch, then bounded up and away, disappearing into the brush.

The dirt track ended at a set of pole-fenced corrals filled with high-headed, platter-footed bucking horses. While Galen checked and noted the brands, David made himself comfortable on the flatbed of the pickup and stared up at the mountains, his brain grinding.

He didn't have a whole lot of options. He'd paid off his debts, but his credit was still in the crapper, and he didn't own anything he could use for collateral other than his worn-out pickup and trailer. And Muddy.

He could've had the money in a single phone call back when the bank in his hometown was locally owned, but it'd been swallowed up by a larger chain. Now they had to follow corporate rules, and a man's character didn't count for much compared to the numbers on a computer screen.

The bank president was still there, though, riding out the last few years until retirement. He was a part-time rancher and sometime roper, and he knew what Muddy was worth. If there was any way, he'd approve the loan.

Then David would just have to be damn sure he won enough to make the payments.

Galen finished up, handed over the blue brand-inspection forms, and collected his fee from the owner, who'd given David a lot of curious looks but hadn't ventured over to chat. Galen climbed in the pickup and pointed it back down the dirt track.

Finally, David couldn't stand the silence anymore. "I assume you didn't bring me along just for the company."

"Nah." Galen hooked his wrist over the top of the steering wheel, squinting into the distance. "I need to ask a favor."

David stared at him in disbelief. "I can't leave Muddy here for another six weeks. Let Mary haul him halfway across the country to Pueblo for nationals. Anything could happen."

"Ain't worth takin' the chance," Galen agreed. "For you or for her."

"Then what was all that about this morning?" David jabbed a finger toward town and the lawyer's office.

Galen contemplated the road ahead for a few beats. Then he sighed. "Don't get me wrong. I got nothin' against Yolanda, but soon as you get the lawyers involved, things go to shit. We'd be goin' about this a whole lot different if I'd stayed in Kalispell until Sunday."

"Why didn't you?" David asked.

"Cissy's aunt fell and broke her hip." Galen gave an eye roll. "Yeah. No joke. But if we'd been there, Mary wouldn't have called Yolanda when you showed up. We coulda handled this amongst ourselves, the way it should be."

David frowned, putting the pieces together. "It wasn't Mary's idea to bring Muddy back here?"

"Nah. That was Yolanda. Always figures you gotta have home-field advantage."

"Mary went along, though."

"She panicked. Wouldn't you, something like that happened with your kid?" Galen's frown dug deep furrows on either side of his mouth. "Mary's scrambling, buying time, wanting to believe she can salvage something out of this deal for Kylan. And Yolanda…she's a lawyer. They figure any time somethin' goes wrong, somebody's gotta pay. She looks at you, thinks, 'Hey, big Colorado rancher, rodeo stud, what's five grand to a guy like him? He can win it back the first time he ropes on Muddy.'"

David did a mental eye roll of his own. If she only knew…

The hell of it was, if all this was happening to someone else, David might think the same. Muddy was worth every cent. Besides, he had put up the reward, and he hadn't rescinded the offer, so why shouldn't he have to pay? And, yeah, Galen was right. David's parents probably would do for him what Mary was trying to do for Kylan. His sister would, for damn sure. She was a hard ass.

"If you don't agree with what Mary's doing, why don't you just say so?" David said. "She seems to listen to you."

Galen shook his head. "I'm not sure she's wrong, and

it's not up to me to judge. Either way, it'd be best to give it some time, let everybody calm down."

"I have to be in Reno by noon on Friday."

"Then you've got a couple of days to spare," Galen said, and his tone said, *And that's that*.

Hot, frustrated words piled up in David's throat, burned all the way down as he swallowed them. Arguing would be a waste of effort at best and antagonize Galen at worst. If Mary wanted time, Galen would give it to her.

"There's more going on here than just roping," Galen said quietly. "Kylan had given up on school, seemed like he was dead set on following in his mother's footsteps. He isn't good at basketball or football or anything like that, but with Muddy to even the odds, he can at least play along in the arena. That's all we want. To keep him interested, give him a reason to keep trying."

David scowled out the windshield. What was he supposed to do, apologize for ruining everything? "So what do you want from me?"

Galen shifted in his seat, rubbed at his thigh as if it ached. "Cissy and I set some money aside for after Kylan graduates, hoping he'd go on and get some kind of schooling. If we put that with what Mary could afford to borrow from the bank, we'd have at least ten thousand dollars. Fifteen if you pay the reward like they're asking."

"You'd spend his college fund on a horse?"

Galen blew out a tired sigh. "Wouldn't be our first choice, but Kylan… Well, it's hard to say what he might do if he gives up on roping, and since he turned eighteen, there's not much we can do to stop him."

Except bribery in the form of a new horse. Ten or fifteen grand might be enough if they got lucky and found just the right one. Nothing close to Muddy's caliber, but that wasn't necessarily all bad. Putting Kylan on Muddy was like handing the kid a grenade launcher when he needed a shotgun. He might be more likely to hit his target, but as often as not the kickback would knock him on his ass.

"You know a lot of people," Galen said. "And you see a lot of horses. I was hoping you'd help us find one to suit Kylan."

Using David's five grand. That rankled, forget all the justifications. But if he could help them, reward or not, he wouldn't be leaving Kylan on foot, and that might keep the guilt monkey off his back.

"I'll call Rusty Chapman first," David said. "He'll know of anybody around here who'd have something."

Galen grunted his approval. David thumbed through the other contacts on his phone, considering and discarding names. He wanted somebody trustworthy, who wouldn't try to take advantage, pawn off a cripple or a head case. "Be nice if you could find a horse in time for nationals, but that would be rushing it pretty hard."

"Good way to get took," Galen agreed. "Once is enough."

Back in Browning, Galen wheeled through the drive-up at the burger joint. "I got this. Least I can do."

David considered arguing, then decided Galen was right and supersized his fries. He propped his elbow on the window frame, watching the traffic rumble past as they waited for their order. "You know, I could just wait until you show up at nationals and have the cops impound Muddy."

"Would you do that to a kid?" Galen asked.

David held back the answer for a long moment. Then he sighed. "No."

Relief flickered in Galen's eyes, and his voice was gruffer than usual. "Good to know."

No doubt. David shouldn't have admitted it, but they would've seen through him anyway. Unlike Galen, he had no poker face at all, and that was probably going to cost him.

Chapter 9

"I NEED TO SEE MUDDY," DAVID SAID AS GALEN PULLED into the fairgrounds and parked. "I barely got a look at him yesterday."

"They'll be here at two. The boys practice on Monday and Wednesday afternoons."

And they didn't bother to ask if it was okay for Kylan to rope on Muddy? David beat down his anger, grasping at his rapidly diminishing patience. The kid needed time to accept that he had to let Muddy go. It had been less than twenty-four hours since David had sprung the truth on them. It only felt like an eternity.

"I'll see you at two," David said, and climbed out of Galen's pickup. As he walked to his trailer, his phone rang. "Hey, Sis."

"Why don't Mom and Dad know about Muddy yet?" she demanded. "I just talked to them, and they have no idea."

"It got complicated." David explained the situation and then held the phone at arm's length while she raged.

She finally sputtered into silence. Then she hissed out a breath. "You want me to call our lawyer?"

"Hiring him would cost more than the reward."

"Better to pay out legal fees than let them blackmail you."

David smiled because it was exactly what he'd expected her to say, and it felt good to know she was ready to kick ass and take names on his behalf. "There's a shock. You, ready for a fight."

"They started it." She paused for a weighted moment. "Don't tell me you're gonna sit back and take this! Let them win?"

He climbed into the trailer and shut the door behind him. "It's not a contest, and no matter what, the kid loses. Paying the reward might be worth it in the big picture."

"The big…" Air exploded out of her like a punctured tire. "Oh, dear *God*. Not another one of your damn curses. For a reasonably intelligent human being…" She sucked in an audible breath before going on with her standard rant. "You know these things are self-fulfilling prophecies, right? You decide you've been hexed, and your subconscious trips you up and makes it come true."

David took a slurp of his Coke, making his tone nonchalant because he knew it would wind her up even tighter. "My luck has been running cold for a month. There's no way I'm gonna risk making it worse by screwing over a kid."

"Geezus, David. *You found Muddy*. Don't you think that's one hellacious big sign your luck is changing?"

"Yep. And that's exactly why I'm not taking any chances on messing it up again."

She made a noise like she was choking on a really bad word. "Honest to God. Next time you're home, I'm scheduling an exorcism, because I don't know what the hell possesses you sometimes." She took a deep breath and a moment to calm down, and her voice leveled out. "Do you need a loan?"

"Yeah, but I'm gonna start at the bank."

"We can help—"

"No. Things are tight enough at the ranch as it is."

"Don't be stupid. This is Muddy. Once you've got him under you, you'll win it back soon enough."

"That's what I thought before."

"You weren't riding Muddy then."

"You said yourself there's no guarantee." David polished off the last french fry and wadded up the paper sleeve. "Muddy might not be what he was. And even if he is, anything could happen. He could get hurt or sick, or I could. Five grand buys a lot of hay, Sis, and you don't know how much you're gonna need, the way things are going."

She was quiet long enough that he knew he'd won... for now. "That's why you haven't told Mom and Dad. Because you want to find the money first."

"Yeah."

"Well, you'd better make it quick. Word's gonna get out."

"I know."

"Call me if there's any way I can help."

"I will."

He called the bank next and caught the manager just getting back from a late lunch. Byron was thrilled to hear the news about Muddy, but his enthusiasm faded when David explained what he needed.

"Well, sure, we could loan you the money if you put Muddy up for collateral, but we'll need a vet inspection to be sure he's sound, and proof that it is the same horse. And you'll have to have him fully insured, with the bank named as a lien holder."

Which meant he wouldn't have the choice of saying no if there was ever another claim to be filed.

David swallowed hard. "Okay."

Byron hesitated and then sighed. "You know if it was up to me, I'd write you a check right now, David. But with your credit scores, management won't give me any wiggle room. I can't approve the loan while Muddy is a thousand miles away. You'll have to bring him home."

And he couldn't take Muddy until he had the money. So there went that plan.

"If your parents cosign—" Byron began.

"I was trying to avoid that. And I'd rather they didn't know we'd talked about this."

Byron sighed again. "I understand. I wish I could bend the rules, but things are really tight for us, too. The longer this drought goes on, the harder it is for people to make their loan payments."

And some were losing the battle, which put a dent in the bank's bottom line and made them less inclined to take even a small risk.

"Well, thanks anyway," David said, his voice stiff with disappointment. "I'll let you know if I figure something out."

"Do that. Call me at home if you need to. I'll push the paperwork through as fast as I can."

"Thanks. I appreciate it."

David hung up and flopped back on his couch to stare glumly up at the ceiling. He was probably being stupid about the loan. In the great scheme of things, five thousand dollars wasn't much money for his parents to borrow. It wouldn't make or break the ranch. But the thought made cold dread curl in his gut, even as he told himself it wasn't logical.

Borrowing against his future with Muddy felt like

asking for trouble, daring fate to do its worst. And, yeah, his sister was probably right. He could be crossing the line from superstition to paranoia, but now was not the time to test the boundaries.

He nursed the last of his Coke and called Rusty Chapman but got the answering machine. He put in three other calls and got to talk to live bodies, but none of them knew of a horse that would fit both Kylan's needs and his budget.

By the time David hung up on the last call, a motley collection of rigs had begun to straggle into the fairgrounds, starting with a rusty, open-sided stock trailer pulled by a mud-caked Dodge dually with one fender tied on with a rope. It backed up to the catch pens behind the roping chutes, and a man around Galen's age bailed out to dump a dozen longhorn roping calves into the alley.

David studied every rig as it arrived, pacing circles in his living quarters, his nerves jumping. One after another, the pickups pulled into line, parked and unloaded, but none of the occupants was Mary or Kylan, and none of the horses was a mud-brown gelding with attitude to spare.

Finally, an older Ford dually pulling a bumper-tow trailer rolled in from west of town and turned into the driveway. David's heart did a quick, hard knock when it got close enough for him to see the driver. Mary was at the wheel, and Kylan slouched so low in the passenger's seat the top of his head was barely visible.

David tossed his Coke cup into the sink and headed outside. They weren't putting him off any longer. He would get his hands on Muddy, and there wasn't a damn thing they could do to stop him.

Mary met him twenty yards from the pickup, feet braced, shoulders squared, making it clear he'd have to go through her. She'd changed into a black-hooded sweatshirt with *Browning Indians* scrolled on the front in red. Paired with black jeans and the expression on her face, the outfit made her look like a very small, very determined ninja.

Hooves thudded on rubber, and David's attention jumped to the trailer as Muddy ejected from the back, scrambling out like the rig was on fire. He flung his head up to survey the rodeo grounds, nostrils flared, his body language screaming, "Bring it on."

David's throat knotted at the familiar arrogance. He was just so...Muddy.

"I need to see my horse," he said, the words coming out sharper, more demanding than he'd intended.

Mary's jaw tightened. "You're not gonna find a mark on him that wasn't there when we bought him."

"What do you mean? What was wrong with him when you got him?" David asked, alarm bells ringing in his head as he remembered the chaos of the night Muddy had escaped. Had he been cut? Injured?

"Nothing," Mary said with an impatient glare. "He was fine. He's still fine. Just that old scar on his shoulder."

"He hasn't been lame?"

"Not a step."

Relief plastered a smile across his face. "Oh. Well, that's good to hear."

Mary stared at him for a beat, eyes narrowed. Then her posture softened and she stepped back, turning as Kylan led the horse around from behind the trailer. The kid was shorter than David had first thought, his skin almost the same shade as Muddy's coat. His stick-straight, jet-black hair poked out from under his hat at odd angles, like a scarecrow's straw wig. His shirt was half untucked again, his jeans hung too loose on his hips, his baseball cap was slightly crooked. Not enough to be a fashion statement, just like he hadn't quite got it on straight. Even his movements were loose, as if someone had forgotten to tighten all the screws in his joints.

He stopped dead when he saw David. "What?"

"Could you hold him there for a minute?" Mary asked. "David wants to check him out."

Kylan clenched his hands, his mouth quivering as if he wanted to shout *no*, but he ducked his head and stepped away to the end of the lead rope, refusing to look at David. "Whatever."

David eased close, reality smacking him square in the chin, turning his knees to rubber now that Muddy was finally within reach. His voice had an embarrassing hitch when he said, "Hey, buddy."

Muddy's ears dropped back, and he narrowed his eyes like he was saying "Oh. It's you."

David choked out a laugh. "What, you didn't miss me?"

He laid a hand on Muddy's neck, savoring the warm, silky hide, laughing again when Muddy shook his head, annoyed. David slid his palm over Muddy's withers, down his back, onto his hip. Muddy cocked his hind leg and gave a warning swipe, but David knew enough to keep his body angled well clear.

He smacked the horse lightly on the rump. "Still up to that old trick, I see."

Muddy craned his head around to glare but let the

foot drop. David bent to slide his hand down, fingers probing bone and tendon. After picking up the foot, studying the hoof and the steel shoe, he set it down and repeated the process with the other hind leg, then the nearest front.

Muddy let out a loud, aggravated sigh, making it clear he was only tolerating the inspection because it wasn't worth his effort to fight it.

"Like I told you, he's fine," Mary said, a softness in her voice David hadn't heard before.

"Unbelievable." David gave a single shake of his head. "If you'd seen the way he tore out of that parking lot in Cody…"

"I can imagine. He doesn't do anything half speed." She smiled. David smiled back, and there was a sizzle and pop in the air between them, two live wires connecting. Mary flinched. David jerked his gaze away, back to Muddy. He picked up the second front hoof, tilting it to inspect the sole, the set of the shoe.

"His feet were pretty bad when he came," Mary said. "Took a while to get them shaped up."

"I'll bet, if he ran barefoot for two years. He's always been prone to quarter cracks." David put the foot down and stepped back, frowning. "He's set kinda low in the heels."

"Our horseshoer thought it would help him slide more when he stops," Mary said.

Slide? Muddy? What the hell? David scowled at her. "You've been messing with his stop?"

Mary bristled. "We wanted to free him up a little. He's so quick… It's hard on someone like Kylan who's still learning."

"I didn't train him to be a kid horse," David shot back.

Kylan made a choked noise, dropped the halter rope, and fled around the back of the trailer. Mary glared daggers at David as she grabbed the loose rope before Muddy could take advantage.

Shit. David gave himself a mental kick in the ass. He'd forgotten the kid was standing there. He glanced toward the arena, the curious faces watching, waiting to see how this little drama would play out.

"I suppose you want to ride him," Mary said, her voice as rigid as her posture.

More than he wanted his next breath, but not here. Not now. If he got choked up just petting the damn horse, who knew how he'd react the first time he got back on Muddy. His luck, he'd start blubbering, and that would end up all over Facebook, too.

Plus, it would be one more kick in the teeth for Kylan in front of all his friends.

"Later," David said. He turned, walked away fast, every fiber of his being screaming in protest at leaving Muddy in Mary's hands. One more day, max. Whatever it took, he'd have his horse back tomorrow.

Chapter 10

DAVID ROUNDED THE CORNER OF THE CATCH PEN, HEADED for his trailer, and came face-to-face with Galen.

"Everything okay?" Galen asked, his gaze focused beyond David's shoulder.

"Just dandy," David drawled, tossing in a sneer for good measure.

Galen gave him a long, level stare.

David was the first to look away. "I've got phone calls to make," he said, angling to step around the other man.

"The kids were hoping you'd rope some with them," Galen said.

David stopped short. "Why?"

"They heard you were pretty good at it," Galen said. "Thought you might show 'em a few things."

A kid sidled up, the youngest and skinniest of the bunch. Couldn't weigh more than a buck thirty-five, all knees and elbows and big, brown puppy-dog eyes. "Sure would be cool, unless you've got somethin' better to do."

David glanced around, found half-a-dozen more pairs of hopeful eyes trained on him. Had they nominated the little kid to speak up, figuring David couldn't say no to the runt of the litter? How would Kylan feel about him butting in to the practice session? On the other hand, Galen wanted him here. David didn't understand exactly why, but so far Galen was the most reasonable person he'd met in this place, so he was willing to play along.

"There's never anything better to do than rope," he told the kid, and went to get Frosty.

They started out flanking and tying on the ground. David held a calf at the end of a rope tied to a post, and the kids lined up to take their turns. Kylan hung back, silent and sullen. David couldn't blame him. He'd probably rather get roping tips from the devil after the hell David had raised with his world.

The calf kicked, nailing David square in the shin. He sucked in a curse and caught a quick glint of amusement in Galen's eyes. The man never missed a beat. The skinny kid—Sam—pushed off the post and ran toward the calf, his left hand sliding down the rope. He grabbed the calf's flank, grunted, lifted hard, and toppled over with the calf in his lap, pinning him down. They wallowed around in the dirt until David got a hold and hoisted the calf up.

Sam staggered to his feet, face red with exertion and frustration. "I'm too little."

"Nah. You just have a low center of gravity." David grabbed his arm, pulled him into position. "Here. Get ahold of him like this. Bend your knees, get 'em down under his body, and roll him up onto your thighs."

On the third try, Sam got it right and flanked the calf cleanly. He grinned up at David, eyes bright. "Cool."

The others took their turns, drinking in David's instructions, faces intent. Then Kylan stepped up to the post.

"I don't need no help," he declared.

"Okay," David said.

Kylan launched from the post, his teeth gritted but his strides sluggish, as if his legs refused to heed the command to move fast. His flank was decent, the tie deliberate but solid until he tried to pull the end through for the half hitch, fumbled, and dropped the string. The calf kicked free. Kylan cursed, untangled the string, regathered and fumbled the tie again. His chin dropped, his shoulders sagging as he sat back on his haunches, letting the calf up.

"Stupid hooey," he muttered.

"Tell me about it," David said. "I missed mine to place in the ninth round at the National Finals."

Kylan's head jerked up, and for an instant, he forgot to be mad. "Really?"

"Yep. Happens to everyone." David paused, considered keeping his mouth shut but couldn't. "Might work better if you didn't wear gloves."

Kylan scowled down at the black nylon batting gloves. "Mary made me."

"Why?"

Kylan shook his head, but Galen stepped up. "Show him."

When Kylan didn't move, Galen reached down, grabbed a wrist, and pulled off the glove. Every knuckle on Kylan's hand was bandaged with blood oozing dark through the tape.

"Before the state finals, he tied the practice dummy so many times he wore the skin right off his hands," Galen said.

Kylan jerked away, clambered to his feet, and stomped back to the end of the line. The kid had practiced so hard he'd made his hands bleed, and he still wasn't any smoother than that? As David watched him shuffle away, the light finally dawned.

Shit. How could he, of all people, be so obtuse?

"Kylan's got some challenges," Rusty Chapman had said. And what had Galen said, about how Kylan wasn't any good at regular sports, but in the arena Muddy could even the odds? David had been too busy sulking to pay attention. He should've seen it right off when he first got a close look at the kid, but he'd been too blinded by his own emotions.

Kylan wasn't sloppy or lazy. His body literally wasn't put together quite right, and probably neither was his mind. The telltale signs were written on his face. The smoothness of it, the odd shape to his eyes. Not Down syndrome—David knew firsthand what that looked like—but something that made his life difficult in similar ways. And now, when he'd finally gotten a break, had a little success, David was going to take it all away.

Hell. *Hell*. Like it wouldn't have been bad enough if Kylan was just a regular kid.

As David grabbed the rope, pulled the calf back into place, and held it for the next roper, he could swear he heard faint hoots of laughter from high in the cloudless sky.

David would've said it couldn't get much worse, but as usual, he was wrong. From the minute the kids climbed on their horses, he could see it was going to be a wreck. Kylan was sulking, his whole body radiating resentment. Muddy fed off his mood and turned cranky, pawing and shuffling, mashing into the other horses. Every time Kylan touched the reins, Muddy grabbed the bit in his teeth and flung his head, damn near yanking the kid's arm out of the socket.

David knew the feeling all too well, and he knew

exactly what would come next, because it always did when Muddy got pissy. The horse ran up on the first calf, barely let Kylan throw before he slammed on the brakes, jacking the kid onto the swells of the saddle. The loop landed wide right, in the dirt.

The next calf, Kylan tried to speed up his rope, slapping it at the calf before Muddy could short him out. The loop nailed the calf in the back of the head.

"Follow through, Kylan," Sam yelled helpfully.

Kylan shot him a glare, but on the next calf, he did try to stand up and rope. The loop hadn't even left his hand when Muddy jammed his fronts in the ground, driving the saddle horn square into Kylan's groin. The air busted out of him in an *uff* they could hear back at the chutes. He folded in two, his face going white and then red.

Ouch.

David's privates puckered in sympathy as Kylan yanked on the reins and spun Muddy around. He rode out the gate and around the back of his trailer before sliding off to hunch on the fender. David glanced at Galen, but the older man didn't move. Up in the bleachers, Mary stood, neck craned, but she stayed put. Only the girlfriend—Starr—hustled down the stairs and out to Kylan's aid.

Well, it wasn't like there was anything they could do, other than pat Kylan on the shoulder and remind him to breathe. Some things a man had to suffer alone.

"Who's been straightening Muddy out when he needs it?" David asked Galen. Because it sure wasn't Kylan. The kid was only along for the ride.

Galen hiked a shoulder. "Even an old team roper like me can tune a horse up a little."

"Pretty well from the looks of it." When Galen's eyebrows shot up, David hustled to add, "I mean, he worked great yesterday. Today..." He shrugged. "Sometimes, he's a real asshole."

Galen laughed. "You got that right. Ready to rope some? I wanna see what that white horse can do."

Chapter 11

DAVID TUCKED THE TAIL OF HIS PIGGIN' STRING INTO HIS belt and clenched the small loop between his teeth as he rode Frosty into the box. He was conscious of the circle of spectators hanging over the fences, the boys plus their parents and a few friends, but only in an abstract way. He was used to having an audience. Years of habit had narrowed his focus to horse, rope, and calf.

He nodded, took two quick swings, and threw, already stepping out into his right stirrup as the loop went around the calf's neck, pulling back on the reins with his left hand as he dismounted to speed up Frosty's stop. His boots hit the ground, five long strides, block the calf, flank, tie, hands in the air. Smooth as silk.

He remounted his horse, rode forward to put slack in the rope, his mind replaying the run, picking out flaws as a pair of boys untied the calf. David built a new loop, put his piggin' string in his mouth, rode in the box and did it again. And again. Three runs in a row because, as he'd explained to Galen and the boys, immediate repetition was important to get your mind and body in the groove. At home he would've run twenty head, but these boys had come to rope, not stand around and watch him all day.

When he pulled his hooey on the third calf and threw up his hands, a smattering of applause broke out. David's concentration broke, and when he turned Frosty around to ride back to the end of the arena, he saw every individual face.

Sam grinned like he'd tied the calves himself. Galen nodded approvingly. Kylan and Starr stood beyond the fence in front of the bleachers beside the roping chutes, both sullen-faced, and Mary sat a few rows up beside a blond woman.

It took David's brain a few beats to switch gears, put a name to the familiar face. Hilary Chapman. David raised a hand in greeting, and Rusty's wife responded in kind with the first welcoming smile he'd seen in days. David smiled back. When Rusty was still on the road, Hilary had been like a den mother, always looking out for the younger, single guys like David who didn't have a wife along to be sure they got a decent meal once in a while.

If David ever did get involved with another woman, it would be with someone like Hilary. Sweet, understanding, possessed of the unshakable faith and infinite patience a woman needed to stand behind a man who made his living on the rodeo trail. Plus, she had a decent-paying job and summers off. Didn't get much better for a cowboy. Hilary made killer blueberry pancakes and lousy coffee, and the last time David had seen her, she'd fed breakfast to a whole herd of starving cowboys in Salinas.

It was a day he'd like to forget, and not just because of the crappy coffee.

The memory twisted a dull knife in David's gut. That morning in Salinas had dawned so bright and full of hope. After a miserable winter, he'd finally put a couple decent runs together at a big rodeo, made the short round, drawn a really good calf. He was on the verge of getting back on track.

But he'd fumbled his slack and knocked the calf off its feet so he couldn't get a clean flank, a small mistake that had cost enough time to take him out of the money. As usual, he'd called Emily, looking for comfort. What he got instead had caught him flat-footed, like a double-barreled mule kick to the chest.

"I'm sorry, David. I know rodeo is the only thing you've ever wanted, but I can't take it anymore."

What she'd meant was she couldn't take *him* anymore...and she'd already found a replacement. Hilary had known all the sordid details. Hell, every roper on the pro circuit had known, plus their wives and kids. David's poker face hadn't been any better back then. The echo of the pain and humiliation, the memory of all those sympathetic looks and wordless slaps on the shoulder had the back of his neck going hot even today.

And now here was Hilary, her head close to Mary's, no doubt telling her the whole sorry tale. David couldn't have felt more naked if he was standing in the middle of the arena in his BVDs. He swung off his horse and led Frosty to an open spot along the fence, loosening the cinches and giving him a rub between the ears before flipping the rein around a post.

Hilary got up and came to meet him. "Nice roping."

"Nice calves. If I could run those little pooches everywhere I went, my summer would be going a lot better."

Hilary reached through the fence to squeeze his hand. "It's good to see you, David. Even better to see Muddy."

"He looks great, doesn't he?" David said, not sure whether to return the squeeze, let go, or just stand there like a lump.

"As good as Muddy has ever looked," Hilary said, a teasing gleam in her eye. David laughed.

"Well, I never hauled him 'cause he was pretty. Do you know if Rusty got my message today?"

She shook her head. "He left early to do some fencing on our summer grazing lease, probably won't be back until suppertime, but I'll make sure he checks the machine."

"I'd appreciate it."

She squeezed his hand again. "If you have time, come and rope with Rusty and stay for dinner if you can. Here…" She reached into her pocket, pulled out a folded piece of paper, and handed it to him. "That's our address, if you have GPS. And directions if you don't."

"Thanks. I'll let you know."

She turned and walked back to Mary, who was standing at the bottom of the bleachers talking to Kylan. David caught snatches of the conversation, Mary telling Kylan it was okay, patting his arm. He shook her off. She lowered her voice, put her hand firmly on his shoulder, and talked up at him, her body language fierce.

Kylan shook his head. "I want to go."

"You need to stay, help push calves and run the chute," Mary said.

David glanced over at their trailer. Muddy was tied to the side, unsaddled. Kylan had packed it in for the day. Might as well. He wouldn't accomplish anything until Galen got on Muddy and made a few tune-up runs.

Except it wouldn't be Galen any more; it would be David, and he wouldn't be worried about whether the horse would work for Kylan. They thought Muddy was strong now. Once David got him dialed up to full speed,

Kylan wouldn't even be able to ride him out of the box, let alone rope on him.

Starr tugged on Mary's arm. "Just this once, Mary. He'll make it up next time. He needs a break." Starr shot a glare at David, in case anybody was unclear on what was upsetting Kylan.

Mary hesitated and then sighed. "Okay. Fine. Where are you going?"

"Over to my house," Starr said. "We're gonna watch some videos and stuff."

Stuff? David could imagine what that might involve with a pair of teenagers in an empty house in the middle of the day. They took off before Mary could change her mind. She climbed up to sit beside Hilary, who wrapped an arm around her shoulders and squeezed. David went back to stand beside the roping box as Sam rode up on an ancient buckskin with knobby, arthritic knees.

"Hey, Dave, should I run this one?" Sam asked.

"David," he corrected automatically.

"Huh?"

"My name is David. I don't answer to Dave. Or Davey."

"Why not?"

"Because I prefer David."

"Oh." Sam's forehead creased. "I don't like it when people call me Sammy."

"Then say so. A man should at least get to decide what name he answers to."

Sam looked startled, then thoughtful, as if the idea was growing on him. "Okay. Should I run this calf, *David*?"

David grinned. Cheeky little brat. "Go for it."

He glanced over and found Mary staring at him, a

perturbed crease between her eyebrows. Their eyes met, held for moment, that same electric charge crackling in the air. The chute banged open, and the calf ducked around to the left and nearly over the top of David. He shooed it away, barking, "Stop, Sam."

Sam stopped his horse, kicking up a swirl of dust that the breeze tossed in David's face. *Geezus. Was it ever not some kind of windy here?*

David walked over to the roping box, gesturing. "That happened because you let your horse break wide out of the corner, instead of straight in behind the calf. A good run starts right here..."

For the moment he forgot about everything but what he wanted the boys to understand. This was his place in the world. Here, inside the arena fence, he knew exactly what needed to be done and how to do it. The rest could wait.

Chapter 12

THE ROPING SESSION EVOLVED INTO A LESSON ON HORSE-manship, the basic skills David's dad and his uncle had pounded into his head while he'd fidgeted in his saddle the same as these kids, impatient to get to the good part. But they listened, did as they were told to the best of their ability. As the day wore on, they relaxed, slapping each other on the back for a decent run, dishing out a good-natured ribbing when it didn't go so well.

Each time David looked up, Mary was there on the nearest end of the bleachers, watching but never alone, even though Hilary had left after half an hour. First, her seat was taken by a teenaged girl who talked fast, with a lot of hand gestures. Mary nodded along, somehow managing to give the girl her complete attention while still keeping one eye on the arena.

"So can you help us?" the girl asked. "Please?"

"Sure. As long as all I have to do is auction off the pies and not make them."

"Thank you. You're the best." The girl gave Mary a hug and then bounced off to share the good news with a gaggle of other girls lounging around on the bleachers, trying to look cool despite the wind and dust.

The seat next to Mary didn't have a chance to cool off before another butt was planted on it, this time a boy no more than eight. He had a fat, fluffy Australian shepherd puppy cuddled against his chest and offered it for Mary's inspection.

"What's its name?" she asked.

"George. Like the pig in the cartoon. 'Cause he's my favorite."

"But...your puppy is a girl."

"Yeah. So?"

"So...um, that's a great name." Her eyes sparkled with humor, and her mouth curled into a tender smile as she stroked the puppy's head. She laughed as it nipped at her fingers. David sidled in closer, leaning on the fence nearest where she sat, pretending his attention was glued to the action in the arena while he shamelessly spied on her. *Hey, the better you know your enemy...*

"Can I bring her for show-and-tell, Miss Mary? Please? She's so little and cute."

Mary tousled the boy's mop of brown curls. "School doesn't start for two more months, sweetie. She'll be half grown."

"Oh." The boy frowned, thinking it over. "But I want them to see how cute she is now."

"How 'bout I take a picture, and we'll put it on my computer in the classroom?" Mary offered. She pulled out her phone and took a few shots, then the boy was off, thumping down the bleachers.

David dragged his attention back to his students, stepping out in front of the chutes to stop the next roper before he rode in the box. "Your reins are too long. Shorten them up, and hold them down close to your horse's neck. That'll help you get up and over the front of your saddle coming out of the box."

Satisfied that the kid understood, David retreated to his spot on the fence as a round-faced little girl in braids and a grubby pink T-shirt plopped down next to Mary, clutching a *Cat in the Hat* book. "Hi, Mith Mary," she lisped. "I been practithing my reading, juth like you thaid. Wanna hear?"

"You betcha."

Dr. Seuss was his cousin Adam's favorite, so David knew most of the book by heart. The little girl stumbled through the rhymes, so painfully slow that he had to clench his teeth to stop from shouting out the right words. Mary murmured encouragement and gentle prompts. When they finally, blessedly, reached the end, she and the girl traded high fives.

"That's amazing, Shalea. I bet if you keep practicing every day, by the time school starts, you'll be able to stay in the first-grade classroom for reading."

The girl's plump bottom lip poked out. "I like being in your room, Mith Mary."

"But you'll get to see your friends more in Mrs. Murphy's room." The girl pooched out her cheeks, thinking it over. "Do I still get to thay the "Good Morning" poem every day?"

"Hmm." Mary made a thoughtful face. "How about Monday and Wednesday? Brendan and Julene like to have a turn, too."

"I thay it better."

"You are pretty tough to beat." Mary's mouth twitched ever so slightly. She put out a hand. "I have to be fair to everybody, though, so...do we have a deal?"

"Oh, aw wight." The girl gave an exaggerated sigh but accepted the handshake. "Deal."

Mary laughed and gave her a hug. "Tell your mama I'm very proud of both of you for all your hard work."

A sharp elbow jabbed David in the ribs, making him jump. He looked down to find Sam smirking at him. "You here to rope, or just check out the chicks?"

A couple of the other kids snickered. David felt his face heating up.

"I was waitin' on you," he told Sam and sent the whole bunch of them down to bring the calves back from the catch pen.

The rest of the afternoon was more of the same. David tried to keep his focus inside the arena fence, but he was fascinated by the endless stream of people who stopped to chat with Mary. Many appeared to be students or their parents, but one woman looked closer to eighty than eight, leaning heavily on a cane as she hoisted herself up the steps.

"You gotta talk to my granddaughter about the boy of hers," the woman declared, loud enough that David didn't have to try to listen. "She don't want to think there might be somethin' wrong with him, and she sure don't want to hear it from me."

She plunked onto the bleachers beside Mary and went on—and on, and on—about all the reasons she feared her great-grandson had a learning disorder, obviously not concerned about the boy's privacy. Or his mother's.

When she paused for breath, Mary patted her hand. "I'll spend some time in his kindergarten class this fall. If I see anything that concerns me, I'll talk to his mom about doing some screenings."

The old lady thumped her cane on the metal bleachers.

"You make sure of it. I don't want him falling through the cracks."

"He won't." Mary's voice was honed steel.

David believed her. The old woman must've too, because she *hmpffed* her approval, ordered Mary to help her down the bleachers, and then stumped off to inflict her opinion on some other poor soul.

As Mary started back up the bleachers, she glanced over and caught David watching. She raised her eyebrows. He gestured toward the old lady, rolled his eyes. Mary smiled and shrugged. For an instant, they were just two people sharing a small joke. Her face was relaxed, her eyes warm, the way she must be in real life.

Then the shutters came down. She ducked her head, turned away, and moved to the other end of the bleachers to join a trio of women near her age who'd been observing both her and David with open curiosity.

It was near suppertime when Galen called a halt. While the boys unsaddled horses and stowed their gear, David accepted a cold bottle of water from Galen and took a long, grateful gulp, rinsing the grit out of his throat. The bleachers were deserted, the parents and girlfriends who'd tagged along with the boys straggling back to their rigs.

"I don't s'pose you're staying a while?" Sam asked, giving him the puppy-dog eyes again.

David shook his head. "I have to leave day after tomorrow."

"Too bad." Sam's gaze slid to Muddy dozing beside Mary's trailer, and he lowered his voice. "Are you taking the horse with you?"

Everyone stopped, waiting for his answer. David was acutely aware that Mary could hear every word.

"We're still working out the details," he said, and went to help load the calves.

Chapter 13

"HAD ENOUGH?" GALEN ASKED, LATCHING THE REAR DOOR on the stock trailer and waving the driver to pull out.

"Yeah." David swiped an arm across his face, grimaced at the smear of dirt on his sleeve. He could feel the grit between his teeth when he bit down. "This wind wears a person down."

"What wind? This here's just a nice breeze." Galen flashed a quick grin and then glanced at his watch. "I better get going. Cissy's still in Great Falls at the hospital with her aunt, so I got all the chores to do."

So did everyone else, judging by the way they'd scattered, headed home to family, chores, dinner. The stab of homesickness was sharp, familiar. Everyone had someplace to be, someone to be with. David glanced up and got an unexpected pang when he saw the bleachers were now deserted. Stupid. Of course Mary was leaving. He wasn't sure why she'd stayed this long.

She came around the corner of the stock pens, marched over to where they stood, and looked David straight in the eye, her expression a perfect match to Galen's poker face. "Are we done for now?"

"Looks like," Galen said.

"I want to see where you live," David blurted.

Her eyes widened, startled, then her gaze shifted to Galen, who frowned at David.

"Where you're taking Muddy," David corrected

before they called JoJo the cop to come arrest him for stalking. "I need to know where you're keeping him."

"Oh." That little pucker appeared between Mary's brows as she considered the demand.

"I don't know…" Galen began.

"All he has to do is ask at the Town Pump, and someone would tell him where we live." Mary leveled a cool-eyed stare at David. "He can ride out with me, and I'll drop him back by here after we get Muddy put up."

"I have time," Galen said.

"No need." Mary transferred her gaze to Galen, and some kind of silent message passed between them. Galen nodded. Either David had met muster, or Mary was nonverbally promising to blast him with pepper spray if he got out of line. Or a shotgun. A woman who'd been to war would know how to pull a trigger.

Galen extended a hand to David. "Appreciate you takin' the time with the boys. They need all the help they can get."

"They've got a lot of try, and they pay attention," David said, accepting the handshake. "There's some real talent in that bunch."

Galen grunted. "Talent ain't the problem. There's a dozen guys on this rez who rope good enough to win the world if they had some money behind 'em or could stay off the bottle and the rest of that shit." He shook his head in disgust. "Don't know if I'll see you tomorrow. Gotta go to Great Falls to pick up Cissy and her aunt, won't be home 'til evening."

With any luck, David would be gone by then, but he only nodded.

"I'll load Muddy," Mary said and turned to walk that direction.

Galen climbed in his pickup, backed out with a final lift of his hand in farewell. David circled around to the nearest spigot and scrubbed the calf manure from his hands the best he could in the icy water, then wiped them dry on his jeans.

Mary fired up her pickup as David walked toward her and had it in gear before his door was completely shut, obviously looking forward to this quality time with him. She didn't have to worry about making conversation. Now that they were alone, his tongue was tied tighter than the best wrap and hooey he'd ever put on a calf.

She swung the rig around and headed for the exit, her gaze glued to the road. The pickup was a four-door dually, diesel engine and manual transmission, at least ten years older than David's but with half the miles. The interior was scuffed and worn but clean except for the inevitable layer of dust.

She turned right out of the fairgrounds, away from town and toward the mountains on the same highway David had jogged that morning. Clouds churned on the horizon, and the wind whipped streamers of snow into the sky above the peaks.

"Gotta wonder how Lewis and Clark ever figured they could cross those," David said.

"They didn't. At least not here. Meriwether Lewis tangled with a band of Blackfeet and had to run south for his life." She cut him a sly glance. "They were trying to steal his horses. Guess it's genetic."

"Uh—"

She laughed, soft and dry. "That was a joke."

Oh. David scraped at a smear of calf snot on his jeans

with his thumbnail. "Thanks for bringing me along. I'll sleep easier."

Mary was silent for a long count of ten. Then she huffed a sigh. "He's your horse. You have a right to know where he is."

She flipped on her turn signal, slowed, and David nearly swore out loud. Son of a bitch. It was the house with the tipi. He'd stood right there beside Mary's mailbox only a few hours earlier, not more than fifty yards from Muddy.

The narrow driveway was pitted and scarce on gravel, but the fences on either side were in perfect repair. The pasture beyond was emerald green, scattered with clumps of willows and some other kind of brushy trees he couldn't name. Twenty acres, he guessed, surrounding the compact manufactured home and a red-tin barn big enough to house a couple of stalls and a tack room.

The deck was freshly stained, the yard fenced and mowed, and the tipi even more gorgeous up close. The buffalo were painted in dark brown, the door flap decorated with handprints of red, yellow and blue. In the broad, black band at the very top, white dots formed the Big Dipper.

Mary followed his line of sight and smiled slightly. "That was my college graduation present from Galen and Cissy. Said I'd always have a home, even on a teacher's salary." She parked in front of the barn and turned off the pickup, swiveling in her seat to face him full on. "So. This is it."

She waited a beat as if he might want to comment. When he didn't, she popped the latch on her seat belt and climbed out. David followed, meeting her at the back door of the trailer. He hesitated, not sure of the proper etiquette. Was it pushy to offer to unload the horse? Rude to stand back and make her do it?

While he debated, Mary flipped the safety catch on the door and swung it open. The trailer was built to haul up to three horses, but the stall dividers had been removed, leaving a single open space. At the front, Muddy bowed his neck and rooted impatiently at the halter rope.

"Yeah, yeah, I'm coming." Mary shoved his nose around so he didn't smack her upside the head while she untied him. The instant she pulled the knot free, he fell back, scrambling out of the trailer and sending the gravel flying when he hit the ground. She gave the halter rope a hard yank to stop him from taking off and shot David an exasperated look. "More of your training?"

"No. He learned that all by himself."

And damned if David hadn't missed even the irritating parts. He held out a hand for the lead rope. Mary hesitated and then reluctantly passed it over, as if he might grab Muddy and run. Not that he wasn't tempted. He reached up instead, intending to pat Muddy on the neck, but the horse dodged away, flattening his ears.

"I wanted to name him Happy. 'Cause of his personality and all. Galen and Otis had to talk hard to persuade me he'd work for Kylan." Mary crossed her arms, eyeing Muddy. "Whatever possessed you to buy him?"

"He was cheap."

"I can't imagine why," she said drily.

David chuckled, letting Muddy tug him toward the open door of the barn. "A neighbor asked me to break a couple of colts and offered me Muddy in payment. I figured I'd start him roping and sell him to a kid or a weekend roper, make a few bucks."

"Guess he had different ideas."

"He usually does." He yanked on the halter rope, forcing Muddy to pause inside the door while David checked out the barn. There were two large box stalls and space for a stack of hay bales. "You don't have other horses?"

"Not here. We had to take Kylan's old kid horse over to Galen's place. Mutt kept picking on him. Then Kylan decided he was lonely and brought a goat home, figuring it could help keep the knapweed cleaned up out of the pasture, but Mutt—um, Muddy—ran it through the fence."

David winced. "He's a hateful little creature."

"He's been a miracle for Kylan." The soft declaration brought David up short. Before he could sort out an answer, Mary spun around. "I'll go unhook the trailer."

David would've watched her walk away—watched a little closer than he should—but Muddy wasn't much interested in standing around admiring the scenery. He rammed his nose against the halter with all his might, nearly yanking David off his feet.

"I was hoping they'd taught you some manners," he said.

Muddy gave him an eye roll, plowed through the open gate of the first stall, and spun around to glare at David, demanding that he take the halter off pronto. David did, then swung the gate shut and fetched a flake of hay. The metal trash can beside the haystack held oats, so he scooped up a coffee can full and dumped it into a bucket tied inside Muddy's stall. The horse jammed his head clear to the bottom, stuffing his mouth as full as possible, then chewed furiously, oats drooling out the sides of his mouth.

Typical Muddy. So exactly the same, every obnoxious inch. David drew a deep, shaky breath. All the memories and feelings he'd been squashing for the past two days balled up to slam into him like a boulder. He folded his arms on the top of the gate, leaning heavily as he gazed upon the horse he'd never expected to see again.

"All this time I was worried sick, and you were living it up. Lounging around fat and sassy in your own private kingdom." David's vision blurred, and the knot in his throat swelled. "You sure didn't miss me."

Emotion got the best of him, welling up and threatening to dribble down his cheeks. He swiped an arm across his damp eyes. The hell with luck and karma and all that crap. He'd scrape up that five grand if he had to sell his soul, the rodeo gods be damned. He could not leave Muddy. Never again.

The scuff of footsteps on gravel alerted David to Mary's return. He swiped at his face again and straightened—but not quick enough judging by the way she hesitated, poised on the threshold like she might turn and run from a grown man's tears. Sunlight angled across the barn door, turning her spiky hair into a golden halo and highlighting the delicate angles of her face, softened by what might have been sympathy.

"It's not just about the roping, is it?" she asked.

"What do you mean?"

She shook her head, dropping her chin to stare at the ground. "I figured for someone like you, a pro, a horse would be a…tool, I guess. What you need to get the job done. But the way you talk to him, touch him…it's more than business, the way you feel about him."

"Yeah. So?" David wasn't sure whether to be offended or embarrassed.

"So…nothing. I didn't realize, that's all." She squared her shoulders, met his eye. "Ready to go?"

No, but he doubted she'd let him roll out a sleeping bag in the haystack where he could keep a constant eye on Muddy. As he walked out of the barn, she retreated, keeping a sizable distance between them.

"I'm not going to attack you," he said, irritated with her skittishness, the contrast between the softness he'd seen earlier with her students and friends and the brittleness he saw now.

She stopped, her pointed chin coming up. "I'm not afraid of you."

"Coulda fooled me."

"I'm not scared. You're just very…um…" Her hands sketched out a large, squarish shape in the air.

"Harmless. I swear." He raised his palms in the classic gesture of surrender, but the shadows that came into her eyes called him a liar. He couldn't argue. Whether he intended to or not, he'd already wounded Kylan's heart, and it was only going to get worse. He grimaced, correcting himself. "I would never hurt anyone on purpose."

Her gaze traveled over him, but her eyes didn't meet his. "You're big enough to do some damage."

Yeah. Sure. And that humiliating night at the bar, he'd had his butt kicked by a man less than half his size. "I'm usually not this cranky."

"Me neither." Her smile flickered like sunlight on water; then her expression went somber. "And you haven't been all that cranky, considering. If it were me, in your place… Well, some shit would be flying."

He shifted on his feet, not entirely proud of the way he'd behaved, especially with Kylan. "I'll get my horse back one way or another, and I hate being a jerk."

Her eyebrows went pointy. "Well, that's refreshing. The world could use more people who don't go around being assholes just for the fun of it."

"I hear that," he said, and their gazes got tangled up again, another zap of connection that had him taking a step forward.

Mary stepped back. "We should go."

Yeah. They should. Before he gave in to the urge to keep moving closer. He didn't try to strike up a conversation on the short drive back to town. What was that old saying? Keep your mouth shut and people will only think you're an idiot. Open it, you'll prove 'em right. Best to just let Mary assume.

But he wanted to talk to her. See more of the softness, that unexpected sense of humor, those mercurial smiles. She was so many things—soldier, teacher, surrogate mother, horsenapper. How did all those pieces fit into such a tight little bundle?

Frosty lifted his head and nickered as Mary pulled up beside David's rig. The Stampede Grounds were once again deserted. David glanced at the dashboard clock. Quarter to six. Four hours to kill before dark. A solitary dinner of cold cuts on stale bread was all he had to look forward to.

"So…" Mary said.

Right. He pushed the door open and stepped out, once again at a loss for words. Big surprise. "I guess we'll talk tomorrow?"

"I have training at the college for the next two days,

eight 'til four. We have to implement a new set of national tests this year, and I got stuck on the work group. If… when…you decide what you're gonna do, you have Yolanda's number. She'll take care of the arrangements."

"I'd rather deal with you."

Mary fixed her gaze on the center of the steering wheel. "Not much sense hiring an attorney if I don't let her do her job."

"That sounds like Yolanda talking."

Mary remained stubbornly silent. David hung there for another long moment, his hand hooked on the top of the door, not wanting her to leave, no reason to keep her. Better to stay clear anyway. The closer he got to her and Kylan, the worse he'd feel about taking Muddy.

"I…um, thanks for the ride."

She nodded. He forced himself to step back, shut the door, turn his back. He took three leaden steps before he heard her door open.

"David?"

He whipped around to face her, hope warring with apprehension. What would she hit him with now?

She tried a smile, uncertain as her voice. "I was wondering… I'm not in the mood to sit around the house alone. I thought I'd drive over to East Glacier, grab a sandwich, and go on up to Two Medicine." Her teeth worked her bottom lip, nervous. "Do you…um, would you like to come along?"

Surprise played in his favor, silencing him for a beat so he didn't sound quite so pathetically eager when he said, "Can I clean up first?"

Chapter 14

HE FOUND A DARK-GRAY HENLEY STUFFED IN THE BACK OF the bottom drawer in his trailer, another winter holdover. It had shrunk in the wash and was a little snug, but the tight fit stretched most of the wrinkles out of the waffle knit. The cleanest of the dirty jeans in his laundry bag would have to do. At least they didn't have calf manure on them.

Before dressing, he scrubbed the dirt off his face and neck and wetted his hair down to get rid of the worst of the hat head. His five-o'clock shadow was more like a blackout, but shaving would be too damn obvious, so he let it go.

He reached for his jacket, then realized he'd left it in Galen's pickup. The afternoon was still warm, but he assumed it would cool off in a hurry when the sun started to drop. The only other coat suitable for evening temperatures was his contestant jacket from the ten days of torture known as his trip to the National Finals Rodeo. No question it was clean, since he'd shoved it clear to the back of the closet before he'd left Las Vegas and never taken it out again. Wearing it now felt both humiliating and boastful, but better than freezing.

Outside, he found Mary sitting on the fence with Frosty's head in her lap, his eyes closed in ecstasy as she scratched behind his ears. She tossed David a smile that softened the angles of her face, warmed her eyes, the kind he'd seen her share with her students. "At least you have one nice horse."

"Too nice."

She cocked her head, questioning.

"Frosty doesn't have a competitive bone in his body," David said. "No killer instinct."

"And Muddy definitely does."

"In spades."

She considered that and then nodded. "I can see how that would matter in a tie-down horse. They have to do an awful lot on their own." She smoothed Frosty's silky forelock. "He's pretty good, though. Will you sell him now?"

"He's not mine. And he's not for sale. My uncle raised him, and my cousin Adam loves him to death." And once Adam got attached, he wasn't capable of letting go. David would never have dreamed of asking to borrow Frosty. The idea had no doubt been planted by his uncle, but the offer had been Adam's. Sweet, empathetic Adam, who had agreed to let Frosty go because he didn't want David to be sad anymore about losing Muddy. He'd been so proud, so determined, David couldn't possibly say no. Even then, he'd had to temper his guilt by bringing Adam a fat, wriggly Labrador puppy to fill the void.

"How old is your cousin?" Mary asked as she climbed down from the fence.

"Thirty-two." Forever going on nine years old.

Out on the highway, Mary made a right onto U.S. 2 to East Glacier. Once they'd climbed the hill out of Browning, rounded a curve, and were rolling straight toward the mountains, she grabbed her cell phone from the center console and offered it to David.

"Look up the Huckleberry Café in the contacts," she said. "If we call in our order, we won't have to stand around waiting." He did as he was told, feeling weird about scrolling through the names listed under H, even if she didn't seem to mind the invasion of her privacy.

"What's on the menu?" he asked as he dialed the number for the café.

"Sandwiches, mostly. On homemade bread. I'm a fan of the smoked turkey and bacon with ranch sauce. And the huckleberry pie, of course."

Since his mouth watered at the description, he ordered the same for himself. Then he stowed the phone in the console and tried to figure out what to do with his hands. He finally settled for clasping them together in his lap while he stared out the window at the rolling green hills, the jagged peaks. No wonder people came from all over the world to visit this place.

The silence began to play on his nerves, so he asked the least personal of the hundred questions whirling around in his head. "You teach special education?"

"Yes."

He waited, but she didn't elaborate.

"You like it?"

"Yes."

So much for that conversation starter. He stared out at the scenery some more, imagining what it would be like to wake up every morning in that cabin on the hillside with that view right in his face. Cold, he decided, exposed to the west wind like it was. Must be a summer home.

"Is that what you always wanted to do? Teach?"

"I toyed around with a few other things, but I wanted

to come home, and education is one of the few degrees that almost guarantees a person a job here." At his questioning glance, she shrugged. "Hard to keep teachers on the reservation."

Yeah, he supposed it would be, between the isolation, that interminable west wind, and the culture shock. "Sure is pretty."

"We like it." She shot him a curious glance. "Did you go to college?"

"Just a farrier program at a trade school."

"Was there book work?" she asked, genuine interest sparking in her eyes.

"Some. Anatomy and stuff."

"Oh." She sighed, disappointed. "I guess that won't work."

"Thinking about taking up a new career?"

She snorted, flexing one arm. "Sure. I can see me propping up a horse. No. Kylan is interested, but anatomy…" She shook her head. "He struggles with book work."

"He doesn't have to go to a school. Someone could teach him. Like an apprenticeship."

She nodded. "I thought about asking our horseshoer if Kylan could follow him around, but I don't think he has the patience."

"Some people aren't cut out to be teachers."

She tilted her head, eyeing him. "You are."

"Me?" David said, taken aback. "Teach what?"

"Whatever you want. You're good with kids."

He tried to picture himself in a classroom and shook his head. "I don't think they make sweater vests in my size."

She gave another of those quicksilver laughs, amused with him, not at him, and he relaxed a little.

"You never wanted to do anything but rope?" she asked.

"Not that I can remember."

"No backup plan?"

"The horseshoeing keeps us fed during the tough stretches. But otherwise…" He shook his head.

"Some people shoe horses for a living."

"Not me." He waved a hand down his body. "I have to fold up like an accordion to get underneath them, especially the small ones like Muddy. Plays hell with my back if I do more than half a dozen horses a week."

That thoughtful pucker appeared between her eyebrows again. "You didn't figure that out soon as you started?"

"Pretty much. But it was something I could do to fill in the gaps while I was on the rodeo trail."

"What about the ranch?" she asked. "No plans to take over for your parents?"

He shook his head. "I'm second in line. My older sister and her husband are partners with my parents."

"You don't sound like you mind too much."

"Not really." He'd always liked not being tied down by expectations, but he hadn't realized how spoiled he'd been, relying on his parents to be there to bail him out… until they couldn't, thanks to the drought and his own poor choices.

"So you really are working without a net," Mary said.

He slid a fingertip along the armrest, studied the results, and then rubbed off the dust on his jeans. "I thought it was better that way. All in, you know? No quitting when the going gets tough, because there's nothing else."

It had seemed like a good idea when he was eighteen. And until Muddy had disappeared, his rodeo career had gone pretty much as planned. Junior rodeo titles, high school titles, earning his pro card and qualifying for the Wilderness Circuit Finals at nineteen. Every goal ticked off his list right on schedule. Yeah, it took four years to break into the top tier, qualify for the Finals, but each of those years had been better than the one before. Success had felt inevitable.

Young, arrogant, oblivious. He wouldn't mind being that clueless again.

"Well, it worked," Mary said.

David blinked. "How's that?"

"You're still out there, entering up and staying afloat. Do you think you would be if you'd had an easier option?"

Yes. Of course. He wouldn't have quit. Couldn't. Could he? Then again, what if that job at the feed store had worked out? Paid a little better, been a little less monotonous…

At the thought of it, his entire soul shriveled in horror. No. That life wouldn't be living at all. "There is no other option for me."

"Well. I hope it works out, then."

Yeah. Him too.

They rolled across a canyon deep enough to make David a tad queasy when he looked down, then rounded the curve into East Glacier. He'd barely noticed the town when he'd barreled through the day before, intent on reaching Browning as quick as possible. Plus, there wasn't a lot to see.

The highway was also Main Street, with all of the businesses on the east side of the street. Motels on either end flanked a market that advertised hand-scooped ice cream cones. The cars parked out front had mostly out-of-state plates, and the people loitering along the sidewalk had tourist all but printed on their souvenir T-shirts.

On his right, David could see nothing but a railroad embankment, a freight train towing a long line of container cars rumbling well above their heads. The highway dipped, and Mary turned right into a tunnel under the tracks.

They emerged into a different world.

Directly ahead, a huge expanse of emerald-green lawn stretched to a wood-beamed hotel built like a massive chalet. The balconies were hung with pots of bright-colored flowers. Shirtless boys and bare-legged girls tossed a Frisbee around, while hikers dozed in the sun, using their packs as pillows. Mary slowed to let a golf cart cross in front of them.

"There's a golf course?" David asked, amazed. All of this, so close to Browning and all of…that.

"Yep. You play?"

"No. You?"

"A few times a year." She tossed him a smile that twinkled with mischief. "It's a fun course, as long as you remember the bears have the right of way."

Past the hotel was a haphazard string of restaurants, rental cabins, and houses. Mary wedged the big pickup into a cramped parking lot beside the Huckleberry Café. "Be right back."

She was gone before David could dig out money for his dinner. He considered following, then sat back to take in the scenery instead. On the patio in front of the restaurant, a girl with greasy blond dreadlocks pounded her fist on a picnic table as she pontificated at a guy in high-tech nylon hiking gear, who seemed mildly amused by her fervor. Ten feet away, a silver-haired couple shared a piece of pie, looking like an L. L. Bean commercial in color-coordinated active wear. Only the waitress appeared to be Native.

Mary came out with a white paper bag, exchanged a few words and a one-armed hug with the waitress before crossing over to the pickup. David liked the way she walked. Brisk, no-nonsense strides, a woman who had places to go and didn't care who was watching her get there.

She passed the bag to him over the console and climbed in after. "We can go to the hotel if you want, have a picnic on the back patio. Great view."

"Better than the other place? What did you call it?"

"Two Medicine. And, no, not better, but closer. I thought you might be tired of sitting in a pickup."

Funny. If anyone had asked, he would've said yes, but he hadn't noticed the miles he'd put on with Galen that morning. Definitely didn't mind a few more with Mary. "Not if you're driving."

She looked at him, really looked, like she was trying to decide if he was being funny or what. When their eyes met, he got another jolt. *Whoa, yeah, definitely a spark there*. Which was the last thing he should be thinking about this woman. As if she wasn't enough trouble.

She grabbed a pair of sunglasses off the dash and shoved them on her face, hiding her eyes. Or just hiding, period. Keeping her distance. Smart. He should try it.

Chapter 15

THE NARROW, SHOULDERLESS ROAD DIPPED AND WOUND around the base of the mountain, through groves of stunted, twisted aspens, their trunks a dizzying maze of paper-white bark and black lines. Once David saw a dark shape that might have been a bear, but judging by the occasional splatters of manure on the highway, it was more likely a cow.

A valley opened to their left, and Mary turned again, onto a highway that skirted an earthen dam and then crawled above the long, narrow, man-made lake beyond. At the gates marking the Glacier National Park boundary, she stopped and held up a tribal ID. The ranger inside the toll booth waved them on through.

"One of the benefits of being Blackfeet," she said. "Free pass to the park."

"Handy," David said. "You come up here a lot?"

"As much as we can, but it never seems like enough."

The highway circled the head of the lake and then tunneled into stands of towering pines. The grass beneath was sprinkled with wildflowers—white, yellow, some kind of bluebells. David could only put a name to the flame-red Indian paintbrushes.

And there was water. Everywhere. Trickling down every rock face, splashing down every gully, fed by the melting snow. Once again, David's chest ached at the contrast between this and the scorched earth back home.

They crossed a river, climbed a set of hairpin curves, and topped a rise to reveal a view that made David's breath catch. The sapphire-blue lake below was roughly circular, framed by sheer-rock peaks. One mountain thrust out into the middle, a towering pyramid carved by the park's namesake glaciers, backed by palisades of rock crowned with stubborn fingers of rock yet to be toppled by the unrelenting assault of the elements.

David caught a whiff of woodsmoke, saw it curling up from the trees in what a sign declared to be the campground. Beside the lake, another chalet-style log building served as the camp store. People strolled along the road between store and campground in pairs and families, licking ice cream cones, slurping drinks, settling in for the evening.

Mary chose the parking lot along the shore. A dock stretched into the water, and as David watched, a low-slung wooden tour boat pulled alongside and tied up to unload passengers. Nearby, rental canoes and rowboats were upended on the rocky beach. Far out on the lake, a pair of kayaks cruised across the gentle chop, reduced to neon-yellow dots by the mass of the mountain behind them.

"This is amazing." David gawked like all the rest of the tourists as he stepped out of the pickup. The narrow strip of beach stretched off in either direction—along the tree line to their left and past the camp store on the right—nearly to the base of yet another mountain where the lake narrowed, funneling into a small river.

"I'd expect a Colorado boy would get his fill of mountains," Mary said.

He shook his head. "I'm a flatlander. Pure prairie out

where we live. We were lucky if we visited the mountains two or three times a year growing up. And now…" He shrugged. "I pass through a lot of scenery. Don't get to stop much."

"You could make a point."

"It's hard when you're hauling horses. They aren't real popular in the campgrounds."

"Hadn't thought of that." She stared out over the water. "Still, I bet you see some amazing places, even passing through. I've never been outside of Montana much."

"Except Afghanistan?"

Her mouth curled down at the corner. "Not exactly a scenic tour."

"What's it like?"

"Hot. Dirty. And it smells." She wrinkled her nose, skimmed a hand over her nape. "My hair was long when I was deployed. After two weeks of grit and sweat, I was in the base barber shop having it cut off. Never got around to growing it out again."

David squinted, tried to imagine her hair long. Picturing her in camouflage and size four Army boots was easy. And oddly sexy. He'd never considered macho women his type. "I bet it looks better now. Short hair suits you."

"Thanks." She flushed slightly but didn't glance in his direction, ignoring what might have been an attempt at flirting.

He hadn't meant it that way—he didn't think—so he followed her lead and pretended he'd kept the observation to himself. "Why did you join the army?"

"College tuition, mostly."

The obvious answer. Which led to the obvious question. "Were you scared when you got deployed?"

"I wasn't thrilled." She tilted her head back, staring up at the mountaintop as it shredded a wispy cloud. "I tried to go into it with a positive attitude. Told myself it would make me smarter. Stronger."

"Did it?"

"I guess. It's just…it's different than you expect. Not all in a bad way. I might've signed on for another stint in the National Guard, but Kylan—" She tossed a look over her shoulder. "Someone probably told you by now about his mother."

David nodded. "How long will she be…gone?"

"Forever if she keeps it up." Mary's jaw went tight, her voice sour. "She was on probation for possession when she got busted for dealing. Then she got more time tacked on for assaulting her cellmate and again for possession inside."

David whistled. "Does she want to be locked up the rest of her life?"

"Like the posters say, there's a reason they call it dope. And she's just plain mean. Takes after her dad." Mary started for the beach, deserted in favor of campsites and cookouts.

David grabbed the bag of food and followed. "She's older than you?"

"Seven years." Mary picked up a flat rock, skipped it thirty yards out across the waves with a flick of her arm. "Her dad is a snake when he's sober, downright scary when he's drunk. My mom was only with him a few months, and he never wanted anything to do with Lori. Didn't matter, though. The mean was bred right into her."

"You aren't close?"

She snorted. "Not even a little."

"So why'd you take Kylan in?"

"He's family," she said as if that explained everything.

"What about your mother?"

"She's got health problems." Mary flicked another rock out over the water, watched it skip. "There was no way she could take on a twelve-year-old boy, and Kylan isn't exactly low maintenance, growing up the way he did."

"Is he the reason you went into special ed?"

Mary froze in the act of picking up another rock and slowly straightened. "Why do you say that?"

"My cousin, the one who owns Frosty, has Down syndrome. You learn to see the signs."

She tossed the rock, watched it disappear, then glanced over her shoulder. "I can see why Frosty's not for sale. They don't take goodbyes very well, these kids."

David ducked his head, guilt grinding like broken glass in his gut.

Mary jammed her hands into the center pocket of her sweatshirt. "That was a cheap shot. I didn't mean it to be. I was talking about the kids I teach, not Kylan." She dragged in a deep breath, let it out slowly. "Officially, he's been diagnosed with fetal alcohol syndrome, but Lori never met a high she didn't like and saw no reason being pregnant should ruin her fun. It's a wonder the poor kid survived, let alone being reasonably functional."

David shifted the bag of sandwiches to his left hand, picked up a rock, curled his fingers around the smooth, water-worn shape. "If you're trying to make me feel better, it's not working."

"I wasn't… I didn't mean…" She cursed and kicked a rock. "You asked. I answered."

"That wasn't a play for sympathy?"

Her chin shot up. "The last thing Kylan needs is pity. People feel sorry for you, it's the same as saying you're weak. You've got no control."

"Does he?"

"Yes!" The word hissed out. She stood arrow straight, her stance defying all that mountains' majesty at her back to overshadow her. "He's impulsive and sometimes he flies off the handle, but he'd never hurt a fly."

"You trust him and Starr together?" David asked. "He's damn near a full-grown man."

Her mouth twisted into a tight smile. "I've lectured him into the ground about using condoms, and Starr's grandmother marches her down to the clinic every three months for birth-control shots. Says she refuses to be a great-grandmother before she turns forty-five, and she's not raising another grandbaby."

Mary picked up another rock, sent it skipping across the waves. "Starr is a smart girl. If I could just get her to believe…" She rolled her shoulders, as if trying to shed the frustration. "She sees her mother and her grandmother scraping by, watches her friends get pregnant on purpose because in some warped way it makes them feel loved and important, and she thinks that's the best she can expect."

"She's got you for a role model."

"I don't count." She waved a hand in front of her face. "I don't look Indian. People off the reservation don't treat me the way they treat someone who looks like Starr."

"And she figures that made it easy for you to go to college?"

"Easier." Mary stood her ground as a rogue wave sloshed right up to the toes of her running shoes. "First thing I did was learn to talk like the white girls so I could blend. Starr doesn't have that option."

David wanted to argue, but who was he to say? He'd never been a minority. He turned the rock in his hand one more time, then reared back and threw it as far as he could out into the turquoise water.

"I appreciate you taking the time to work with the boys today," she said. "It's good for them to spend time with someone like you."

"Like me?" David echoed.

"You have a dream, and you stick with it. You have no idea what it means to a kid like Sam to have a man he admires look him in the eye and say he doesn't have to let other people tell him who he's gonna be."

"I wasn't trying to preach."

"That makes it even better." Her smile caught him off guard and sent a pulse of warmth through him like a stray beam of sunshine breaking through the clouds, and just as fleeting. "These kids see so much failure. People who give up or never even try. It's contagious. But so is success, so we try to expose them to it on a regular basis."

Success? She must be thinking of someone else. "I haven't exactly set the world on fire."

"You bought that jacket at the Salvation Army?" She cocked her head toward the pickup, where they'd left their coats.

"No." He gave a stiff shrug. "I qualified for the National Finals once. Big deal."

"Yeah. It is. Ask all the guys who've been busting their butts for years and haven't made it."

He shrugged again, uncomfortable with her implied compliment. "I just gave the boys a few roping tips."

"Not just that. You gave them your time. Not because you were paid to or had to, but because they asked. That means a lot."

"I couldn't just walk away."

"Sure you could. People do it all the time."

He met her gaze, held it. "Not me."

She studied him for a moment, that little pucker in her forehead again, as if she couldn't decide if he was for real. Then she waved at a pile of logs that had washed up on the beach, stacked at angles like straws tossed down by a massive hand. "Take the sandwiches down there. I'll run into the store and grab something to drink."

"Only if you let me buy."

He dug a five-dollar bill from his pocket, surprised when she took it without protest. Once again, he couldn't help watching as she walked away, her butt twitching with each purposeful stride. Yep, it would fit right in the palm of his hand.

And damn it all, he had to stop taking measurements.

Chapter 16

THE SOMETHING SHE FETCHED WAS ROOT BEER IN OLD-fashioned brown bottles, brewed just over the mountains in the Flathead Valley. David had chosen a spot to sit where they could use the bottom log as a backrest. Several more were propped across it at an angle, providing shelter from the breeze.

Mary handed over his root beer and sat down beside him, leaving a safe distance between them, he noticed. She twisted the top of her bottle and then scowled. "Crap. I forgot. These aren't twist tops."

"Here." David set his root beer aside and took the bottle from her hand. Lifting his shirt, he unhooked his belt buckle, clamped the prong over the edge of the cap and popped it off. He held the bottle out to Mary. "Old cowboy trick."

Her gaze was stuck on the front button of his jeans and the swatch of exposed stomach. Her eyes came up, saw that he was watching, and color stained her cheeks. She snatched the bottle from his hand. "Thanks."

"You're welcome." *To the root beer and anything else that strikes your fancy.*

She buried her nose in the bag of sandwiches, rooting around in there twice as long as she needed to, considering both sandwiches were the same. He squelched a grin, taking his time to pop the top of his bottle of root beer and buckle up his belt. So…he wasn't the only one taking notice of things he shouldn't. And damned if he wasn't dumb enough to feel a little cocky about it.

Mary handed him his sandwich without meeting his eyes. He took the first bite and momentarily forgot everything else, his appetite roaring to life at the yeasty perfection of the bread, the tang of ranch dressing and salty crunch of bacon. He barely paused to breathe while he wolfed down the rest.

Mary fished a pair of white Styrofoam containers from the bag. "This is the best huckleberry pie you've ever tasted."

"Guaranteed, since I've never had it before."

She widened her eyes at him. "What, were you raised by wolves?"

"Worse. Flatland farmers."

She laughed, and it made him tingle in places that had no business getting tingly with this woman. The same way he shouldn't watch how the breeze ruffled her spiky hair, or how the reflection of the water made her eyes look almost green.

He pulled his gaze away and settled back, tipping his head to inspect the nearest sheer rock face. Were any of the white spots up there mountain goats? He stared, waiting to see if they moved, until all of the spots began to dance in front of his eyes.

"Did you know the guy who took Muddy?"

She stiffened. "Not personally. Why?"

"I was curious, that's all. I wasn't accusing you of anything." This time.

She eyed him for a long moment, then relaxed, popping open the top of her pie container. "Most people who follow rodeos in Montana had heard of Jinks. He roped tough, won a lot when he was sober. Sometimes even when he wasn't."

"Rusty said no one would be surprised that he'd picked up a good horse somewhere. Legally, I mean."

"Depends on your definition of legal." Mary forked up some pie, lifted it toward her mouth, and then set it down again. "You were right. I suspected something was fishy about Muddy. But I never dreamed he was stolen. You gotta understand… Jinks dealt a lot more than horses. I assumed some cowboy had snorted more than he could afford, and Jinks took the horse as payment."

David stared at her, dumbfounded. She talked about drug deals as if they were an everyday occurrence. Maybe in her world they were, along with street people and sisters who did prison time. *Cripes*. David felt like a country hick on his first trip to town.

Mary caught him staring and flushed. "I suppose it sounds ridiculous, knowing the truth. I have a bad habit of seeing things the way I want them to be."

Things, or people? He saw the memories that passed behind her eyes, like the cloud shadows that skimmed across the lake.

"Have you ever been married?" he asked.

"No."

"Me neither." He forked in a bite of pie and took a moment to savor the explosion of sweetness on his tongue, tarter than blueberry, more intense than blackberry. It would be killer with a scoop of vanilla ice cream. Might even cover the bitter taste of the words when he added, "I assume Hilary told you why."

Mary hesitated and then nodded.

"So that's my excuse," he said. "What's yours?"

He expected her to shrug off the overly personal question, but maybe she figured fair was fair since she knew his story. "There aren't many men who want to raise someone else's *problem child*."

She added air quotes, echoing words she'd heard too often, or from the wrong person, judging by the hint of venom. Sore subject. Not sure how to back away, David kept quiet.

"That wasn't fair, blaming Kylan." She stabbed at her pie, pulverizing a section of the crust. "It's not like I was any good at relationships before he came along. When it comes to men, my judgment is questionable at best."

David took another big bite of his pie, a legitimate excuse to avoid answering, since he once again had nothing to add. He attempted to change the subject. "What happens when Kylan graduates next spring?"

"He'll still be mine." Her voice went fierce, her eyes hot. "No matter how old he gets, he will always be mine. I'm not booting him out the door the minute he graduates, and anybody who wants a piece of me will just have to deal with it."

David blinked, taken aback by her intensity. "I, uh, meant…is he going to college?"

"Oh." The color burned hotter in her cheeks, and her gaze dropped to the pie plate in her hand. "Yeah. We're looking at classes at the community college."

"In Browning?"

"He's not ready to go off on his own." She licked the tines of her plastic fork, the dart of her tongue momentarily distracting David from the subject at hand. "Kylan is very…naive. Easily led. He wants so bad to belong, he doesn't see when people are using him. Ninety-nine percent of the time, if he gets in trouble it's because he let someone talk him into doing something he knows shouldn't."

"He'll have to learn to take care of himself someday."

Her mouth flattened into an obstinate line. "He's got plenty of time."

He was tempted to ask how long she planned to keep the kid under her thumb. The rest of his life? Or just until she found the right girl to take over babysitting duties? Starr, or someone like her, who craved a place to belong, someone who needed her, didn't mind being as much mother as lover as long as she had a man who treated her decent. Nice plan, but David figured Kylan would eventually have other ideas, if he didn't already.

When that happened, where did it leave Mary?

"You can have the rest." Mary shoved her pie box toward David and jumped up, that firm little butt directly in his line of sight as she brushed the sand off her jeans with brisk slaps. David clenched his fists, fighting the urge to help her out. "I should quit boring you with all our troubles." She turned, avoiding his gaze as she reached for the empty sandwich bag. "I also have a bad habit of…uh…" Her eyes went wide. "Bear."

David squinted at her, confused. Bear what? The responsibility for Kylan? Or did she mean bare, like her soul?

"*Bear!*" she whispered, making a jerky motion toward the trees with her chin.

David froze. *Oh. Shit.* "How close?" he whispered.

"Too damn," she whispered back, her lips barely moving.

Ever so slowly, he turned his head to look over his shoulder. Less than twenty yards away, a bear stood at the edge of the trees. A big bastard, with broad, muscular shoulders and a head the size of a tree stump, sunlight gleaming off his blond coat.

"That's not a black bear," David whispered.

"Grizzly." Mary breathed the word like a prayer. "What do we do?"

"You're asking me?" David kept his eyes locked on the bear. "I'm the prairie boy. What do they teach you mountain people?"

"Mostly to hope I'm faster than you."

David choked off a nervous laugh. The bear's nose came up, twitching as he tested the air.

"He smells the food," Mary whispered. "We have to get rid of it."

David rotated his head inch by inch, eased a hand out to grab the paper bag and slide both pie boxes inside. The bear sniffed again, its beady eyes watching every move. David rolled the top of the bag to secure it, then in one swift move, pivoted onto his knees and heaved the whole thing as far as he could, toward but not directly at the bear. It flinched but didn't give ground as the bag skidded over the rocky beach. The bear looked at the bag, then at David, head swinging side to side as it debated which it would rather snack on.

David grabbed Mary's wrist and yanked her down beside him.

"Hush!" he said when she yelped in protest. He scooped one arm under her knees, slapped a hand on top of her head, folded her in half and shoved her into a space beneath the crossed logs. "Get under there."

She pushed back, trying to resist. "No. We'll be cornered—"

"We can't outrun him." He gave her another shove, wedging her all the way under the logs, and then dropped down behind her, still watching the bear, who stared back at him with what David hoped was a curious gleam in its eye as opposed to hunger.

"What about you?" Mary protested. "We won't both fit—"

"I'm not snack-sized. And I've heard something about playing dead. Covering your head and curling up to protect your vitals."

"I guess it is our best bet." She sounded dubious, but she wiggled farther into the crevice under the logs.

David eased his body flat, hating when he lost sight of the bear, praying it would lose interest when it couldn't see him anymore. If it came around to their side of the log pile, they were screwed. David slid his arms around Mary and scooted his body as far under the logs as he could, curling his knees up and his head down until they were spooned so tightly together he could feel every shallow breath she took. Under other circumstances, it would be a real turn-on, but right now all of his parts, manly and otherwise, were more concerned about staying attached.

She squirmed, twisting her head and using one hand to carefully scoop away the coarse gravel. "There's a gap under this log. I can see him."

"What's he doing?"

"Nothing. Yet."

They waited, every second an eternity, every sound magnified. The shush and splash of the waves. Distant voices calling out, too far away to hope for help even if any of the tourists had witnessed their dilemma. The bear snuffled and grunted, grinding rocks under his weight as he moved.

David's lungs ached with the effort to corral his panic into slow, silent breaths. His heart pounded so hard he was sure Mary could feel it. He fought the rising swell of adrenaline that urged him to jump up and run, tried to block the image of claws raking his exposed back, those huge teeth clamping down on his leg, his shoulder, his neck...

"He's moving," she whispered. "Oh God, he's coming this way."

Go for the pie, dammit. Weren't bears supposed to be crazy about huckleberries?

Mary whispered a jumbled mix of profanities and prayers as claws clicked against the rocks. "Wait. He stopped... He's turning..." David felt her body tremble. "He found the pie."

Paper crumpled and tore. Styrofoam crunched as the bear helped himself to their dessert. There was slurping and the smacking of very large jaws, then David jerked, smacking his head on the log as the sound of a car horn blasted into the evening air, long and loud. The bear snorted. Rocks scattered under his retreating steps when the horn sounded again.

"He's gone." A shudder of relief racked Mary's shoulders, her body going limp as the horn blared once more. "Some guy in the parking lot must've seen we were in trouble. And there's a park ranger headed this way."

David let go of Mary and rolled out from under the logs, flopping onto his back to gulp in air. "Holy shit.

That was…" He slapped his free hand onto his thundering chest. "I think I'm having a heart attack."

Mary's laugh climbed the scale into the hysterical range as she squirmed free of the logs and rolled over, David's arm still pinned under her. "Lucky for you, I know CPR."

He turned his head, intending to make some kind of joke, and found her nose only inches from his. They both froze, awareness sizzling through the tiny space between them.

"Oh hell," she said. And then she kissed him.

Shock paralyzed him for a beat. Then he curled up his arm, dragging her against him while their mouths tangled, hungry and hot, adrenaline and desire crashing together and exploding into white-hot flame. He angled his head, intending to go deeper with the kiss, until he heard a shout.

Mary jerked away, pushing herself upright as footsteps rattled down the beach, coming fast.

"Are you okay?" a woman called out.

"Yeah." Mary skimmed an unsteady hand over her hair and scrambled to her feet. "We're fine, thanks to that guy and his car horn."

David sat up, propping his elbows on bent knees and taking long, deep breaths, not sure whether the fear or the kiss had made him dizzier.

The ranger was a tall, bony woman, her brown hair pulled back into a neat braid and her finger on the trigger of a canister of bear spray. "Quick thinking with the car horn," she said, nodding her approval. "And smart of you to get down and lie still."

"Not bad for a prairie boy," Mary said, flashing David

a smile that melted what was left of his brain cells. She jerked her gaze away, brushing at the dirt on her clothes. "We should get out of here, in case the bear decides to come back for seconds."

They gathered their wits and the remains of their dinner and quick-stepped with the ranger back to the parking lot. A cluster of onlookers had gathered, eager to hear the story and offer backslaps to their rescuer. With every word, every moment they spent working through the crowd, David could feel Mary retreating, putting distance between them.

Finally, they escaped to the pickup, closed the doors, and sat in shell-shocked silence for a few beats.

"Don't say anything," Mary warned, her eyes fixed on the mountain in front of them. "Just…don't."

"Okay." Like he had any idea what to say anyway.

Her hands clenched the steering wheel. "I overreacted, all right? It's not every day a man puts himself between me and a grizzly bear. I was…grateful." She nodded once, then again, as if satisfied with that explanation. "I got carried away. I do that sometimes. Doesn't mean anything. We'll drive back to town, I'll drop you off, and we'll pretend this never happened, okay?"

No. Not okay. But a whole lot smarter than any of the ideas running wild in his head. "Mary—"

"Don't." She gave a quick, hard shake of her head. "It was a huge mistake. If Kylan knew…"

Her words brought David back to earth with a bone-rattling thud. Of course. It was all about Kylan with her. Always would be. Something David would do damn well to remember, not that he intended to stick around long enough to risk forgetting.

Fatigue rolled over him in a dense gray wave, blurring his mind. He slumped down in the seat, tilted his head back, and closed his eyes. "Just take me home."

She did, and left him standing beside his cold, dark trailer to watch her taillights disappear into the dusk. *Just as well*, he told himself.

And he damn near believed it.

Chapter 17

DAVID WOKE UP AT EIGHT THE NEXT MORNING, SWEATY and irritated. The nose of the trailer was stifling because he'd gone to the Town Pump and filled the propane bottles when he got home, then cranked the thermostat too high because he was chilled through and through. Even after he'd kicked off all the blankets, he hadn't slept for shit, his mind too full of Mary and bears and where he could possibly find a horse for Kylan in less than forty-eight hours.

He showered, shaved, and then checked his phone for missed calls. Rusty had left a message while David was at Two Medicine dancing with grizzlies. He'd promised to call back after he'd had a chance to look into a couple of likely prospects for Kylan. Sure enough, the missed-call icon was lit up on the screen, but the number wasn't Rusty's.

David stared at the phone, trying to line his thoughts up into some kind of order before he returned his dad's call. The smart thing would be to ask him to cosign on a loan, but everything inside David balked. He couldn't exactly say why. He just knew he wasn't ready to give in. Not yet. He didn't have to leave for Reno until Thursday morning. That gave him until tomorrow to figure out another way. And two more evenings he could possibly spend with Mary.

Right. Like she was gonna go for that. She'd made

her opinion crystal clear the night before, when she'd booted him out in the cold without so much as a backward glance.

He splashed water on his face to rinse off the shaving cream, rubbed it dry with excessive force. Forget mooning over a woman. He'd wasted enough years and tears recovering from the last one. He had to keep his head on straight, take care of business. The first order was to tell his parents about Muddy before they found out on their own.

His dad must've had the phone in his hand, because he answered before the end of the first ring. "Hey, David. How's it going?"

"Well, um, I have news. Good news." Weird, how hard it was to get the words out. His throat went painfully tight, and his heart pounded as if this was the moment that finally made it true. "Dad, you're not going to believe—"

"What?" his dad demanded, alarmed.

David drew a shaky breath. "I found Muddy."

There was a moment of stunned silence. Then a sharp intake of air. "You're kidding."

"No." David gave a shaky laugh. "Would I kid about this? It's him, and he's…" No, not fine. Better. "He looks great."

Their words jumbled together, questions and answers running over the top of each other as David explained where and how and as many of the details as he knew. His father's silences grew longer and more thoughtful when David told him about Kylan.

"Hell of a thing, having to take a horse away from a kid," his dad said. "What's he going to ride at nationals?"

of a lot more. So did Galen, even if he did feel bad about it. And David...well, he'd rather not take any chances. If the rodeo gods were determined to whittle out one last pound of his flesh, he'd pay up, one way or the other. Then he'd move on, free and clear, with nothing more than the memory of one heart-rattling kiss to tug at his sleeve at odd moments.

He tried Rusty's number but got the answering machine. Hilary would be in the same teachers' training as Mary, he supposed, and Rusty was probably out doing chores. No sense sitting in the trailer, staring at the walls. David's phone worked just as well outside, and as long as he had time to kill, he might as well put it to good use.

Frosty's shoes were due for a reset, so David pulled his portable anvil out of the tack compartment. Then he stopped, considered, and shoved it back in, slamming the door behind. Hell with it. Muddy belonged to him, and that shoeing job was driving David crazy.

He jumped Frosty into the trailer, unhooked the water and electrical lines, and headed west out of the fairgrounds. Within minutes, he was turning into Mary's driveway. As expected, her pickup was gone, but the sound of David's engine brought Kylan out of the barn, pitchfork in hand, hair sticking out every which way from under a backward baseball cap. Out in the pasture, Muddy raised his head long enough to give the rig a brief, dismissive glance, then went back to grazing.

David climbed out of the cab, debating how best to approach Kylan. The kid didn't give him a chance to open his mouth. He gripped the pitchfork in one hand and held up a cell phone with the other, his voice quivering.

"You better not try to take him. I'll call JoJo, and they'll pick you up before you get a mile down the road."

David raised both hands. "I'm not gonna steal him back."

"Then what are you doin' here?" Kylan demanded, waving the pitchfork with enough menace to make David decide he'd best keep his pickup door open.

"I want to reset his shoes."

Kylan's eyes narrowed, suspicious. "He don't need shoeing. We got it done right before I went to state."

"I don't like how he's set."

"Why not?"

David stifled a growl. "Get him in, I'll show you."

"Uh-uh. You're tryin' to trick me." The pitchfork wobbled again, the tines long, shiny, and very sharp.

"It's not a trick. Here..." David reached into the pickup, pulled the keys out of the ignition, and heaved them across the yard. They chinked onto the ground in front of Kylan. "Take my keys. Then I can't leave."

Kylan stared at the keys for a moment. His gaze bounced to his phone, then the pitchfork, then back again, stymied. He had to put something down in order to pick up the keys, but what?

David breathed a sigh of relief when he chose the pitchfork, jabbing it into a nearby bale of hay. Kylan snatched up the keys and stuffed them in his pocket, his expression still skeptical. "You really just want to shoe him?"

"Really."

"And you'll show me why before you do anything?"

"Yes."

Kylan considered, then nodded. "Okay."

While the kid went out to catch Muddy, David unloaded Frosty and tied him on the shady side of the trailer out of habit. Then he realized it was damn chilly there and moved the horse around into the sun. *Criminy*. Did they ever get actual summer here?

He set up his anvil and hoof stand just inside the barn door where he could also catch some warmth from the sun and buckled on a pair of short, heavy leather chaps to protect his thighs.

When Muddy was tied to the stall gate and munching from a bucket of grain, Kylan squinted at his feet. "I don't see nothin' wrong with them."

"That's because you don't know what to look for." David pulled out a hoof rasp, a twelve-inch length of flat steel, covered on both sides with curved teeth sort of like an industrial-strength cheese grater with a wooden handle on one end. He used the rasp as a pointer, tracing a line down Muddy's cannon bone, around the ankle, and to the midpoint of the hoof. "See here, how his heels are low and his toe is a little long, so it makes this angle sharper?"

"Yeah. So?" Kylan looked over at Frosty. "It's no different than your other horse."

"But they're not built the same. Look at Muddy, how straight he is through the shoulder. Then look at Frosty. See how his shoulder slopes more? With most horses, the natural angle of their pastern is the same as the angle of their shoulder." He used the rasp again to trace the flex of Muddy's ankle—which technically was a toe, not an ankle as compared to human anatomy—but he didn't intend to go that deep in this impromptu lesson. "If they're not lined up right, it can cause problems."

"Like what?" Kylan leaned in to look closer, suspicion elbowed aside by curiosity.

"In Muddy's case, you're putting more stretch on the flexor tendons, which wrap around the navicular bone like a rope around a pulley. Too much stress can cause bone spurs, arthritis, or even navicular disease."

Avascular necrosis, in veterinary terms— degeneration of the bone due to loss of circulation.

Kylan frowned. "That's real bad."

"It can be," David agreed. "Which is why I'd like to fix it sooner rather than later."

"Oh. Okay." Kylan flipped a bucket upside down and sat, elbows on knees, watching intently as David pulled the right foot up between his thighs and propped it on the hoof stand. He rasped off the bent ends of the nails on the outside of the foot, then used the hoof nippers— long-handled, industrial-strength toenail clippers—to pry the steel shoe off.

"I bet it took a long time to get good at that," Kylan said as David set the first foot down and moved to the other side.

David paused, arching the kinks out of his back while he looked from horse to kid. For all his other quirks, Muddy was civilized about shoeing, and Mary had said Kylan was interested in learning. "Want to give it a try?"

Kylan snapped upright, eyes widening. "Seriously?"

"Sure."

"What if I screw it up?"

"I won't let you." Kylan eased around, sneaking up on the horse like he might turn into a grizzly bear.

Muddy flicked an ear, rolling his eyes as though he was saying, "Oh, for God's sake. Get on with it."

"You've picked up his feet before, right?" David asked.

Kylan bristled. "Of course. I clean them all out every time I ride him, before and after."

"Good. Face toward his head, pull the foot up and hold his shinbone between your knees so his foot stays on the stand."

Kylan did as instructed, more smoothly than David expected. "Looks like you've done this before."

Kylan hunched a shoulder. "I been watchin' our horseshoer, and I tried it a few times."

More than a few, David guessed. He held out the rasp. "Here. Take off the bent ends of the nails."

The first few strokes were jerky, the nails catching the teeth of the rasp and stopping it short. Kylan swore and tried again, with no better results. David hesitated, not sure how the kid would react if he got too close. Guess he'd find out. He crouched, putting his hands over Kylan's on the ends of the rasp. The kid didn't flinch away.

"Like this." David tilted the rasp to the correct angle, demonstrating the proper amount of force needed to grind off the nails. "See?"

"Yeah. I got it."

David stepped back. The rasp snagged again, but Kylan corrected himself, and the next stroke was smooth and steady. He clamped his bottom lip between his teeth, concentrating hard as he carefully removed the rest of the nail ends. He finished the last one and flashed a triumphant grin at David. "Like that?"

"Perfect." David took the rasp and handed him the nippers. "Now pull the shoe off."

Kylan struggled a little but pried the shoe off without

help. Then David took over, the rest of the job requiring more finesse. Muddy dozed, bored as a socialite getting a pedicure, while David nipped off just the right amount from the front of the hoof, set the foot on the ground to inspect the angle, and showed Kylan the result. Then he used the rasp to plane the bottom flat and tacked on the new shoe. He let Kylan finish it off, clinching the pointed ends of the nails down and under on the outside of the hoof to clamp the shoe firmly in place.

They repeated the process on all four feet. While Kylan clinched the last set of nails, David stretched out his back, groaning. "Short horses kill me."

"Doesn't seem so bad to me," Kylan said, setting the foot down and popping upright with a cheeky grin.

"Say that after you've shod a couple thousand head."

Kylan's expression went sober. "You think I could?"

"Sure. Seems like you've got a knack for it."

"Really?" A delighted smile spread across Kylan's face. "I'm not usually good at stuff."

A lump the size of a bowling ball swelled in David's throat. His phone rang, and he could barely choke out a "Hello."

"Hey, David. It's Rusty. I've got a horse that might work for Kylan. Can you track him down and come out this afternoon?"

"He's standing right here. How long will it take us to get there?"

"An hour."

"See you in an hour and fifteen, then," David said, and hung up.

Kylan stepped back, suspicion flaring in his eyes. "Who was that?"

"Rusty Chapman. He's got a horse for you to try."

Kylan's gaze flicked to Muddy, his face going sullen. "I already got a horse."

"Kylan—"

The kid took another step back, shaking his head. "Mary said she had it worked out so I could still use him at nationals."

Dammit. Why had she told him that when she didn't know for sure? "She offered me a deal," David said, forcing the irritation out of his words. "But I have to say no. I can't leave Muddy here."

"Why not?" Kylan demanded, his voice pitching higher.

"My dad won't let me."

Kylan blinked, momentarily surprised out of his sulk. "Your dad still bosses you?"

"Parents never quit bossing you," David said. Or sisters, for that matter. "I listen, 'cause he's a smart guy. Plus, I need Muddy pretty bad right now if I want to make the National Finals this year."

Kylan's lip poked out, his voice going sulky. "I guess that's a bigger deal than the high school finals."

David took a deep breath. *Patience.* "It could be worth a lot of money to me."

Kylan stared down at his feet for several long moments. Then his shoulders rose and fell on a defeated sigh. "You'd have to be kinda stupid to leave a horse that good standin' around here."

"That's what my dad said. So…are we gonna go rope or what?"

"I have to ask Mary."

"So ask."

"I can't. She's in that training thing, and they're not allowed to have their phones."

"Then we'll have to go without asking her."

"She won't like that."

Oh, for God's sake. The kid was eighteen years old, and he was afraid to leave home in broad daylight without permission? David took another calming breath. "Call Galen. He's the one who asked me to help find you a horse."

Kylan dialed the number, listened, and then frowned. "Voicemail. I'll try Cissy's number." He did and frowned again when he got another voicemail. "They're prob'ly at the hospital with Aunt Mona. We'll just have to wait."

"I'm only here until Thursday," David said, hanging on to the last shreds of his temper. "We can't sit on our asses all day. Besides, Galen already knows I was gonna call Rusty. And you know the Chapmans, right?"

"Well, yeah, but—"

"No but. We're going. And…" He paused, aware that he was railroading the kid, but it was in Kylan's best interest as much as his own. "I'd like to take Muddy along."

"To Rusty's?" Kylan threw out his hands, shaking his head. "Uh-uh. You can't."

"Why not? You'll be right there to keep an eye on me." Hell with it. He wasn't too proud to beg. "Please, Kylan? I've been waiting four years. I never thought I'd get to rope on him again, and now he's right here…"

Kylan's forehead crinkled, fear, uncertainty, and a hint of sympathy flickering across his face. "But Rusty's place is, um…you know."

"What?"

"Uh…kinda far."

"An hour, he said. It's only eleven o'clock. If we get a move on, we could hustle out there, rope, and be back before Mary gets home."

"Well..." David saw the teen wavering and pushed the advantage. "Grab your stuff and let's go. Time's a-wastin', and I don't have much to spare."

Kylan hesitated for another few beats, then squared his shoulders and fixed David with a decent imitation of Mary's cold-eyed soldier stare. "First, you gotta promise you'll bring Muddy back."

"Cross my heart," David said, and didn't think twice about sealing the deal with a slash of his fingers across his chest.

Chapter 18

WHEN THEY FINALLY PULLED IN ALMOST TWO HOURS LATER, Rusty was out in his yard roping a plastic calf head stuck into the end of a hay bale. He hadn't changed a bit, still raw-boned and redheaded, with a permanent sunburn on his neck and oversize ears. He coiled up his loop and crossed to meet them as David stepped out of the pickup.

"What took you so long?"

"Kylan thought he knew a shortcut." David didn't bother hiding his exasperation since he'd already given the kid a raft of shit about the detour.

"I forgot there's not a cut-across from the boarding school road to Meriwether." Kylan hunched his shoulders, but he didn't seem all that apologetic. "At least we didn't have to go through town."

"Yeah, that saved us a bunch of time," David drawled.

Rusty frowned at the empty cab of the pickup. "I thought Galen would be with you."

"He's out of town," David said.

"It's just the two of you?" Rusty asked, his eyebrows shooting up in disbelief.

"We're big boys," David said. "We thought we could handle it. Which horse are we looking at?"

Rusty stared at him for a beat and then waved a hand toward the three horses tied to a rail in front of the barn. "The dun on the end. My wife's cousin took him in on a trade, says he works good out in the arena but he's a little tricky in the box."

That didn't sound promising, but it couldn't hurt to try, especially when it had given David an excuse to bring Muddy.

"Let's give it a shot," he said, and went to unload his horses.

Frosty backed out slowly, deliberately, one foot after another. David handed the lead rope to Kylan. Then he released the next swinging divider inside the trailer and jumped out of the way, snagging the lead rope as Muddy ejected. He followed the horse out.

Rusty stared, dumbfounded. "Holy shit. That's Muddy."

"In the flesh," David said.

"I didn't expect... How did you get Mary to—" Rusty cut himself short and looked at Kylan. "Why don't you grab your saddle and put it on the dun?"

Kylan looked from David to Rusty and back again, then he handed off Frosty's lead rope and did as ordered. The instant he was out of earshot, Rusty stepped closer and lowered his voice. "Mary and Galen don't know you're here, do they?"

"Uh, no." David tried hard not to look guilty, but was pretty sure he didn't succeed. "Why?"

"Because I don't live on the reservation, David."

David sucked in air as he grasped the significance of Rusty's statement. "Why didn't Kylan say something?"

"Maybe he forgot."

No. He didn't forget. David remembered the hesitation. *"Rusty's place is...kinda far."* Kylan knew what he was risking and did it anyway. Why?

Rusty glanced over his shoulder at the kid, who was tossing his saddle blanket onto the dun's back. "We could call the sheriff's department right now. They'd be out here lickety-split. If you've got your papers and stuff along, you could leave here with Muddy today and settle the thing with the reward later."

David went dizzy at the possibility. Without even trying, he'd managed to smuggle Muddy off the reservation. All he had to do was jump him into the trailer and drive away.

"My attorney friend called back," Rusty went on, talking low and fast. "In her opinion, Mary doesn't have a leg to stand on. Your posters said the reward was for information leading to Muddy's return, but Mary didn't come forward. You found her. If anybody deserves the reward, it's Shane Colston."

David's brain felt like it had been dropped into a blender. Too much information too fast. Rusty had put his finger on what had been bothering David about paying the reward. Mary hadn't returned Muddy to him. In fact, she'd done the opposite.

He was off the hook. Legally, ethically, he didn't owe Mary or Kylan a damn thing. Except...

"I promised," he said.

Rusty squinted, bewildered.

"You what?"

"Kylan made me promise I'd bring Muddy back to his place." David let out a long, resigned breath. "I even crossed my heart."

Rusty stared at him like he'd grown a second head. "You're shitting me, right?"

"'Fraid not. I gave my word, and I gotta stand by it." Even if it might likely kill him. Or his sister would when she found out. And she would find out. She always did.

Rusty gave his head a slow shake, side to side. "You're either the most stand-up guy I've ever met, or the dumbest."

"I'm an idiot. Ask my sister." David clapped him on the shoulder. "Let's go rope."

Before he grabbed his saddle from the tack compartment, David paused to scowl up at the cobalt-blue sky. *Happy now, you cranky old bastards?*

By the time Muddy was saddled and bridled, David's chest was so tight with anticipation he could barely breathe. He led the horse into the arena, stuck his foot in the stirrup, and swung his leg over. Muddy jumped ten feet sideways and nearly dumped him right back off again, just to see if he was paying attention.

"Nice try," David said but grinned. Geezus, the little shit could move.

Muddy snorted and shook his head, then shoved at the bit, raring to go. David gave him some rein and Muddy took it, churning and puffing around the arena like a miniature steam engine, all stoked up.

"These first three calves are a little juicy for Kylan," Rusty said. "Why don't you rope them?"

David checked his cinches, remounted, fumbling as he readied his rope and piggin' string. *Criminy*. He was shaking worse than the first time he'd ever roped at a rodeo, when he was eight. He rode into the box, turned around, and laughed out loud when Muddy kicked up his heels.

Rusty grinned. "He's ready. Are you?"

"You betcha." David cocked his loop and nodded his head.

Muddy blasted out of the corner so hard the cantle of the saddle slapped David on the ass, and he let his loop go before he was ready. Muddy slammed him into the swells as the rope spun around the calf's ears and off.

"He's kinda short on the stop," Kylan called out, all helpful-like.

David ignored the jibe, recoiled his rope, and rode back into the box. This time, he was ready for the start. He took three swings and threw, standing out in the right stirrup and pulling back on the reins, same as he'd been doing on Frosty for the past two years.

Not a good idea.

The first thing that hit the ground was the back of his head. Muddy spun him around and slammed him down so hard and so fast, David didn't even feel it coming. Stars burst in front of his eyes, and every molecule of air was forcibly expelled from his body. He rolled over, scrambling to his hands and knees just in time to collide head-to-head with the calf as Muddy dragged it over the top of him.

Rusty came running, grabbing the rope and flanking the calf to the ground while David forced oxygen into his flattened lungs. He heard a snicker and turned his head to glare at Kylan. "You should at least make sure a man's not hurt before you laugh at him."

Kylan flattened out the grin. "Are you okay?"

"Yeah."

"You might not want to hang out on the side of this horse," Rusty said, fighting a grin of his own.

Kylan burst out laughing.

David knocked the dirt off his hat, flattened out a brand-new crimp in the back of the brim and staggered

"That's why I'm still here." David sashayed right past the part about Mary kidnapping Muddy and the ransom demand and on to the next excuse. "His uncle asked if I'd help them find another horse."

His dad considered that for a long moment. "Frosty would probably work great for him," he said slowly. "But you know how Adam feels about that horse, and how he tends to fret. He's okay as long as Frosty is with you, but I don't think I could ask them to let you leave him with someone Adam doesn't know."

"You shouldn't," David said. "If I'm going to leave a horse here, it should be my own."

"You can't do that." His dad's voice hardened, the sympathy leaching out. "I feel bad for the boy, but Muddy is worth too much. And I don't need to tell you what it could mean, having him for the Fourth of July rodeos."

"I know." But it was good to hear his dad confirm that David wasn't just being a selfish bastard.

Female voices sounded in the background, followed by a burst of laughter. "Your mom is back from the bakery. Do you want to tell her yourself?"

"You go ahead."

"Figures. You know she's gonna cry." His dad blew out a gusty breath, sounding a little choked up. "Send us a picture, would you? I'm not gonna believe it's him until I see his ugly little mug."

David laughed. "He hasn't gotten any prettier."

"I don't imagine, but he'll still be a beautiful sight. And David…don't beat yourself up. All considered, it's damn good of you to do what you can to help the boy out. No one can expect any more."

His dad was wrong about that. Mary expected a hell

back to Muddy, who, damn his evil heart, looked like he was smirking, too.

Gotcha.

David built a new loop and took a couple of deep breaths, closing his eyes. This was not how he'd pictured his first runs when he got back on Muddy. He was too jazzed, too emotional. *Focus*. Inside his head, he replayed the best runs he'd made on Muddy, how it felt. The speed, the power. *Gotta be aggressive*. He took another cleansing breath and then opened his eyes.

Muddy's ears pricked, as if he felt David's resolve. His butt had barely touched the back corner of the box when David nodded his head. Two swings and *zap*. He roped the calf clean. David was off the right side and gone, holding the slack so the calf switched around on the end of the rope without losing its feet. It jumped into David's arms, helped along by Muddy hustling backward. David snatched the calf out of the air and dropped with it to the ground, the flank, gather, and tie flowing so smoothly into one another it was a single, continuous motion. He slapped on a wrap and hooey and threw up his hands.

Rusty hooted his appreciation, clapping as he jogged out to untie the calf. "That'll punch your ticket to Vegas!"

David glanced over at Kylan. The kid stood slack-jawed.

"Whaddaya think?" David asked.

Kylan jerked a shoulder and turned his back. "It'll work, I guess."

His lack of enthusiasm stung, and David couldn't exactly say why. It wasn't like he needed the kid's approval. He knew a good run when he made one. But still...

He coiled his rope, adrenaline surging in his system, blasting away the momentary gloom. Muddy hadn't lost a beat. Images raced through David's head, the places they would go, the things they could do. His muscles twitched, and his heart raced in anticipation. He wanted to load up and go now. This minute. Find a rodeo, any rodeo, and rope.

All of a sudden, Friday's run in Reno was an eternity away.

He tied Muddy to the fence, breathing deep to settle his revved-up system. Kylan climbed on the dun and loped a few circles. The gelding handled pretty nice and wasn't tough to look at. Could they actually be lucky enough to find the right horse on the first try? David was so pumped, he felt like anything was possible.

Kylan rode into the box and eased the horse back into the corner. The dun stood square, ears at attention, until Kylan cocked his arm back, ready to nod. The horse slumped, dropping his right shoulder to lean against the side of the box.

"Tighten up your left rein," Rusty said. "And try to push him over with your right foot."

Kylan tried, but the dun just leaned harder into the side of the box.

"Ride him forward and reset him," David suggested.

Kylan pushed his reins forward and kicked with both feet. The dun obliging walked to the front of the box, stood calmly beside the chute, then backed into the corner when Kylan picked up on the reins, but as soon as the kid cocked his loop back and got ready to nod, the horse slumped over against the side of the box again.

"Maybe if you quarter him more," Rusty said.

Kylan rode up and back again, angling the horse more to the left the way Rusty had instructed. The horse still leaned, so far his left hind foot came off the ground, and David thought he might flop onto his side. *Crap.* No wonder someone had wanted to get rid of him.

They tried circling him, first one direction and then the other. Didn't matter. The horse would stand perfectly straight until Kylan cocked his arm back to nod, then he'd slouch over like he'd decided to take a nap.

"Well, at least he's pretty calm about it," Rusty said.

"He gets much calmer, he's gonna doze off." David walked into the box, grabbed the breast collar, and pulled, dragging the horse upright and holding him there. "Nod your head."

Kylan nodded. Instead of running straight out of the box, the horse moved sideways and then forward. The delay made them a mile late, the calf wandering out of the chute, then squirting ahead when he heard them coming. They caught up just as the calf reached the end of the arena and ducked left. Kylan threw a loop that sailed like a Frisbee, three feet above the calf's head.

Rusty said a bad word. David silently concurred. "Come on back," Rusty yelled. "We'll try it again."

And again. And again. No matter what David did, the horse wouldn't run straight out of the box. After six attempts, Kylan was red-faced and panting from frustration. He hadn't had a single decent throw.

"I guess we know why he's cheap," David said.

Kylan slid to the ground and tugged his rope off the saddle horn with angry jerks, his head bowed and his face set. He'd barely said a word the whole time. David followed him across the arena where Kylan tied the dun down the fence from Muddy and crouched to unstrap the skid boots from his hind legs. David would've liked to pat the kid on the back, reassure him, but he wasn't sure he dared.

David erred on the side of caution and kept his distance. "Well, I guess it was worth a shot."

"Yeah. Whatever." Kylan stuffed his rope into his can and slapped the top on, showing David his back.

Okay, then. The kid didn't want to chat. David backed off, retreating to the roping chute and leaving Kylan to loosen his cinches and stow the rest of his gear.

"What else have you got?" David asked Rusty, already knowing the answer.

"Nothing that would suit Kylan. The sorrel horse is too green…"

David listened with half an ear while he watched the kid, puzzled. He'd explained on the way over that this was a long shot and not to get his hopes up, and Kylan had said he understood and he wasn't expecting much. So why get all upset?

"What's that?" David asked when he realized Rusty had said something and was waiting for an answer.

"Do you want to run a few on your white horse?" Rusty repeated.

Kylan shuffled over, his gaze glued to the dirt, and slouched against the fence, still mute. The brim of his cap was yanked down so far David couldn't see much of his expression. Was he sulking? Embarrassed? Disappointed? Impossible to tell.

"You go ahead and get on your horse," David said. "Kylan and I will push a few for you."

And while they were at it, maybe he could figure out why Kylan wouldn't even look at him.

Chapter 19

KYLAN REMAINED STUBBORNLY SILENT THROUGH THE REST of the practice session, responding to all attempts at conversation with grunts and shrugs. After a few tries, David left well enough alone.

When Kylan did speak, it was a whole four words. "Shouldn't we go now?"

David checked the time on his phone. Crap. It was after three. "He's right. We'd better scat."

"You sure?" Rusty asked, shooting David a loaded glance that clearly said, "You can still take Muddy and run."

"I'm sure," David said. Almost sounded like he meant it, too.

They took the direct route, rather than Kylan's short-cut, and David kept one eye on the clock, tapping his fingers in a nervous beat on the steering wheel. He'd meant to get home before Mary even knew they were gone. No chance of that now. She'd have time to stew before they got back to her place. To think about where they'd been. Didn't take a fortune-teller to predict how she'd feel.

It was four thirty when they rolled into Browning. As the community college came in sight, Kylan spoke up. "Could you drop me off at Starr's place? We're sup-posed to go to a movie tonight."

"Oh, sure," David grumbled. "Let me take all the heat."

"It was your idea," Kylan said.

David shot him a narrow-eyed glance. "You aren't gonna take care of your horse first?"

"He's not my horse anymore," Kylan said flatly.

The kid had a point. He also had some serious attitude. David wasn't sure how much more of it he could tolerate, so he said, "Fine. I'll handle it."

Kylan ignored his snide tone, pointing to a street across from the Town Pump. "Turn up there."

David followed Kylan's directions to a white clapboard house with peeling paint and a rickety woven-wire fence. The yard was clean, though, the grass mowed, a pot of pink geraniums on the front step. Kylan bailed out and slammed the door, buried his hands in his pockets and slouched his shoulders as he circled the front of the pickup without a glance in David's direction. David watched him go, kneading the steering wheel with his hands. What the hell? Everything had seemed fine on the way out to Rusty's place and while they were saddling up to rope. Kylan had even laughed when David got slam-dunked. What had got up his ass all of a sudden?

David shook his head. This was exactly why the wild idea that had been brewing in the back of his mind was impossible. He was not equipped to handle any kid, let alone this one.

He eased away from the curb. A right at the next street took him down to the main drag. He turned left, toward the fairgrounds, and was deep in contemplation of just how damn good that last run on Muddy had felt when a siren shrieked behind him. He glanced down. Nope. He wasn't speeding. Maybe they were after someone else. But the cop car stayed right on his bumper when he turned into the casino parking lot to get off the street.

David peered in his rearview mirror and swore when he saw the stocky form behind the wheel. Oh hell. JoJo.

Then the car stopped, the passenger door flew open, and David realized the cop was the least of his problems. He barely got both feet on the ground before Mary was in his face, her voice climbing the scale into a panicked shriek.

"Where have you *been*?"

David put out his hands, ready to ward her off if she went for his throat, which seemed likely the way she was frothing at the mouth. "We were roping. At Rusty's. Kylan was supposed to leave you a note."

"You mean this?" She slapped a yellow sticky note onto his chest hard enough to make it sting.

He peeled it off and read the childish, blocky print. *WENT WITH DAVID.* Seriously? *What the hell, Kylan?* David crumpled the note in his hand. "I'm sorry. We thought we'd be back before you got home."

Mary's hands fisted in the front of his shirt, and she did her damnedest to shake him. "*Where is Kylan?*"

"I dropped him off at Starr's." David pried her fingers loose, wincing as they ripped out a few chest hairs. "What did you think, I sold him into slavery?"

"Great. Make jokes." She clenched her fingers on the hem of her blazer as if in dire need of an anchor. Her voice shook, her breath hitching like she might hyperventilate. "I come home, Kylan is gone, Muddy is gone, your rig is gone. What am I supposed to think?"

David scowled. "The worst, obviously."

"That's generally the safest bet." She spun on her heel and ran square into JoJo.

The cop caught her shoulders, steadying her. "You want me to arrest him, Mary?"

"What for?" David demanded.

JoJo glared at him over Mary's head. "Child abduction. Horse theft. Whatever else I can think of."

"It's my horse. Kylan is an adult. And in case you didn't notice, I brought both of them back." Although David was beginning to regret that decision.

"It's okay, JoJo." Mary shook off his hands and pressed a fist to her mouth as if it might steady her voice. "I can handle it from here. And since Kylan doesn't seem to have his phone turned on"—she glared at David as if this was somehow his fault—"I'll call Starr to make sure he's okay."

"For Christ's sake!" David threw up his hands, exasperated. "We drove across the county to rope a few calves. I don't think he's traumatized for life."

Mary's stare could've cut glass. "Kylan gets upset more easily than most kids."

David squelched a twinge of concern. No sense telling her about Kylan's mood after the roping session; it would only set her off again. And besides, Kylan had said he and Starr had a movie date. That should cheer him up.

"Can you talk while we drive?" he asked. "All I got for lunch was some beef jerky and a Coke, and my belly is starting to think my throat's been cut."

Mary's expression suggested she wouldn't mind if he keeled over from starvation. She stomped around the front of the pickup, hopped into the cab, and slammed the door. David did likewise. He was extra careful pulling out of the parking lot, praying all of his trailer lights were in working order since JoJo stayed on his tail and would love any excuse to write him a ticket.

Mary jabbed at buttons on her phone and then pressed it to her ear. "Hey. It's Mary. David said he left Kylan there."

She listened, lips pressed tight as Starr's voice chirped through the phone. Then she frowned. "Oh. Yeah. I forgot. But you should have called me first. I don't think it's a good idea, driving over to Cut Bank when Kylan's had such a rough couple of days…"

Starr's voice rose, insistent. Mary's frown deepened. Then she sighed. "Go ahead, since you're already on your way, but come straight back after."

She hung up after what sounded like Starr's assurances that they would be fine.

"Satisfied?" David asked.

"No." Mary swiveled in her seat to squint at him. "What did you do at Rusty's?"

"We roped. The horse Kylan tried was a pig in the box and we couldn't figure out any way to get by him, so we gave up and came home." David paused, debated whether to confess he'd broken the news to Kylan that he wouldn't get keep Muddy until nationals, decided against it. Was it his fault Mary had misled the kid?

Mary gave him a long, narrow-eyed stare, as if trying to see through his words to the truth, whatever she imagined that might be. Her face was pinched with worry, the shadows dark in her eyes.

"Listen, I am sorry we scared you," David said, his conscience giving him a sharp jab as he imagined her coming home, finding nothing but that piece-of-crap note from Kylan. "We would've waited until after you were done with your work thing, but we couldn't waste a whole day."

"Plus, you knew I wouldn't let you take Muddy."

David started to object, but they would both know it was bullshit. Hadn't he been relieved when Galen didn't answer his phone and there had been no one to order Kylan not to go with him? "For what it's worth, I didn't know we'd left the reservation until Rusty told me."

"I can believe that. But Kylan…what was he thinking?"

"That he could trust me?"

She snorted. "Right. Like he knew one way or another."

"I'm here, aren't I?"

She stared at him for a beat, then buried her chin in her chest and slumped in her seat, pressing her fingers to her temples. "God. I have to stop and breathe. I'm so… I was really… I just need a minute."

David gave her several, listening to her slow, deep breaths and feeling the tension begin to ebb in the cab of the pickup. She was slumped bonelessly in her seat by the time he pulled the rig around and parked in front of her barn. "I'll take care of Muddy. You can…whatever."

"Go to hell?" she said quietly.

He paused, his hand on the door. "I didn't say that."

She dipped her chin, her teeth pulling at one corner of her bottom lip, eyes downcast. "You have a right. I… um…might've overreacted a little."

"You called the cops on me." He couldn't wring all of the outrage from his voice.

She rubbed a hand over her forehead, as if to massage away a pain. "I called Kylan's cousin, who happens to be a cop. It's not like we put out an APB on you…exactly."

"Uh-huh. In other words, every cop on the rez was looking for my rig."

"Actually, JoJo had already told them all to keep an eye on you." She gave a puzzled shake of her head. "I don't know how you made it out of town without getting stopped."

David did, but he wouldn't tattle on Kylan and his *shortcut*. "Might as well slap one of those electronic ankle cuffs on me while you're at it," he said, unable to let it go. He wasn't the one who had a stolen horse in his corral. Why was he being treated like a criminal?

Mary hunched lower into her seat, her shoulders creeping toward her ears, and for the first time, David saw a resemblance between aunt and nephew. "I'm sorry, okay? I didn't mean to imply that you're not trustworthy. But Kylan… Sometimes he does stuff."

"Like what?"

"Like when he got mad at me for not letting him watch TV until he got his math grade up, and he decided to hitchhike to Billings to see his mother. Galen found him at two thirty in the morning, twenty miles out in the middle of nowhere on Highway 89." She shuddered, remembering. "Anything could've happened to him out there. Today, when I had no idea where he'd gone…"

Fear bubbled in her voice, defusing David's righteous anger. He'd taken her reaction personally, an insult to his character. He hadn't considered there might be good reason Kylan was required to check with her before leaving home. Hadn't thought about much of anything except finally having the chance to rope on Muddy.

For the first time since this whole mess started, he truly did feel like a selfish bastard.

"That was stupid of me," he said, shame lowering his voice. "I should've called your cell phone and left a voicemail. And I did sort of railroad him into going, so don't be mad."

"I'm not. At him anyway." Her voice was tart, but the look she gave him held more exhaustion than anger. The delicate skin under her eyes was smudged purple, a clear sign he wasn't the only one who hadn't had much sleep.

David's stomach rumbled. Before he could think twice, he asked, "Can I make it up to you?"

She frowned, instantly suspicious. "How?"

"I could really go for another piece of that huckleberry pie, since I didn't get to finish the first one." He tried a cautious smile. "Come with me. I'll buy you dinner."

She hesitated, long enough that he guessed she wanted to agree and was lining up all the reasons she shouldn't.

"Just sandwiches and pie, Mary. Maybe some ice cream on top, if we really want to get crazy."

"I won't be very good company."

"You don't have to be anything. Just relax and come along for the ride." He put a little more warmth into his smile, coaxing. "And the pie."

Chapter 20

WHILE MARY WENT INSIDE TO CHANGE OUT OF HER WORK clothes, David unloaded the horses and watered them at the tank behind the barn, smacking Muddy on the neck when he nipped at Frosty. "Play nice. The two of you are gonna be spending a lot of time together."

He put Frosty in the extra stall in the barn, fed both horses and unhooked his trailer. Maybe it wasn't exactly a date, but it seemed like he should drive since he'd done the asking. He hopped into the living quarters, stuck his dented cowboy hat on the rack, scrubbed off today's layer of grit and dust and changed into the semiclean clothes he'd worn for the previous evening's trip to the mountains, once again pulling his Finals jacket on over the gray Henley to ward off the cool edge of the breeze.

Mary was standing beside his pickup when he stepped outside. She'd swapped the khakis, blouse, and jacket she'd worn to the seminar for jeans and a soft green fleece pullover. Her sunglasses were firmly in place, hiding her eyes. She stared at him for a beat, and one corner of her mouth curled into an off-kilter smile.

"What?" he asked.

She shook her head and climbed into the pickup. David followed suit. When they were rolling over the hills toward East Glacier, he asked, "How are JoJo and Kylan related?"

"Kylan's dad and JoJo's sister were together for a few years when Kylan was little."

David had to think about that for a minute. "So they're not really cousins."

"Technically, no, but JoJo's sister treated Kylan like he belonged to her. Even when she wasn't with his dad anymore, she'd look after him when his mother didn't. If I hadn't taken custody of him, she would've." Mary's mouth curved into a soft smile. "JoJo gets carried away, but he's got a good heart and we can always count on him."

"What about Kylan's dad?" David asked. "Where is he?"

"Last I heard, down east at Fort Belknap. That's where he's from."

"Does Kylan ever see him?"

"Once in a while. He's not the kind to provide a kid with a stable home, if that's what you're wondering."

"Actually, I was surprised when you mentioned him," David admitted. "I thought maybe Kylan didn't know his dad."

Mary snorted. "A fair assumption where my sister is concerned. She only insisted on a paternity test because his dad is Assiniboine, so Kylan gets benefits from both tribes if there's any money being handed out."

"Does that happen often?"

"Now and then. We get a few bucks at Christmas, and a couple of years ago there was a big oil-rights settlement and everybody on the Fort Belknap rez got a thousand bucks." Mary tilted her head back against the seat and rolled it sideways to look at him. "I should warn you, I had a killer headache so I took one of my migraine pills. They make me kind of loopy."

"I'll watch so you don't end up facedown in the pie."

She laughed, and it eased his mind to see her relax a little. If these past two days had been rough on him, he could only imagine what they'd been like for Mary.

They opted out of the ice cream because Mary suggested they get their sandwiches and pie to go and take them to the hotel. She swayed when she stepped out of the pickup, and she didn't seem to be tracking quite right for the first few steps. Must be the medication. David kept a hand ready to catch her, but she got lined out all right as they crossed the gravel parking lot.

Inside, David gazed in awe at massive lodgepole pine pillars, three feet in diameter and three stories tall, soaring clear to the wood-beamed ceiling of the huge open space at the heart of the hotel. Mary led him through a doorway in the corner and out onto a veranda that overlooked the pool, bringing them face-to-face with a mountain.

They found a pair of vacant patio lounge chairs sheltered from the breeze and warmed by the sun. David shrugged out of his coat and hung it on the back of his chair. As he made himself comfortable, he caught Mary watching him with that same inscrutable half smile. He raised his eyebrows.

"Oops. Busted." She gave a sigh that might've qualified as dreamy. "That shirt fits you really well. But I'm sure you already knew."

He glanced down at the too-snug waffle knit and then back at her. "I knew it was clean."

"Sure you weren't showing off?"

Showing off? Looking good? This was not the Mary he'd known over the past two days. He leaned over and pushed up her sunglasses. Her eyes were slightly glassy. "You're stoned."

"Nah. Just really, really relaxed." She swatted his hand away and slouched into her chair, unwrapping her sandwich to nibble at one corner. David watched her for a moment and then glanced down at his chest, stifling a grin. It was a start, wasn't it, even if she'd only admitted it under the influence?

A start toward what, he couldn't say.

And he didn't intend to figure it out on an empty stomach. He ate his sandwich, half of hers, and his slice of pie in record time, making damn sure he didn't have to share any of it with the local wildlife. After gathering up the wrappers and dumping them in the nearest trash can, he returned to find Mary slumped forward, kneading the muscles of her neck.

"Stiff?" he asked.

She rolled her head to one side, grimacing. "Some people carry their worries on their shoulders. According to my chiropractor, mine are a pain in the neck."

David hesitated, but really, it was only good manners. Since he'd been the biggest pain in her neck today, the least he could do was offer some relief. He leaned over, grabbed Mary around the waist, and slid her forward on the chair.

"What are you doing?" she protested.

"Offering my expert services." Which sounded vaguely obscene if you were prone to thinking that way. He stepped over the chair, sat down, and rested his palms on her shoulders. "Relax. I'm not going to molest you."

But having that firm little butt cradled between his thighs was giving him all kinds of ideas. "David—"

"Shhh. I know what I'm doing. Emily—my former fiancée—was a nursing student, and she had a lot of trouble with trigger points in her neck. She taught me how to do acupressure." He probed with his thumb, found a knot just below the base of her skull. "There?"

"Yeah."

He pushed.

"Ow!" Mary squirmed, hissed out a curse word. "That hurts."

David clamped his hands down on her shoulders. "Hold still. And tell me when it doesn't hurt so much."

She muttered another curse but stayed put. After a few seconds, she said, "Okay. Not so bad."

He pushed harder.

She cursed some more. "Damn. And here I thought I was getting a nice, relaxing neck rub."

"This will make you feel better in the morning."

"Like I've never heard *that* before," she grumbled.

David laughed and then moved on to the next trigger point, ignoring curious stares from the tourists around them as Mary groaned. When he'd worked his way up and down both sides of her neck, he let his hands drop. "There. How's it feel?"

She tipped her head forward, then sideways, then back. The spiky tips of her hair brushed his jaw, sending a prickle of awareness over his skin that heated as it spread, exploding into miniature fireworks at every point of contact between their bodies.

She angled a look over her shoulder. "Feels better. Thanks."

"You're welcome." That should've been his cue to get up, move away, but his body and his brain were not in agreement. She felt too good nestled so close to him. Smelled good, too—a tart, citrusy scent with a touch of sweetness underneath. So very Mary. From this angle, he could see behind the sunglasses to the lines of fatigue around her eyes and a vulnerability she would never admit. David's heart pinged again, and it was more than guilt that had him lifting his arms, wrapping them around her.

She stiffened. "David—"

"Shhh." He whispered it into her hair, ruffling the gold-tipped spikes.

"But we can't—"

"For the treatment to work, you need to lean back and relax. Let the muscles unwind." Total bullshit, of course, which she'd know if she felt his heart thumping. "Don't worry. We're in a public place."

She was still for a painfully long count of five. Then she sighed, tilted her head back against his shoulder, and closed her eyes. "Just so you realize, I wouldn't be doing this if it weren't for the drugs."

"I'll keep that in mind." He pulled her more snugly into his arms, marveling at how well she fit there. As if the space had been waiting for someone exactly her size and shape. But that thought was a scary sort of crazy, so he tried to distract himself. "There's more to the story with Kylan, isn't there?"

She stiffened again. "What do you mean?"

He closed one hand around her upper arm, massaged the muscle gently. "You're a teacher who's used to dealing with tough kids. You've been to war. You wouldn't have reacted the way you did today without reason."

He waited, but she only stared off at the top of the nearest mountain, impenetrable as the rocky crags.

Fine. If she was gonna be that way, he'd forget about being tactful. "How many times has he run away, Mary?"

She was silent for a very long moment. Then she shook her head with a tired sigh. "I couldn't even tell you. The first time I heard about was when he was four. He got out of the yard while Lori was in the bathroom, went next door, and hid in the neighbor's doghouse. Didn't come out for hours. And once, when he was seven, he crawled in the back of a stranger's car at a rodeo and ended up clear over in Box Elder."

David rubbed her arm with slow, soothing strokes. "Why does he do it?"

"It's like an anxiety attack, or claustrophobia. Sometimes, everything is just so hard for him. He gets wound tighter and tighter until he comes undone and has to get away." Her voice faltered, and she swallowed before going on. "The worst was a couple of years ago. We had a fight because he came home drunk. He climbed out of his bedroom window in the middle of the night and walked to town. JoJo found him two days later, passed out in an abandoned building down by the tribal offices with some of the street people. I just can't…" She swallowed again, squeezed her eyes shut, her voice fading to a whisper. "I'm so afraid we're going to lose him for good one of these times."

David folded his arms close around her, an ache settling in his chest as if he'd absorbed it from her. "I'm sorry. All the times I imagined finding Muddy, I never dreamed it would cause so much pain."

"It would be easier if you were an asshole," she said

softly. "Big and mean and scary like you looked in Kalispell."

"Big I can do, but mean… I can't fool anybody for very long. I can manage scary, though, if you catch me first thing in the morning."

Her laugh verged on a sob.

He fought the temptation to press his cheek against her hair. "When everything was going to hell and I couldn't rope to save my life, somebody told me I needed Muddy back in the worst way. As if I didn't know. All I could think was that's the stupidest saying I'd ever heard. There couldn't be a bad way to get Muddy back." He puffed out a sigh. "I was wrong."

Mary put her hand over his, tracing her thumb in a line across his knuckles. "Why did you come back today?"

He could've explained about the promise to Kylan, but the truth was even simpler. "I had to."

"Because?"

"The usual." He tried for a casual tone that wouldn't make him sound like a total sap. "You reap what you sow, what goes around comes around, that sort of thing."

She cocked her head to squint at him from under her lashes. "You were afraid stealing Muddy back would give you bad karma?"

"Dunno. Maybe." He shrugged, embarrassed. "My sister says I take that stuff too seriously. Karma, superstition, whatever you call it."

"Me? I call it being Catholic."

He tipped his head to look at her face. "Really?"

"Yeah. Why does that surprise you?"

"I thought the Blackfeet had their own religion. Drums, dancing, sweat lodges, and stuff."

"That too, but the Catholic missions educated most of the Indians around here in the early days, and for most of the families, it stuck. We do a little of this, a little of that, but both are pretty heavy on the 'do unto others.'" Her smile was edged in disbelief. "You're serious? You and Muddy could be halfway to Colorado by now, but your conscience wouldn't let you?"

"Guilt is a powerful force."

She was so close he could feel her breath against his cheek and see the doubt stamped as clearly on his face as the scatter of freckles. Her eyes searched his for an ulterior motive she seemed determined to find. As if that was easier than believing him. Maybe it was for Mary. Someone—or a lifetime of someones—had done a number on her. Were the effects irreversible? Was she capable of trusting anyone?

Then again, who was he to talk? It'd been four years since Emily had dumped him, but he was still alone, and the absence of a woman in his life wasn't an accident. He was in no rush to play the fool again, to stick his heart out there for someone else to drop-kick into the nearest trash bin.

Especially a woman who was looking for an excuse.

Mary jerked her gaze away, braced her hands on his thighs, and pushed free of his arms. The cool evening air rushed in to take her place. He shivered. She stood and looked down at him.

"I think I had it right the first time I saw you." This time, the off-center smile had a sharper edge, but it was turned inward. "You are a dangerous man, David Parsons."

Chapter 21

MARY WAS QUIET UNTIL THEY WERE IN THE PICKUP HEADED toward Browning. She stared resolutely out her side window as she spoke. "You're taking Muddy when you go."

"I have to."

She nodded once, abruptly. "Yeah. I suppose you do."

The silence hummed between them for another couple of miles. David stared at the white center line flickering past—*zip, zip, zip*—marking the distance between being with her and being alone. Mary stared south, toward the mountains that marched off to meet the horizon, no end in sight.

"What about the reward?" she asked.

Yeah. What about it? He hadn't called the bank again to try to change Byron's mind, and he hadn't asked his dad to cosign on a loan. How did he figure on leaving day after tomorrow with Muddy in the trailer?

"I'm having a problem with the reward."

Mary finally looked at him, poker-faced behind her sunglasses. "What kind of problem?"

"Well, first off, I don't have that much money sitting around. Neither does anyone else in my family." He flexed his fingers on the steering wheel, like he could get a handle on the words he needed. "The thing is, if I fight you, I'll win."

She flinched, and her mouth trembled for an instant before she pressed it flat. "You're sure of that?"

"Yes." He drew in a breath, lining up the rest of what he had to say. "The reward was intended for someone who helped me find Muddy. If you'd seen an old picture, recognized him, and called to say, 'Hey, we have your horse,' there would be a check in your hand tomorrow."

Her chin came up a notch. "You're splitting hairs."

"Am I?" He took his eyes off the road long enough to give her a hard stare. "You think you've been helpful?"

Her gaze dodged his, going back to the vast spread of prairie that now rolled out to the south, uninterrupted.

David couldn't let her off the hook. "It's up to you, Mary. You can force me to miss the next few rodeos, hire a lawyer, and camp on your doorstep until it's settled. If you think that's what's right."

Because he would. He hadn't known it for sure until this very moment, but the hard kernel of resistance had been there from the beginning. It had sprouted when Rusty had shared his lawyer's opinion and grown stronger every moment since, the roots winding deeper into his gut. Not logical. Not even smart. But there it was.

"And what do I tell Kylan?" Mary asked, her voice shaking. "Sorry, kid, you get the short end of the stick. Again. How does your conscience feel about that?"

Like shit.

If she hadn't been on the verge of tears, he might've snapped back at her, but he knew her anger came from guilt, failure, frustration. She was hurting for Kylan, beating herself up for letting him down. She needed to lash out, and he was a big target. Fine. He could take it.

Mary's phone rang. She had to clear her throat, take

a steadying breath before she answered. David heard Starr's agitated voice on the other end, saw Mary's expression shift into alarm.

"We were up at East Glacier. There's no service," she said. "What's wrong?"

There was more shrill chattering that made Mary's face go grim. "Dammit. I should have known... No, it's not your fault. Take a breath, calm down, and for God's sake, drive safe. We'll meet you at the casino in a few minutes."

She jammed the cell phone back into the cup holder and cursed.

"What happened?" David asked.

"Kylan took off."

Oh geezus. David's stomach clenched, remembering what Mary had said about the last time. "How? Where? Can we catch him?"

"I don't know." She tilted forward in her seat, pressed her palms to the dashboard as if to make the pickup go faster. "They went to Cut Bank to a movie. The sequel to one of those stupid alien-invasion movies that Kylan loves. He's been waiting weeks for it to come to town, so I thought maybe it would be good for him to go. Cheer him up, you know? I thought it would be okay—"

Her voice broke, and she had to gather herself before she could go on. "Afterward, they stopped for snacks and ran into one of his other cousins from Lori's dad's side. Weasel." She spat out the word, made it both name and description. "The scuzzbag figured out Kylan had some money and talked him into going to a party."

"Starr didn't go with him?"

Mary shook her head. "She hates Weasel, and she

doesn't want any part of that crowd. She tried to talk Kylan out of going. They had a huge fight, and he left with Weasel." Mary raked trembling hands through her hair, so it was as wild as the fear in her eyes. "Weasel's crowd is older, and some of them…" She bit her bottom lip when it started to tremble, too. "Kylan's not safe with them. And if he gets caught drinking, he'll get suspended and won't be able to go to nationals."

So they wouldn't be calling JoJo. If it had been any other kid, David would've said it served him right. But Kylan wasn't any kid, and intentionally or not, David had had a big part in whatever set him off. "Does Starr know where they went?"

"A tire party somewhere north of town."

"Tire party?" David echoed.

"Like a bonfire, except they're too lazy to gather wood so they just burn old tires."

David grimaced, imagining the stench of burning rubber. "I'll go with you."

"You don't have to—"

He ignored her, taking a right into the casino parking lot. "If this crowd is as rough as you say, you shouldn't go alone."

And if Kylan didn't want to come home, Mary wasn't physically capable of making him. David was. She wanted to argue—he could see it in her eyes—but good sense and concern for Kylan won out. She nodded reluctantly.

As he pulled into a parking spot, Starr leaped out of her battered car and came running, her face puffy with tears. She jerked open Mary's door. "I called my cousin Janelle. She parties with Weasel sometimes." Starr gulped, her dark eyes fixed on Mary. "She said they were going to Freezeout Ridge."

Mary's face went pasty, and she clenched her hands into white-knuckled fists.

"Janelle said she wasn't going because the border patrol's been on a tear," Starr added. "Bustin' up any parties they run across and callin' in the tribal cops."

"Shit." Mary squeezed her eyes shut for a moment. Then she dragged in a deep breath and opened them again, setting her jaw. "We'll go get him."

"Maybe me and him should go," Starr said with a doubtful glance at David. "I know the way, and that place…"

Mary shook her head. "I'm going."

"Me too," Starr said.

"No. You know those guys—"

"Yeah. I'm related to most of 'em." Starr settled the matter by climbing in the back seat and slamming the door.

Mary hesitated only a beat. Then she nodded at David. As he wheeled around, she said, "Take a left and go to the end of Main Street. Then take another left at the stoplight by the concrete tipi."

He followed her terse instructions and ended up on Highway 89, heading straight north out of town, past the hospital and signs that said *Port of Piegan* and *Canada*. A couple of miles out, Mary said, "Take a right up there."

The smaller highway angled to the east for a bit before cutting north again, getting narrower with every mile until the pavement ended completely. The gravel road started out broad and well maintained but degenerated into rutted dirt pocked with mudholes. The pickup bounced and rattled, jarring David's bones and slamming his shoulder against the door as they jolted through yet another washout.

Starr kept up a running monologue from the back seat, cursing Weasel, all of his crowd, and Kylan's hard head. How he could believe those jerk-ass scumbags were any friends of his? Was he trying to lose his chance to rope at nationals?

"I told him." She sniffled, the tears starting up again. "I said he'd get suspended if he got caught, but he said it didn't matter, 'cause if he didn't have Mutt, he couldn't rope for shit anyway." She punctuated the sentence with a glare at David.

"That's no excuse," Mary said tightly. "I've told Kylan flat out to stay away from Weasel and them."

"But—"

"No *but*." Mary braced one hand on the dashboard as David wrestled the pickup over a set of axle-dragging ruts that didn't fit his dual rear tires. "He won't have to worry about having a horse for nationals. I'm not hauling him down there if this is how he acts."

David's head bounced off the ceiling hard enough to make him see stars as they lurched over a cattle guard. Would Mary really refuse to take Kylan to nationals? Or was that just bravado, anger easier to handle than fear?

And curse David's selfish soul, he couldn't help but think—just for a second—that if Kylan couldn't go to nationals, taking Muddy away from him would be a whole lot simpler.

"Take that road," Mary said, pointing to the left.

"What road?" David braked almost to a stop, squinting at what appeared to be a dried-up mud bog.

Tire tracks ran through it to a packed dirt trail on the other side. But since it obviously saw little or no traffic, at least it wasn't as rutted. The so-called road circled the flank of a long, high ridge, backlit by a sun that had only now dropped low in the western sky.

"Is that Freezeout Ridge?" he asked.

"Yeah." As Starr leaned forward, peering between the front seats, a column of black smoke billowed ahead. "Those dumb shits. They ain't even smart enough to wait 'til it's dark to light their fire. If there's border patrol anywhere close, we're screwed."

The draw narrowed, squeezing the road into a tight S curve. Out in the open, the prairie gleamed with slanted golden sun, but in the dense shadow of the butte, it was twilight.

Mary wrapped her fingers around the door handle. "Stay in the pickup, Starr."

"I'm not scared—"

"Kylan's still mad from your fight," Mary cut in. "If he sees you, it'll be harder to get him to come with us."

And David wasn't absolutely sure they could force him, especially if Weasel and the others decided to interfere. David's hands bunched in reflex, his body tensing for a possible fight. His last attempt at brawling had been an embarrassment, but he was sober now and a whole lot more motivated.

Chapter 22

FLAMES GLOWED AHEAD AS THE DRAW WIDENED TO FORM a small bowl carved into the base of the butte. Two battered cars were parked near busted-up chunks of concrete that looked like the remnants of a foundation. A cabin or possibly a barn. Hard to tell through the haze of oily black smoke.

One thing was obvious—it was a dead-end road. They were bottled up like flies in a jar if any kind of cops came along.

Starr hunched down, peeking from behind the headrest of Mary's seat. In the smoke and the shadows, no one outside would see her. And they were all looking. Only half-a-dozen people, David saw with relief. Two guys and three women, all in their twenties, David guessed, though the years had been hard enough they could've passed for forty. Kylan was a soft spot in the crowd, standing toward the rear with a beer bottle in one hand.

Mary took a deep breath, squaring her shoulders. "Let me do the talking."

"No problem," David said.

Starr ducked lower as they kicked open their doors, triggering the dome light. The *thud*, *thud* of the doors closing was as loud as a thunderclap in the now-silent clearing. As David and Mary approached the fire, a couple of the guys stepped forward to meet them, one wiry with a narrow, ferret face and hair slicked back in a greasy ponytail. The other weighed at least four hundred pounds, none of it muscle.

Okay. They could maybe take these two as long as the big guy didn't fall on them. David put himself behind Mary's left shoulder as she stopped a few paces short, just out of reach. Even over the stench of burning rubber, David caught a whiff of body odor.

"Hey, Mary," the fat guy said with a sloppy leer that was missing a couple of teeth on one side. "Never figured you'd show up here."

"Hey, Weasel."

The fat guy was Weasel? David eyed him in amazement. Either the nickname was based solely on his personality, or he'd been a lot skinnier as a kid.

"If you wanna party with us, you better've brought your own booze," Weasel declared.

Mary spread her hands, showing they were empty. "I guess we're outta luck, so I'll just take Kylan and go home."

"Maybe Kylan don't want to leave. And you ain't even introduced me to your friend." The nod toward David sent a ripple through multiple chins. "Or is the hotshot cowboy too cool for us rez boys?"

David shifted onto the balls of his feet, uncomfortably aware of how flashy his Finals jacket looked compared to the other men's cheap, greasy windbreakers.

Mary tilted her head toward him. "Weasel, this is David." She kept her voice cool, her stance firm but not hostile as she shifted her gaze to the huddle of people. "Come on, Kylan, let's go."

Kylan didn't move. His face was set in the usual stubborn, sulky lines.

"He's tired of bein' a sissy boy, always under your thumb," Weasel taunted. "He's gonna stay here, party with the grown-ups."

David slid his gaze from Weasel to his buddy and on to Kylan, let his disgust show as their eyes met. *Is this what you want?*

Kylan couldn't hold his stare. But he didn't budge. Neither did Weasel.

The skinny guy smirked. "Guess you can go on back to town, Mama Mary."

"Guess so."

To David's astonishment, she stepped back, started to turn. Then she paused. "Oh, by the way…when we were driving out here, JoJo called to warn me. He heard on the scanner that the border patrol saw your smoke and they're headed this way."

For an instant, they were frozen. Then they burst into frenzied movement as if the grass beneath their feet had gone up in flames. The women scurried around, fumbling for bottles and cans that weren't empty yet, while Kylan made a futile attempt to kick dirt on the fire. Only Weasel hesitated, like he might call her bluff.

"Shit, Weasel," the ferret-faced guy said, joining the stampede toward the cars. "Cops got a warrant on me. I gotta get out of here."

Weasel grunted, gave Mary one last leer. "Later, bitch."

The car sputtered and then roared, the skinny guy revving the engine as Weasel lumbered over and wedged his bulk into the passenger seat. Kylan started after them.

"No, Kylan, you can't—" Mary jumped to intercept him, but he shoved her away. She stumbled, going down to one knee as Kylan broke into a run.

David didn't bother to talk. He launched his body at Kylan like the defensive tackle he'd been back in high school. His shoulder slammed into Kylan's chest, and they went down in a heap, David on top. He heard the air go out of Kylan's lungs in one big *oof*. The kid squirmed, but between lack of oxygen and David's weight, it was a weak effort.

His buddy Weasel wasn't waiting around anyway. The car whipped around in a ragged, bouncing arc, the back bumper swinging close enough that the tires spat dirt in David's face as the skinny guy gunned it. They hit the road at an angle, lurching over the grassy berm. The rear end slewed sideways, first one way and then the other. One tire caught in some brush on the shoulder and sent the car careening up the side of the draw. The driver yanked at the wheel, and the car swung sideways, slid downhill, and caught, the uphill tires coming off the ground.

For an instant, it hung there, a breath away from rolling down the embankment and into the draw below. Then the tires slammed down and the front end came around. The car bounced onto the road and away, skidding through the bend in the draw and out of sight. The second car followed more cautiously.

Kylan jerked, driving an elbow into David's gut. He rolled off, turning the kid loose.

Starr ran up to crouch beside Kylan, tears streaming down her face. "Ky, baby, are you okay? Oh my God, I don't know whether to hug you or kill you." She chose the first, flinging her arms around him and burying her face in his chest.

At first, David thought the girl was making the weird moaning sound. Then he realized it was coming from behind him. He twisted around, alarm shooting another spurt of adrenaline into his veins. Mary was still on the ground where she'd fallen, crouched into a tight ball with her fists pressed against her eyes, face screwed up tight. She rocked slowly, rhythmically, her lips moving, another low, guttural moan coming from deep in her throat.

David scrambled over to her on hands and knees and reached out, but he stopped short of touching her. Was she injured? Having some kind of seizure? "Mary? Are you hurt?"

She gave no sign of hearing him. He leaned in closer, straining to hear the words she mumbled. "Eighteen, nineteen, twenty…" She was…counting?

"Mary?" he said again, letting his hand rest lightly on her shoulder.

She flinched away, shaking her head, counting louder. David pulled his hand back.

"Starr," he called softly. "What's happening to her?"

Starr peeled herself off Kylan and stood. With oily smoke swirling around her, face smeared with black makeup and hair wild, she looked as if she'd emerged from the apocalypse. She stared at Mary, edging closer. "Flashback, maybe? I heard she used to get them, and this is the worst place…"

"What do I do?" David asked, helpless.

"I dunno, but we gotta get out of here before the cops really do come."

Kylan stumbled to his feet, hunched over, his breathing labored. He shot a glare at David. "What did you do to her?"

"I didn't do anything!" David snapped. "You're the reason she's here."

"She din't have to come after me," Kylan shot back, but there was a whine under the bravado.

"Oh, shut up." Starr punched him hard in the arm. "You're such a jerk."

Mary didn't seem to hear any of it, still rocking and counting.

"Can you carry her to the pickup?" Starr asked, with a panicked look over her shoulder at the road.

Mary was small enough, for sure, but would she freak out if David grabbed her?

"We have to *go*," Starr said.

She was right. They couldn't get caught here with the fire still burning, remnants of the party scattered on the ground around them, and beer on Kylan's breath. David sent up a quick, silent prayer, then scooped Mary into his arms and staggered to his feet. *Damn*. For a little thing, she was packed pretty solid.

She stiffened, her head rearing back, her eyes popping open but not seeing.

"Easy, Mary," he murmured in her ear. "It's okay. I've got you. You're safe."

He strode toward the pickup, as fast as he could in the dim light, hoping to at least get her in the back seat before she came unglued. She strained against his hold, strong in her panic. David stumbled, nearly lost his grip, but suddenly she went limp, curled into him, and buried her face inside the open front of his jacket like a frightened kitten.

Starr hustled ahead and opened the door. David tried to settle Mary on the seat, but her fingers clutched his coat, refusing to let go.

"Can you drive?" David asked Starr.

"A stick shift? Uh…maybe."

"Not very good," Kylan said. "I'm better."

"You've been drinking," David said. "Get in the pickup. Starr can manage."

David ducked his head and slid into the back seat, Mary on his lap. Starr shut the door behind them and jumped behind the wheel.

"Put it in first gear and let the clutch out slow," David said as she fired up the engine.

She did as instructed. The pickup lurched, but she didn't kill the engine. She eased it around and onto the road. Kylan slouched on the passenger's side, sneaking worried glances at Mary as David coached Starr through shifting into second gear and then third, which was as fast as they could go on the god-awful road.

The pickup rocked through a set of ruts, and David cupped Mary's head to keep it from bouncing against his shoulder. A sigh shuddered through her body, and her hands released their death grip on his coat. She flattened one palm against his chest. The other fell into her lap. The harsh lines smoothed from her face.

She was the only one who could relax. The air inside the pickup crackled with tension as the rest of them strained their eyes for any sign of a vehicle bearing down from any direction, but the visible lights were all stationary, orangish outdoor security lamps that had flickered to life as the sun sank behind the mountains.

David's adrenaline began to fade, slowly pushed aside by awareness. Mary's warmth, the soft press of her body against his, the friction generated by the rocking and bouncing of the pickup. His body responded, his blood heating and his pulse rising.

Stop. Geezus. He had to think about something else. Anything but how perfectly she fit there in his arms. How easy it would be to tip her head back, put his mouth on hers…and get his throat ripped out in return. He tried to conjure up depressing thoughts. Picture the withering, sunbaked prairie back home. That was always guaranteed to deflate his…mood. Dry. Dust. Desert…

Afghanistan. What had happened to Mary over there, bad enough that reliving it could completely disable her? David had only vague impressions of news reports, half-heard stories of roadside IEDs and suicide bombers. He'd never paid attention. Had never wanted to know.

Wasn't sure he wanted to know now.

After a five-minute eternity, they reached the main road. David breathed a sigh of relief as they bounced over the cattle guard and then sucked it back in when headlights popped over the hill behind them, followed immediately by an explosion of blue and red flashers.

Starr said a very bad word as she pulled over. "Still think you shoulda drove?" she asked, shooting Kylan a spiteful glare. "Woulda been real smart, getting a DUI when you don't even have a license."

"You said you could drive," David said, adding a glare of his own.

"I can," Kylan shot back and then hunched his shoulders, burying his chin in his chest. "I drive good. I just can't pass the stupid written test."

"Everything is just so hard for him."

Even getting a driver's license. Christ. No wonder the kid wanted to run away from himself, be someone, somewhere else. If he couldn't get a license, how could he get a job? Any job. Especially in a place like this, where he couldn't exactly hop a bus or a subway to work. So many little stumbling blocks, stacked up one by one. To Kylan, they must seem like a solid brick wall he'd been bashing into his whole life.

Starr finger-combed her hair and swiped at her smudged eyes, managing to look less disastrous by the time the white SUV bounced to a stop behind them. They waited, but it just sat there, lights spinning.

"What's he doing?" Kylan asked, darting a scared glance out the back window.

"Running my plates," David said. Or so he guessed.

"They're real suspicious of out-of-state vehicles on these back roads," Starr said. "In case you're running drugs. Or smuggling guns into Canada."

Oh great. David imagined them all dragged into an interrogation room at the nearest border crossing, held for hours while the pickup was torn apart as they looked for secret compartments. The door of the SUV opened, and a broad-shouldered male figure stepped out, flashlight beam skimming over the ground as he walked. A light-colored uniform, not black like JoJo's.

Starr rolled down her window and pasted on a smile. "What can we do for you, officer?"

"Agent," he corrected. "Border patrol. What are you doing out here so late tonight?"

Late? David glanced at the dashboard clock, stunned to see it read ten thirty.

"We was showing him around," Starr said, jerking a thumb over her shoulder at David. "He's visitin' for a couple of days. Wanted to see some ranch country."

The flashlight beam swung around, full in David's face. "Name and residence?" the agent asked.

"David Parsons. Brush, Colorado."

"This is your vehicle?"

"Yes."

The officer nodded, as if that jived with his information. "Reason for visiting?"

"Business. A, um, horse deal."

The flashlight beam settled on David's jacket, the National Finals logo with his name stitched underneath. Then it slid down to Mary. Her head jerked up and she blinked, her eyes unfocused. She burrowed deeper into David's jacket, digging her fingers into his chest as if she wanted get under his skin.

David tightened his arms around her, stroking the back of her head.

"What's wrong with her?" the agent asked.

"Migraine," Starr said. "They come on real sudden, so bad we have to take her to the hospital to get a shot. Light and noise are super painful for her," she added, with a pointed look at the flashlight.

The agent took the hint, switching the beam over to Kylan, who stared back like the proverbial deer in the headlights. "I don't suppose you happened upon a party while you were touring around?"

"We seen the smoke," Starr said. "But we din't want nothin' to do with them guys."

"Which *guys* would those be?" the agent asked, suspicion sharpening his tone.

"The kind that have tire parties," Starr retorted.

David probably should speak up, help her out, but she was handling it better than he would, so he buttoned his lip. Kylan seemed to be going with the silent approach, too, thank God. Or he was too terrified to speak.

"Where was this party located?" the agent asked.

Starr pointed back over her shoulder. "Last road west. Least that's where it looks like the smoke is coming from."

"But you didn't drive up there."

"Mary don't go on that road," Starr said. "It's where her brothers died."

Kylan made a choking sound. The flashlight beam swung around to his face.

"Something wrong, son?"

"I…uh…forgot. About the wreck bein' there." His voice started to quake, and he clamped his mouth shut.

"Was it recent?" the agent asked.

Starr shook her head and lowered her voice, injecting some drama. "It was awful, though. All four guys in the back of the pickup got killed. And Mary seen it happen, so, you know…"

Mary *saw* it?

David tightened his arms around her in reflex, as if he could protect her from the horror, but it was much, much too late. Now he didn't have to wonder what she'd seen during that flashback. Dear God. And she'd gone to war *after* that?

The border patrol agent lowered the flashlight, gave each of them a long look. Then he stepped back, face inscrutable. "I won't keep you, then. Drive safe."

"Will do," Starr said.

He got in his SUV, switched off the flashers and bumped through a U-turn. Starr waited until he was headed back toward the smoke that still billowed from the base of the butte before easing out the clutch, so he wouldn't see the pickup lurch when she fumbled the clutch.

Smart girl.

As she worked her way up through the gears, David felt a different sort of tension building in Mary's body. Awareness. She shifted, tipped her head back, and stared up at him.

"You," she whispered.

He nodded, bracing himself for her reaction.

"I… Why…" She trailed off, her body still curled into his like a missing piece as the haze cleared from her eyes. Then she moved so fast he had no chance to react, scooting off his lap and across the seat.

The motion caught Starr's attention, and she eyed Mary in the rearview mirror. "You okay?"

"Yeah."

Her voice was husky, her face pale and sharply drawn in the dim-green glow of the dash lights. She looked very young, and very alone way over there on the other side of the pickup. David ached to gather her up again, shelter her until the monsters inside her head crawled back into their hiding places.

He reached out and cupped his hand over hers where it rested on the seat. Her startled, wary gaze jumped to meet his. He gave her icy fingers a gentle squeeze. She stared at him for a long moment and then slumped so her head rested against the back of the seat. Her eyes drifted shut while he cradled her hand as carefully as an injured bird.

Chapter 23

THEY ALL SANK INTO THEIR OWN THOUGHTS FOR THE NEXT few bone-rattling miles. Then the road noticeably improved, and Starr shifted into fourth gear without prompting. Beside her, Kylan began to snuffle, turning his face into the collar of his coat. Starr didn't say a word, just flipped on the radio and turned the staticky country station loud enough to mask the noise.

If Mary noticed, she gave no indication. She made no movement or sound whatsoever until the pickup bumped from gravel onto pavement. Then she slid her hand from under David's and straightened. "Pull over, Starr. You shouldn't try to drive this thing in town."

Starr pulled over, and she and David swapped places. As he slid behind the wheel, Kylan swiped an arm across his eyes, trying to erase the signs of his tears. David took his cue from the women and pretended he didn't see. Starr scooted across the seat, wrapped one arm around Mary, and put the other hand on Kylan's shoulder, forming a tight little nucleus that left David firmly on the outside.

Right where he belonged. So why did he care?

When they passed the old gas station on the main drag, the street people were still huddled in front, half-a-dozen dogs milling around them. By contrast, the casino and adjacent hotel looked surreal, the parking lots an oasis of brightly lit, pristine concrete. David parked next to Starr's compact Chevy and killed the headlights.

"You need anything tomorrow, let me know," Starr said with one last squeeze of Mary's shoulders.

Mary worked up a weary smile. "We've got another day of curriculum training at the college, so I won't be at home." She tapped Kylan on the shoulder. "Walk her to her car."

"But it's right—"

Mary smacked him harder.

"All right. I'm going." Kylan slouched out of the pickup.

David didn't pretend not to watch as the kid cowered like a whipped pup while Starr read him what appeared to be the riot act. Then she relented, wrapping her arms around his neck and bringing her face close to his. He nodded at whatever she whispered in his ear. She patted his damp cheek and then kissed it for good measure before shoving him away toward his pickup.

"Did you apologize?" Mary asked when Kylan climbed into the passenger's seat.

"I tried, but she was too busy yelling at me. She said if I ever pull anything this stupid again, she's done with me." His eyes filled with tears. He tried to sniff them back. "I din't know that was where they was going, Mary. And I forgot about your brothers. Honest. I din't mean to—"

"I know." That was it. No *It's okay* or *I'm fine*. Her tone suggested that life would be considerably less than okay for Kylan when they got home.

"Should I follow Starr to be sure she gets home safe?" David asked as the girl backed her car out of the parking slot.

"That would be nice." Mary tilted her head back and closed her eyes, as if the little bit of conversation had worn her out.

David saw Starr safely into her driveway, then circled back to the main drag and pointed the pickup west out of town.

"How come your trailer is parked here?" Kylan asked as they turned into the driveway.

"David and I had dinner. We, uh—"

"Had things to talk about," David cut in. *Geezus*. She acted like she was confessing to adultery instead of huckleberry pie.

Kylan grunted. The pickup barely came to a complete halt in front of their house before he was out the door, slamming it behind him.

"Thank you for driving and...everything," Mary said stiffly, pushing her door open but not getting out. "I, well...it's good you were there."

She kept her head down, undoubtedly embarrassed that he'd seen her flashback, or whatever that was she'd had.

"Want me to stay and knock some sense into Kylan for you?" David asked, only half joking. Not that he would ever smack a kid, but looking at Mary's pale, drawn face, it was hard not to want to give him a good, hard shake.

She laughed, the sound thin and brittle. "Thanks, but no. I can manage."

"Are you sure?" David unbuckled his seat belt and twisted around to look at her straight on instead of in the mirror. The shadows in her eyes had crept down to darken the circles beneath them. "You look whipped. Maybe you could leave it until morning."

She shook her head. "We'll both be better off if we have it out before we go to bed. I won't be able to sleep for a while anyway. I need to…unwind."

Chase the demons back into their hidey-holes, she meant. David wanted to say he understood, but of course he didn't. The worst thing that had ever happened to him was nothing compared to what Mary had been through. And no way in hell was he leaving her and the kid alone out here tonight. What if Kylan took off again?

David turned off the pickup. "I think it'd be best if I stayed."

"Here?" Her eyes widened.

"In my trailer. Just in case."

"We don't need a watchdog."

"Then humor me. I'll sleep better if I'm close by." He flicked off the headlights and stepped out into night air that felt like it had lost twenty degrees since sunset. "Do you mind if I check out your tipi? I've never seen the inside of one."

She shut the pickup door, her brows drawn together as if trying to figure out what weird game he was playing. Finally, she shrugged. "Go ahead. There's an electric lantern to your right just inside the door."

"Thanks."

"You're welcome. I'm just going to—" She gestured toward the house.

"Okay."

Good night seemed stupid, considering, so he said, "I'll see you in the morning."

She gave him another of those searching looks, then nodded and turned to walk to her house. Her strides were slower than usual, as if she dreaded the confrontation to come. She paused a beat with her hand on the doorknob, shoulders squaring and chin coming up. Battle mode. David doubted Kylan would appreciate the butt-kicking he was about to receive, even if it was for his own good.

The tipi loomed, ghost-white in the darkness, but David went the other direction first, to check on Muddy. Just a quick peek in the barn, because he still had trouble believing the horse would be there. But he was—square, solid, his eyes slitted with annoyance at the intrusion. In contrast, Frosty nickered softly in welcome and stuck his head over the stall gate in search of the horse treats Adam liked to feed him and insisted David keep on hand.

"No luck tonight, buddy," David said.

Frosty nuzzled his hand to be sure and then sighed, disappointed. David scratched behind his ear in consolation. He would miss Frosty. The gray might not have Muddy's talent, but he was a lot better company.

David propped his elbow on the stall gate, combing his fingers through Frosty's long, silky forelock as he replayed the scene out there on Freezeout Ridge. *Christ.* No wonder Mary was so prickly and overprotective. She'd watched her brothers *die.* A person didn't get over something like that. Then tonight, Kylan had come damn close to repeating history, making all her nightmares come true.

Which begged the obvious question… What would the kid do when David took Muddy?

Somewhere not far away, a coyote howled, setting off an eerie chorus of yips and yowls that hit a crescendo, then faded into silence, leaving only the soft snuffle of horses breathing. David listened to the night breeze sifting through the trees while he probed at his emotions.

Seeing what he'd seen, knowing what he now knew about Mary and Kylan, had set him back on his heels, that was for sure. But was it enough to change his mind?

Not about leaving Muddy. That would never be an option. But the reward? How much was his peace of mind worth? A hell of a lot more than five grand. Still, the sour taste gathered at the back of his tongue when he considered paying Mary off. It felt wrong deep down in his gut.

Not unjust, he realized. Not unfair. *Wrong*.

Wrong answer. Wrong move. The money and a new horse weren't what Kylan needed. Not in the long run. Or even the short run. Certainty shot through David's veins, hot and heady as bourbon. He didn't know the right answer, not yet, but the reward money wasn't it. He felt it the same way he'd known he couldn't collect the insurance money for Muddy, no matter what it cost him. Instinct? Or a helping hand from the old boys upstairs?

An idea that had been floating around tried to take root in his head—one that might solve all their problems—but David shook it loose. It was way too risky, especially after what had happened tonight.

David stared at Muddy as if the horse could somehow give him a clue. Muddy rolled his eyes back until the whites gleamed, yawning as if to say, "Are you still here?"

"Yeah, yeah. I can take a hint." David gave Frosty a final scratch and then double-checked the stall latches before he left.

Not that he was paranoid or anything.

Chapter 24

OUTSIDE, A SILVERY QUARTER MOON HAD CLIMBED INTO A sky dense with stars. It seemed odd to see the same familiar constellations, but comforting, a reminder David hadn't landed on a completely different planet. Bending over double to step through the circular entrance to the tipi, he found the lantern and turned it on as he let the canvas door flap fall shut behind him, frowning at the harsh blue glow of the LED bulb.

It was cozier than he'd expected. The walls didn't slant outward clear to the ground. A four-foot-high canvas liner circled the inside, forming a near-vertical wall decorated with a parade of crudely painted animals, most of which were vaguely recognizable as horses, wolves, buffalo, deer, or elk. The ground was also covered by canvas and a hodgepodge of rugs, but the center had been left open for a pit circled by rocks. Logs and kindling were stacked inside, and the tipi smelled of woodsmoke from fires past.

A trio of lawn chairs were scattered around the interior, and against the far wall a low camp bed was piled with pillows, blankets and what appeared to be a buffalo hide. Half of one anyway, David saw when he lifted it from the bed. One side tanned, the other covered with coarse, curly hair. And heavy. The weight of it would go a long way toward sealing out the chilly night air. He folded it in half and set it aside, then spotted a blue plastic cooler.

The evening's drama had left him with a powerful thirst, so he flipped open the lid. Inside, half a dozen cans of store-brand soda floated in melted ice. David contemplated the selection and then picked grape because it was Adam's favorite and he had a sudden, intense need to feel closer to home.

He stacked up the pillows and sleeping bag on the camp bed and sat down, using the bedding as a backrest so he could recline and stare up at the converging poles of the tipi above him, a tiny slice of jet-black sky visible through the smoke hole at the top. Fatigue pooled like lead in his muscles. Geezus, what a day. He closed his eyes, let his tired brain go blank to everything except the skitters, squeaks, and sighs of the night.

He was on the verge of dozing when Mary's front door opened and then closed. David's pulse jumped. He hadn't expected to see her again tonight. Or was it Kylan sneaking out? David listened intently but couldn't hear footsteps. Whoever had come outside, they must be crossing the lawn, not the gravel driveway.

The tipi flap rustled, and Mary poked her head in. "Oh. Hey. I guess I don't have to tell you to make yourself at home."

"Hope you don't mind." He should sit up, but he felt like his bones had melted.

"The least I can do is buy you a drink." She stepped through the door, letting the flap fall behind her. "I just wanted to tell you that there's an electrical outlet inside the door of the barn, if you want to plug your trailer in."

"Thanks. I will."

She clasped and unclasped her hands, then cocked

her head, eyeing him. "It's weird, seeing you laid back. You are a very upright sort of person."

"I try to be."

"I noticed. You've swooped me up and out of danger twice now." She fluttered one hand over her heart and faked a smile. "My hero."

He toasted her with the grape soda. "Dudley Do-Right, at your service."

Her eyebrows arched, questioning.

"Like the movie." Damn. Why did he bring that up? "Someone called me that once, because I'm so... upright."

Make that uptight. At least, that's what the blond interviewer in Cody had implied when he'd turned down her offer. And he'd been so self-righteous, so smug because he was so much better than that and Emily deserved nothing but the best. Lucky for her, she'd found it. Too bad for David it wasn't him.

"The bravest of the Canadian Mounties and his trusty horse. I can see you playing that part." Mary laughed softly. Because the humor chased some of the strain from her face, he didn't mind that it was at his expense. She glanced around, as if deciding which of the chairs to take.

He surprised both of them by patting the camp bed next to him. "Sit with me."

She eyed the spot like it might be booby-trapped. "Why?"

"I like it when you're close." Crap. What was he saying? The tipi must be working some kind of weird voodoo on his brain, because he patted the space beside him again. "You look like you're about to fall over. Trust me. Would Dudley lead you astray?"

She narrowed her eyes at him. "How do I know you aren't Snidely Whiplash in disguise?"

"You'll have to take my word for it."

She wavered, the doubts chasing across her face, one after another, as she pondered all the reasons she should stay the hell away from him. He didn't suppose trust came easily for Mary at the best of times, and their whole situation was anything but. Air backed up in his lungs when she moved toward him like she was a wild fawn and he might frighten her away if he took a breath. She eased down on the camp bed, perched on the very edge, not exactly beside him but better than across the room. Or tipi, in this case.

"How'd it go in there?" he asked, tilting his head toward the house.

"The usual. He's sorry. He never meant to scare me. He feels terrible." She blew out a troubled sigh and then angled a questioning look at David. "He's afraid you think he's dumb and irresponsible, and you won't let him help you shoe Frosty tomorrow like you said. Obviously, the two of you spent more time together today than I realized."

Wow. Was that just this morning? It seemed like a week had passed since Kylan's impromptu shoeing lesson. "We're still on."

She dipped her head, lacing and unlacing nervous fingers. "Thank you. Knowing how precious Muddy is to you…it meant a lot to Kylan that you trusted him to help. I guess that's why he went along to Rusty's. He felt like he owed you."

"That wasn't why I let him help me." David bristled, insulted by the implication. "Is it impossible for you to believe a person could do something without an ulterior motive?"

"Not impossible. But not exactly easy, either."

"Why is that?"

She clasped her hands and pushed her thumbs up to form a steeple. "I have a mother who only calls when she needs someone to listen to her problems, a sister who'd trade me and her son for a dime bag of anything with a decent kick, and the army…" She wrinkled her nose. "If you have any illusions about humanity before you enlist, you can bet they'll be gone by the end of your first overseas deployment."

David frowned, studying her profile. "Why do you stay here? With your credentials, you could go almost anywhere, get Kylan away from people like Weasel."

"I'd also be taking him away from Galen and Cissy. JoJo." She rubbed one thumb against the other, up and down, eyes focused on the motion. "There are bad people everywhere, and they seem to gravitate toward Kylan. Or he gravitates toward them. Either way, at least here I know who they are."

"The devil you know?"

"Yeah." She rubbed one thumb across a smear of dirt on the knee of her jeans where she'd fallen when Kylan pushed her. "There are plenty of good people around here. We take care of each other. Everybody keeps an eye out for the kids."

A whole network of spies to help her keep track of Kylan. But the watchdogs couldn't be on guard every single minute. Look at tonight. At some point, somehow, Kylan had to learn to handle himself. If he didn't…

David would rather not think about the alternative.

"Did you live with Galen and his wife, the way Kylan lives with you?"

"Yes." A fond smile came and went, the sadness creeping back into her eyes. "After my brothers died."

"What about your mother?"

"She was a mess. She could barely take care of herself."

"Does Galen have kids of his own?"

"Yep." She held up four fingers. "The last daughter had just graduated from high school and left for college, and along I came to foul up their empty nest."

"I bet they didn't think of it that way."

"You might lose that bet." She shook her head. "I was a handful before the accident, let alone after."

"Really? I would've figured you for the straight-A student."

"I was. Didn't mean I wasn't a wreck lookin' for a place to happen." The expression in her eyes was so bleak that David had to work at keeping both hands on his soda can and off her.

"The accident was bound to have some effect."

"You'd think so, wouldn't you?" Her mouth twisted. "Didn't teach us a damn thing. The day of their funeral, we all went out and got drunk *in their honor*. Like it couldn't happen to us. Probably would've, if it hadn't been for Cissy. I stayed out all night, came stumbling in expecting her to chew my ass, but she just looked at me and said, 'Please don't make me have to bury you beside your brothers. I don't think I could stand it.'"

Mary shivered, rubbing her hands up and down her arms as if to chase away a chill. "I actually saw myself in the coffin. And it finally hit me that I could die, and I really didn't want to." She wrapped her arms around her waist, staring into the cold fire pit as if she could see the scene playing out there.

"Can we light the fire?" David asked.

She started and then frowned. "It's late."

"You said you wouldn't be able to sleep for a while." He ran his gaze around the inside of the tipi. "Artificial light doesn't do this justice."

She shrugged. "Go ahead. I could use warming up."

David refrained from offering his body as a ready and willing source of heat, peeling himself off the bed instead. Much safer to keep the flames inside the fire pit.

Chapter 25

DAVID KNELT BESIDE THE FIRE RING, STRUCK A MATCH from the box Mary had found for him, and held the flame to a cluster of tiny, dry pine branches. It took hold with a greedy crackle.

"I suppose you were a Boy Scout, too," Mary said.

"Nah, I was an ag nerd. I showed a steer every year at the county fair until I was fourteen, then I got too busy with the junior rodeos."

"You started early."

He fed a slightly larger twig into the fire, watched the flame lick around it. "My uncle gave me a rope for my second birthday, and I slept with it instead of a teddy bear."

"You must've had to work pretty hard to get so good."

David nudged another twig into the growing fire. "When you love what you're doing, it doesn't seem like work."

"Even when it's not going so well?"

"Even then." He flashed her a wry smile. "You know what they say, the worst day roping is better than the best day of honest work."

"You treat it like a real job."

"I have to. Otherwise, I'd be pretty skinny by now." He carefully crossed a pair of larger chunks of kindling over the hungry fire, thinking of how patient and connected she'd been with her students the day before. "I bet you feel the same way about what you do."

She smiled, her face going soft. "Yeah. Some days it's so frustrating you wonder if you're accomplishing anything, but when I get up in the morning, there's nothing I'd rather do."

"Exactly."

Their eyes met, and this time the ping of connection was different. Deeper. Soul to kindred soul.

Mary looked down at her hands, lacing her fingers together again. "Are you over her? The one who left you?"

"Yes." His response was abrupt enough to raise Mary's eyebrows. David poked at the fire with a stick and then threw it onto the flames. "I wouldn't take her back if she showed up on my doorstep tomorrow."

"That's not the same as being over what she did."

He shrugged. "Some lessons can't be unlearned."

Mary was quiet, staring into the fire. Then she sighed. "It would be nice, wouldn't it? If you could just wipe the slate clean, start over?"

For himself, David would have said no. He didn't want to be that stupid, that vulnerable, all over again. For Mary…knowing the memories that haunted her, if he could clear the shadows from her eyes for even an hour, a day, he'd do it. He stacked a couple more logs on the fire and then switched off the lantern, leaving the firelight to dance over the creatures that ambled around the walls. "Nice drawings. Do them yourself?"

She shook her head with another of those soft smiles. "I took the canvas into my classroom and turned the kids loose on it."

"That explains the purple dinosaur. I didn't think they were a big part of Native American culture."

She laughed. "They were a big part of Crystal Little Bear's culture at the time."

He stood, brushed the wood shavings from his jeans and sat down beside Mary, close enough to feel her tense. Every inch of skin on that side of his body tingled, as if the very molecules were straining to reach out and touch her.

"What are you doing, David?" she asked quietly.

"I don't know, but I can't seem to stop." He angled a glance at her, but she turned her face away. "If it doesn't feel right to you, I'll back off."

"Doing something because it feels good has never worked out very well for me."

"Maybe you were doing it with the wrong guy."

She looked at him, caution and humor fighting for the upper hand. "Are you the right guy, Dudley?"

"There's only one way to find out."

She went still, her eyes locked on his as he reached up to cup her face. He rested his little finger against the fluttering pulse in the curve of her throat as he lowered his head and brushed his mouth over hers. Just a taste. A test. When she didn't pull away, he went back for more, gentle, coaxing kisses that she returned in kind. They eased into each other, feeling their way, lips, then tongues, touching, tasting, but not taking more than was offered.

He felt her smile against his mouth and pulled back to look at her. "What?"

"The first boy I ever kissed tasted like grape soda."

He touched a fingertip to a freckle on her nose. "I hope it's a good memory."

"It was very sweet." Her eyes twinkled with mischief. "And not just because of the grape soda."

"Then I'd best be sure I match it," he said and kissed her again.

This time he gave himself more rein, asked for the same in return. She leaned in to him, sliding her hands inside the open front of his jacket to press her palms to his chest. The contact set his blood pounding. He ached to haul her hard against him, press her into the softness of the bed and find the release his body craved. He settled for working his fingers beneath the bottom band of her pullover, peeling up the clingy cotton shirt underneath until he found bare flesh.

She breathed a sigh into his mouth as he spread his fingers over warm, silky skin, able to span the width of her lower back with one hand. The muscle beneath was firm, her body petite but not fragile. A spine of steel, like her name.

And if he kissed her much longer, he was gonna have a permanent kink in his back from bending in half.

He moved his hand down, cupped her butt, the curve of it fitting his palm exactly the way he'd known it would. He eased back onto the pillows, lifting her so she sprawled across his chest, her thigh between his. David groaned at the rub of denim on denim, over the hard and ready flesh beneath.

She nibbled at the corner of his mouth, her tongue playing hide-and-seek with his as she trailed her hand down, along his side to the hem of his shirt. The muscles in his stomach tensed in anticipation. A reflex, dammit; he was not sucking in his gut. But man, was he glad he'd ditched the spare tire. It was worth every drop he'd sweated to hear that hum of appreciation low in Mary's throat when her fingers trailed across his navel, then back to his chest, combing through the hair she found there.

He cupped the back of her head with one palm, capturing her teasing mouth while his other hand reluctantly gave up possession of her butt and went exploring under her shirt, tracing the curve of her spine. She arched into him, made him groan again, and then laughed at his pain. He slid his palm higher, thumb and pinkie finger skimming the delicate angles of her shoulder blades, the impossibly soft skin between.

Completely bare skin. His hand froze, and he broke free of the kiss to blink up at her. "You're not wearing a bra."

Her smile raised his internal temperature another ten degrees. "It's not like I need one."

Holy. Crap. She was naked under there. He lost his breath, his lungs flattened by a tidal wave of lust. All he had to do was slide his hand around to the front, and he'd be holding a piece of heaven. Even better, he could push her shirt up and taste it…

No. He couldn't.

He pulled his hand from under her shirt, smoothed both layers into place, willing his heart to stop thundering. She tipped her head back to give him a puzzled frown, dropping her wandering hand to his waist.

"What? You don't approve?"

His laugh was three-parts groan. "Hell, yes, I approve, but I don't want to take advantage."

"Of me? You're a little late for that." But her words were slightly blurred around the edges, her eyes a tiny bit glassy. He guessed it was from more than lust. He ran his hand up her spine—on the outside of her pullover, unfortunately—and kneaded gently.

"You've been put through the wringer twice today. You're exhausted…and I'm betting you popped another migraine pill."

Her gaze dropped to his chest, and her bottom lip poked out. "Only half."

"Enough." And he'd bet she'd needed it. If she'd had a killer headache before dinner, it must feel like she'd been whacked with a sledgehammer now. "How often do you have flashbacks?"

She extracted her hand from his shirt, avoiding his gaze. "Not since high school. I thought I was over them."

"Did you get professional help?"

"Sure. Sad to say, our school district has a lot of experience in grief counseling, so they've got all the resources in place."

He massaged a slow circle at the base of her neck. "The counting… Is that something they taught you?"

"Was I counting?" Her forehead puckered as she tried to remember. "It's a coping mechanism. A way to try to stay grounded in reality. But tonight it came on so fast, I couldn't hold it off."

David stared at her, confounded. How could she go through something like that and choose to enlist? "I can't believe they let you in the military."

"They didn't know. I was a minor when my brothers died. My mental health records are sealed."

"Weren't you worried you might have a flashback in the middle of a mission or something?"

"I cruised through basic training without any problems, so I figured I'd be okay. And I was…until tonight." She blew out a long stream of air. "It was damn near inevitable, I suppose. Same place, same stupid shit."

Same man, at least inside her head? He hesitated, but he couldn't resist asking. "Who did you think I was when I carried you out of there?"

"I don't know. His name, I mean." She twisted one of the buttons on his shirt, the friction setting off little explosions of desire in spite of the depressing turn in the conversation. "After the accident, I went into shock. I freaked out when they tried to put me on a stretcher. One of the EMTs carried me to the ambulance and held me on his lap all the way to the hospital." She smoothed a hand over David's chest. "He was big, solid, like you."

David slid his hand up and down her back in long, soothing strokes, all he could offer to ease the pain of remembering. "I thought it might have been the guy who left you because of Kylan."

"You say that like there was only one," she quipped and then bit her lip as if she regretted the words. Instead of hiding her face, though, she leaned in closer, nose to nose. "Did you know your eyes are the exact same color as the mountains right before sunset?"

"In other words, you don't want to talk about this anymore."

"Not tonight, thanks."

"Fair enough." He had no right or reason to pry. Just a burning need to know everything about this woman he'd never see again once he left Browning. He went back to kneading her tense muscles.

She arched into his caress like a cat. "Keep that up for an hour or two and I bet you'd get good at it."

"Practice makes perfect."

He moved up to massage the base of her neck again, enjoying how her hair tickled his fingers even if it did nothing to help his body settle. Like that was going to happen anyway with Mary draped over him. She nestled her head into his shoulder. He liked the weight of it there, the trust it implied.

"You must have plenty of opportunities to practice," she said, tracing the line of his jaw, her fingertip rasping against the stubble. "And don't try to tell me Emily is the only girl you've ever kissed. You're not that pure of heart, Dudley."

He rolled his eyes. "I'm gonna wish I never told you that stupid nickname."

"Yep," she agreed with a quick grin. "And you're changing the subject."

He sighed, wishing they could skip this part of the getting-to-know-you routine. Women always got weird when they realized how backward he was about sex. "There were other girls before Emily. And after she left, I was mad at the world and dead set on getting even. I did some things…" He shrugged, assuming she could fill in the blanks.

"But not anymore?"

He tilted his head back, gazing up at the point where all the tipi poles converged. "It didn't feel right, being with someone when there were no feelings involved."

"Have you had feelings for anyone since Emily?"

"Not really." *Unless you count now*.

His hand froze on Mary's back again. Where in the hell did that thought come from? Mary was…different. Unlike any woman he'd ever met. Fierce. Vulnerable. Brave. And even more head shy than he was. Could he find a woman more likely to bolt at the first sign of trouble?

"So…what? You're celibate?" And there it was. The disbelief, as if he was some kind of freak.

"It's not like I made a vow," he said, unable to keep the defensive note out of his voice. "It takes me a while to get comfortable with a woman, that's all. So if being with someone is just a way to get off, I'd rather, um… you know."

"Handle it yourself?"

"Uh…yeah." And he was not exactly comfortable with where the conversation was going, so he turned it around. "What about you?"

Her eyebrows quirked. "Girls have ways of handling things, too."

Heat flared in David's face and then washed over his entire body at the mental picture she conjured. "I wasn't asking… I meant… Shit. Are you trying to kill me?"

She laughed, taking way too much pleasure in his discomfort. "If you meant how long has it been since I've been involved with anyone? A while."

"Because?"

"Same reasons as you, pretty much. More trouble than it's worth, and it's hard on Kylan when they leave."

"Just Kylan?"

Her gaze fixed on a point somewhere below his chin. "We're fine how we are, just the two of us."

Questions piled up at the back of David's throat. *Are you sure about that? Do you really think you can keep him forever?* And a dozen others. But it wasn't his business to question her choices, criticize her for wrapping her life around the kid and her work. Like he could talk. Besides, nothing he said would change her mind, so no sense ruining what was turning out to be a damn fine moment.

She settled deeper into his embrace, her eyes drifting shut. "God, this feels good. Just being here."

Being held. Holding on. A basic human need that went much deeper than sex. "Then stay." Because right or wrong, he didn't want to let her go.

"Can't," she mumbled through a yawn. "Kylan… He'll think…"

"How 'bout this one time you don't worry about Kylan?"

She dragged her eyes open, tried to scowl. "I can't just stop. And you still have to decide about Muddy—"

"We'll figure something out." He feathered his fingertips down her forehead, stroking her eyelids shut. "Give yourself a break, Mary. You need it."

Her protest was lost in another yawn. She gave in to exhaustion and the medication, her hand going limp on his chest, her body going liquid as fatigue pulled her under. "Just for a minute," she mumbled. "But tomorrow…"

"Tomorrow," he promised, kissing her forehead.

He eased around so they were stretched out on the camp bed, pulled the buffalo hide over them and closed his eyes, contentment wrapping around him like a cocoon. It had been so damn long since he'd had this— the sharing of warmth and comfort at the end of a hard day. It was worth the deep, grinding ache of unfulfilled physical desire. As much as the sex, the laughter, and even the conversation, he'd missed this moment between wakefulness and sleep, when everything he needed was right here in his arms.

Until tomorrow.

That same crazy idea fluttered at the edge of his consciousness, like unseen wings in the darkness, but he was too tired to latch on to it. His thoughts drifted up and away, wafting out through the top of the tipi with the woodsmoke to evaporate into the night sky. Tomorrow, he'd gather them up again. Tonight, he wanted only to feel the soft weight of Mary's body against his as he sank into oblivion.

Chapter 26

DAVID WOKE TO THE SOUND OF MARY CALLING HIS NAME. He had a hazy memory of grumbling in protest when she'd left him some time in the wee hours, tucking the buffalo hide around him to replace her warmth. Sleep had claimed him again, dense and dreamless, and it wasn't letting go without a fight.

"David?" Mary's voice was closer, more insistent.

"Yeah?" he grunted.

One side of the door flap peeled back a few inches. "Is it safe to come in?"

"Yeah." He shoved up onto one elbow, squinting as brilliant sunlight followed her inside.

"That's the trouble with a tipi. Kinda hard to knock on the door." She flashed a nervous smile, got a good look at him, and burst out laughing. "Hello. There's the man who scared the shit out of us in Kalispell."

He swiped a hand over his hair, and yep, it was sticking up all over. Nice. Mary, on the other hand, looked as dewy fresh as a woman could after the day and night she'd had, all primped and prim in her work clothes. She probably smelled good, too, but no perfume could match the scent wafting out of the mug she held.

"I brought coffee," she said, holding up the mug and a napkin-wrapped square. "And a bacon-and-egg sandwich."

"You didn't have to bother."

"I know." She left it at that, watching with an amused expression as he fought free of the buffalo hide. She handed him the coffee first, and he took a careful sip. "If you need cream or sugar, I can get some from the house."

"Black is great." He took another sip and then stood, scrubbing a hand over his face to try to wake up. Stubble rasped under his hand. *Oh yeah. Looking good.* "Are you leaving for work?"

"Uh-huh. Gotta be there in about fifteen minutes, so…" She held out the sandwich at arm's length, as if she was feeding a dog she didn't quite trust.

David stepped closer, taking perverse pleasure in seeing the nerves jitter in her eyes. "Sleep well?"

"Uh, yeah. Not bad. You?"

"Great. Thanks for lending me your tipi."

"Anytime. Except, um, I guess this will be the only time, but—" She dragged in a breath and huffed it out. "Wow. Who knew the morning after was this awkward when you *didn't* have sex."

"Maybe this will help." He scooped his arm around her waist, hauled her in, and kissed her. She gave a little squeak of surprise, then relaxed and kissed him back. She'd had her morning coffee, too, and now he knew she took it sweet and with cream.

When he lifted his head, her eyes were warm and amused. "That's one way to break the ice."

"The best way."

She smiled, pushed him away, and slapped the sandwich into his hand. "I have to go. We'll, um, talk later, okay?"

"Okay." He waited, watching, and was rewarded with an excellent view when she bent to duck out the door.

Then that first shot of caffeine hit his brain and triggered an actual thought. "Mary?"

Her head popped back through the door. "Yeah?"

"I want to go back to Rusty's today. I'd like to take Kylan with me."

The doubt sprang into her eyes. "He's not supposed to be going anywhere after last night. And he doesn't have a horse."

Yet. The idea that had been nudging at David was back, three dimensional and fully fleshed, as if it had incubated in his mind while he slept. But it was still more than half-crazy, so he didn't go blurting it out.

"We'll do some groundwork," he hedged. "Flank and tie a few calves, work on his technique."

Mary's gaze dropped away from his. "I s'pose you want to take Muddy."

"Yes."

His pulse thudded as she considered, then nodded. "Okay. I'll see you when you get back, then."

His head went a little loopy with relief, and something more. She trusted him. Mary, who didn't trust much of anything. She started to leave, but he stopped her again. "Mary?"

"What?" She peeked in at him again, even more wary.

"I'll make sure Kylan takes his phone. We'll call if we're going to be late."

Her face relaxed. "Thanks. Can I go now?"

"Yeah. Have a good day."

"You too."

She disappeared, leaving him with the triumphant knowledge that he'd faced a moment of judgment and passed. A foolish grin spread over his face. He flattened it, as if someone might see and know how much Mary's faith mattered to him.

He took another gulp of coffee and a big bite of his sandwich, heard the rumble of her pickup engine fade as he stepped out the door. Sunlight poured down a crystal-clear sky, beginning to take the edge off the breeze. The air smelled of dew-soaked grass and the sharper tang of new leaves with a hint of pine. His muscles twitched, primed and ready after a decent night's sleep.

A smile pushed onto his face. And why not? The sun was shining, the birds were singing, and today they would rope. Plus, he finally had a plan, for what it was worth.

He polished off his breakfast as he walked to his trailer. Once inside, he dialed up a number from his contacts. "Hey, Uncle Pete. It's David."

He endured another round of congratulations and explanations about how he'd found Muddy and then worked his way around to the reason for his call. "I assume Dad told you about the kid who's been roping on Muddy?"

"Yeah. Tough deal. Any luck finding him something to ride at nationals?"

"No. But I was hoping you'd be willing to help us out…"

He hung up ten minutes later, the first step of his fledgling plan complete. Now it was a matter of whether he had the balls to go through with the rest. And whether Mary would hand them to him on a platter if he did.

He swung open the door and stopped dead. Kylan was slouched on the hay bale in front of the barn, the brim of his cap pulled low over his eyes. As usual, he looked like a half-made bed, hair poking this way and that from under the cap, the tail of his shirt slopping out of his jeans, one pant leg caught on the top of his boot. David stepped down, shut the trailer door behind him, and walked toward the kid. He stopped a few yards short, and they sized each other up like a pair of gun-fighters at high noon.

David waited for Kylan to ask what he was doing there, but the kid didn't say a word. Just sullen silence and the sound of both horses munching the hay Kylan had fed them.

"You took us on that detour on purpose yesterday," David said. "So we wouldn't get caught leaving town."

"Yeah. So?"

So Kylan had known exactly what he was doing, letting David take Muddy off the reservation. Not only knew, but aided and abetted. Trusted David to keep his promise. That counted for a lot in David's book.

"How much trouble are you in for last night?"

Kylan hunched his shoulders. "I'm grounded until nationals. Can't go anywhere with my friends, can't even hang out at Starr's place."

"Tough."

Kylan pulled an alfalfa stem from the bale and crimped it in half with a thumbnail. "It was stupid. I don't even like Weasel."

"Why'd you go with him?"

"I dunno. Sometimes, everything in my head gets so—" He fisted his hands, shook them, crushing the alfalfa into bits.

"Does running off make it better?"

"Sort of. At first. I just… I get so tired of feeling

stupid and stuff, and it seems like it would be better to be somewhere else."

Somewhere that wasn't his own life. A different place. A different person. A boy who didn't have to try so damn hard and fail so often. David yanked his gaze away and stared at the snowcapped mountains while he waited for his eyes to stop stinging.

Kylan's head jerked up, his voice harsh. "Why don't you just say it?"

"Say what?"

"That I'm not good enough for a horse like Muddy." Kylan lurched to his feet and jammed his hands in his pockets. "That run you made on him yesterday... Shit. I could never in a million years rope like that. It must really piss you off knowing he's been stuck here, wastin' his time with me."

So that's what had set him off. Pretty damn obvious, now that David didn't have his head up his ass. Watching David rope on Muddy must've really brought it home to the kid that the horse was no longer his.

"I'm not pissed," David said. *Anymore.*

"Why not?"

"Because I think things happen for a reason."

Kylan snorted. "Yeah, right. Everybody gets exactly what they deserve."

"No. Life isn't that fair. But sometimes, the powers-that-be even things up a little." David's thoughts crystallized with the words, and he spoke the truth as he had come to see it now that he understood Kylan's situation. "Maybe you needed Muddy more than I did. Or maybe I needed a lesson."

"Like what?"

"To appreciate how lucky I was, for starters. To buck up and keep going, even when it's really hard." David made a wry face. "Mostly, I learned I'd rather have a lousy day roping than a great day doing anything else."

"Me too." Kylan pulverized a dried-out horse turd with the toe of his boot. "It doesn't matter what horse I ride, I can't beat those guys at nationals."

"Is that the only reason you want to go? To win?"

Kylan frowned, like it was a trick question. "That's why everybody goes."

Okay. Treacherous ground here. David didn't want to imply that Kylan didn't stand a chance, but the kid wasn't stupid. He knew his own limitations. "When I was in the ninth grade, I was so excited just to be there, I didn't expect to beat anyone."

Kylan stared at him in awe. "You made it to nationals in the ninth grade?"

"I was, uh, big for my age."

Kylan ducked his head again. "The only reason I qualified is 'cause a couple of the guys who were supposed to win had bad calves."

"That's rodeo. Luck of the draw. You still had to rope and tie your calves to beat them." David paused, tried to put together the right words, borrowed some instead. "My dad told me to focus on catching both of my calves at nationals. He said most years, no more than a third of the ropers will get a time on both runs, so if I just did that, I'd be in the top forty in the country, and that wasn't half bad."

"Did you do it?"

"Yeah."

Actually, he'd ended up third, not thirtieth, but that wasn't anything Kylan needed to know.

Kylan's forehead puckered as he thought it over, then he puffed out a sigh. "I miss a lot of calves."

"Muddy can be hard to rope on."

At the sound of his name, Muddy raised his head, looked from David to Kylan, then decided neither of them were worth his time and went back to his hay.

Kylan stared into the barn, working his bottom lip in and out. "Are you still gonna take him?"

"Why wouldn't I?"

"I thought maybe since you and Mary…"

"Since we what?" David asked, his voice hardening.

"Um, you know." Kylan waved a hand toward the tipi. "You were in there together last night, and she didn't come in the house until real late."

"And you assume we had sex?"

Kylan's face went red, but he didn't back down. "That's usually how it works."

"Not for me."

Kylan shot him a look of patent disbelief. "You don't like sex?"

"No. I mean, yes, of course I like sex." David felt his own face heating up. "But not with a woman I've just met."

"Why not?"

Oh, hell. David did not want to go through that whole song and dance again, so he kept it as simple as he knew how. "I don't like being naked in front of a stranger."

"Oh." Kylan pondered that for a moment. "I guess I never thought of it like that. It is kinda scary, huh?"

"I've always thought so." He gave the kid a severe look. "And you have no right to judge Mary."

Kylan tucked his chin into his chest, scuffing at the dirt with his foot. "I heard her tell Galen she'd do anything to make sure I had Muddy for nationals."

The doubt demon jumped on David's back, dug in its claws. He tried to shake it off. "I don't think that includes seducing me."

"Yeah. I guess not."

Probably. Silence fell again, heavy and awkward. Even the horses stopped chewing, eyeing them as if waiting to see what would happen next.

David cleared his throat. "About nationals…how would you like to try roping on Frosty?"

"Your white horse?" Kylan's gaze shot to the stall. "You mean you could leave him—"

"I haven't entered any rodeos yet for that week," David cut in. "And it's not that far to Pueblo from where I live. I asked my uncle, and he said I could haul Frosty down there for you to ride."

Kylan stared at Frosty. The horse lifted his head, gazing back with his usual placid expression. "He looks really smooth to ride."

"He is."

Kylan stepped closer to the stall. Frosty stuck his head over the gate to greet him. "I bet he hardly ever hurts you."

"Hasn't yet."

Kylan held out a hand, smiling when Frosty nuzzled his palm. Then his face fell. "But if you don't leave him here, what am I gonna practice on between now and then?"

"I'm still working on that part." And there was no

sense getting anybody excited until they saw how Kylan and Frosty got along. "Before we do anything, we have to reset his shoes."

Kylan's eyes brightened. "You're gonna let me help you again?"

"I was counting on it," David said, and went to get his tools.

Chapter 27

"I HOPE YOU KNOW WHAT YOU MIGHT BE GETTIN' YOUR-self into," Rusty said as they watched Kylan and Frosty lope circles at the far end of the arena, warming up.

Since thinking too hard about it made his stomach buzz like it was full of bees, David just shrugged. Would've been nice if Rusty had been more encouraging. He and Hilary might not know Kylan real well, but damn sure better than David did. If he was smart, he'd listen to them. Too bad he was operating on instinct instead of brains. The idea that had planted itself in his brain refused to be beaten down, no matter how much logic David threw at it.

Kylan loped up and pulled Frosty to a stop in front of the chute. David handed him a rope with a breakaway hondo, so it would pop off the calf's neck when the loop came tight. "Let's start out easy, so you can get a feel for him before you have to step off and go flank and tie a calf."

The kid looked almost as tense as he had at the state finals. His nerves had no effect on Frosty, who settled into the corner of the box dead calm. Kylan nodded. The horse flowed out of the box, those long, effortless strides eating up the ground.

Kylan took one extra swing over the calf's back and threw, a quick jab of his arm that shouldn't have worked, but the loop went around the calf's neck anyway. Frosty dropped his butt, back feet sliding, fronts pedaling, pretty to watch, even more fun to sit on if you weren't worried about shaving off tenths of seconds.

The breakaway hondo snapped free, the rope flinging out to the side. Kylan sent David a wide-eyed grin. "Whoa. That was awesome."

"Looked good," David agreed. "Run another one."

They ran a dozen more, switching to a tie-down rope after the first four. With every nod of his head, Kylan got more confident, more aggressive. And with every run, the pressure inside David's chest built, a growing certainty of what he had to do coupled with the gut-wringing fear that he might not be up to the job.

What did he know about teenagers, let alone a kid like Kylan?

Kylan flanked the last calf and tied him pretty well. As he threw up his hands, an awestruck grin split his face ear to ear. "I didn't miss a single calf! That's the first time ever."

"Good job." Rusty waited for Kylan to mount up and ride forward, putting slack in the rope so he could pull the loop off the calf's neck. "Looks like that horse suits you to a T."

Rusty fired a weighted look at David. *Well, now you did it, smart guy.* David felt like a hand had clamped around his windpipe. *Shit.* He was going to have to follow this through to the end. A small, selfish part of him had hoped Kylan and Frosty wouldn't click and he'd be able to shrug and say, "Well, I tried." But it had worked, better than he could've dreamed. He had the means to repair the damage he would do by taking Muddy. All he had to do was say the words.

Hey, Kylan, how 'bout you come with me when I go?

Kylan would say yes. What teenager wouldn't? A month on the road, traveling to the biggest rodeos in the country, hanging out behind the chutes with the best calf ropers in the world? Plus, free horseshoeing lessons and riding Frosty at nationals. Where was the downside?

Other than David having full responsibility for a kid who might run for the hills the first time they butted heads.

And Mary. At best, she'd be skeptical. At worst, furious. She barely trusted him to take Kylan across the county. Could he make her believe, as he did, that loosening her grip on the kid was best for Kylan, both long and short term?

Plus, there was the not-so-small matter of the reward money. If she was still hell-bent on collecting, she'd throw this whole scheme back in their faces and they'd be back to square one.

As he tightened up his cinches and tied his rope on his saddle, David's mind played out the inevitable argument. What he'd say, what she'd say, trying to account for every possible angle of attack. His body moved on autopilot, loping Muddy through a few warm-up laps, stopping to drop his rope on the ground and then coil it up and rebuild a loop from scratch, making sure there were no kinks. He tucked the tail of his piggin' string in his belt as he rode toward the box.

He had one more night in Browning. What were the chances Mary would still be speaking to him once he'd said his piece? Was there even a remote possibility he'd get to kiss her, hold her again? His body pulsed with heat at the thought. He had to find a way to talk her around. Charm had never been his strong point, but he was gonna have to give it his best shot.

Muddy jammed his nose into the bit, ripping the reins through David's hand. *Pay attention, dipshit.*

"What?" David asked, realizing Rusty was talking to him.

"I said, this calf'll run pretty hard, so get a good start," Rusty repeated.

Muddy cranked his neck around to shoot David a disgusted glare. He blinked and gave himself a mental slap. *What the hell?* Here he was, rope in hand and Muddy underneath him—exactly what he'd fantasized about for four damn years—and he couldn't concentrate? He had this one practice session before Reno, but instead of focusing on his horse, his rope, and the calf, his head was full of Mary.

And he'd invited her in. As if he hadn't lost a big enough chunk of his heart and soul the first time around. Every championship dream he'd ever had was laid out in front of him, suddenly attainable again, and he was on the verge of giving another woman the power to cut him off at the knees. Wasting the second chance he'd thought he'd never get.

He stuck the loop of his piggin' string in his mouth and clenched it hard between his teeth. Roping was his job. His life. Like he'd told Kylan—if nothing else, the past four years had taught him how much he was willing to sacrifice to live his dream. If he wanted to make the most of his last night in town, he'd be a damn sight better off doing his laundry.

With the skill born of long practice, he cleared his mind, tucked his rope under his arm, and rode in the box.

"All set?" Rusty asked.

"You betcha," David said.

And then he went out and proved it.

An hour later, they sat at Rusty's kitchen table, sipping Cokes and brainstorming. Kylan slouched in his chair, his mood on the downside of one of the swings between elation at being invited to go with David and the morose certainty that Mary would never let him.

"'Specially after last night," he said, staring glumly into his soda can. "She said it was gonna be a long time before she could trust me again."

Rusty came back from his office with two sheets of crisp white paper fresh off the printer. He set them in front of David. "That should do the trick."

David already knew the gist, but he read it through to make sure Rusty's attorney friend had put it all down just like he wanted.

> *I, David Parsons, agree to provide Kylan Runningbird with a horse on which to compete at the National High School Rodeo Finals in Pueblo, Colorado, beginning on the twentieth day of July. In return, the horse registered as Mister Nicker Bar, known as Muddy, will be returned to me immediately, and reward monies that might have been applicable will be forfeited.*

There was more legal mumbo jumbo, but for the most part, the contract was brief, to the point. David would take Kylan along with him, cover his expenses, and coach Kylan when he practiced on Frosty. In addition, he would teach Kylan how to shoe horses. In a month's time, the kid could master the basic skills. Where Kylan took it from there was up to him.

And David would get Muddy back with his bank account intact.

David's heart pounded...slow, painful thuds against his sternum as he stared at the contract. Once this paper was signed, he was committed. Four weeks of living in a trailer with a kid he barely knew. What if they were a thousand miles down the road, and Kylan had a major meltdown? Or health problems? For all David knew, he could have asthma or a heart defect, or who the hell knew what.

But the vision that flashed in front of his eyes wasn't any of the potential disasters. It was those damned old codgers up there on their front porch, nodding their approval.

He folded the paper and put it in his shirt pocket. "Looks good."

"She strongly advised that you have the signatures notarized," Rusty said. "Assuming you can get Mary to sign it at all. What are you gonna do if she holds out for the reward money?"

Kylan's head came up, his expression puzzled. "What reward money?"

David did a double take and then looked at Rusty, who looked equally astonished. Hadn't Mary told Kylan how she hoped to coerce David into letting them keep Muddy until nationals?

Rusty leaned back and folded his arms. "When

Muddy disappeared, David put up a five-thousand-dollar reward for anyone who helped get him back. Mary wants to collect."

"We didn't help you find him," Kylan said.

Exactly. "The reward money would go toward buying another horse for you," David said.

Kylan framed his soda can in both hands, pushing a dent into the side with his thumb. "But why should you pay if we didn't earn it? And besides, I don't want another horse. I want to ride Frosty."

"That'll only get you through nationals," David persisted, bound and determined to shoot himself in the foot. "What then?"

"I dunno. We'll figure it out." Kylan set his jaw, defiant. "If you teach me how to shoe horses, I can earn my own money."

In the kid's eyes, David saw the stirrings of what he hadn't seen before. Pride. Determination. The belief that he could make his own way. All the things David hoped he could give Kylan in exchange for Muddy.

"You have to convince Mary," David said.

Kylan stared at the soda can for a long, weighted moment. Then he said very quietly, "No, I don't."

"What do you mean?" Rusty asked.

Kylan's voice was barely more than a whisper, as if he was afraid to say the words out loud. "Before Mary bought Muddy, she made me promise I'd take care of him, clean the barn, all that shit. And to make sure I understood he was my responsibility, she put the bill of sale in my name." Kylan lifted his gaze to meet David's across the table. "Mary doesn't have to sign that paper. Muddy belongs to me."

Chapter 28

DAVID PEELED HIS CLENCHED FINGERS OFF THE STEERING wheel one by one for the hundredth time since they'd left Rusty's. Then he thought about Mary, and his knuckles went white again.

She lied. She lied. She lied. The refrain rang inside his head like a hammer on steel.

She'd been lying to him all along, playing him for a fool. No wonder she didn't want him anywhere near Kylan. She was scared shitless what the kid might say. And now her worst nightmare had come true, damn her perfect little ass. Had she meant any of it? The kisses, the heat he'd seen in her eyes—had any of it been real, or had she just been humoring him?

"She told Galen she'd do anything."

David pried his fingers loose again, rubbing clammy palms down the front of his jeans, first right, then left, as he steered the rig down Browning's main drag. Kylan was mute with anxiety in the passenger's seat. The stores and restaurants seemed as familiar as David's hometown. He even recognized a couple of the stray dogs hanging around the grocery-store parking lot. Geezus. He had definitely been here too long.

Well, that was fixin' to change. They'd swung by the county courthouse in Cut Bank on the way back. He had one signed, notarized copy of the contract stashed safely in his trailer, the other in his pocket. Muddy was officially his again, and there was nothing Mary could do to stop them both from leaving in the morning.

It remained to be seen whether he'd be traveling alone. Kylan was determined to go along, but his bravado was pretty thin. Hell, he was so scared David could hear his teeth rattling from across the cab. Could he really stand up to Mary? David wouldn't bet on it, but he knew one thing for sure. She was gonna blow a fuse when she saw what Kylan had done.

Bring it on, sweetheart.

As if in response to his mood, clouds had built up behind the mountains, churning gray and white around the peaks and sending a bitter wind whistling down across the plains. Gusts slapped at the pickup as they cleared the west end of town and made the short drive to Mary's house. Her pickup was parked in front of the house, and she stepped out onto the deck as they rumbled down the driveway. David swung his rig around and stopped by the barn.

"We can do this, right?" Kylan asked, his voice small.

"Sure." David stepped out of the pickup and slammed the door hard enough to rattle the mirror.

Mary met them halfway, her shoulders hunched against the wind, her steps tentative, as if she sensed trouble. Or maybe she could see the expression on David's face. Her smile flickered and then faded, her worried gaze darting to Kylan. "How'd it go?"

"Awesome," he said in the same tone of voice he might use to announce a terminal illness.

"Really?" Her gaze bounced to David, then back. "How come you both look so serious?"

Kylan shifted on his feet, sucked in a deep breath, and

then blurted out, "I roped on Frosty and we did great and I'm gonna ride him at nationals."

Mary blinked, confusion digging a furrow between her brows as she shot David a questioning look. "But... how? Frosty isn't yours, David. You can't leave him here. Can you?"

"No." His face felt stiff, layered in plaster, his lips barely moving for fear the mask would crack wide open and all his rage would come pouring out. He pulled the contract from his pocket and shoved it at her. "Consider this my counteroffer."

She fumbled, the wind trying to tug the paper from her fingers as she unfolded it. Her eyes followed the lines, left to right, left to right, the color draining from her face as she read. The paper crumpled in her fist, her voice climbing the scale as she stared at Kylan in disbelief. "You signed this without talking to me first?"

He ducked his head, unable to hold her stare. "It's what I want," he mumbled.

"What *you* want? Or what *he* talked you into?" She jabbed a finger at David.

"He din't talk me into nothin'," Kylan insisted. "We made a deal."

"Oh, yeah, it's a hell of deal. For David." When Kylan opened his mouth to protest, she stuck up a hand, shaking her head. "Go in the house. We'll discuss this later."

"But—"

"Go!" she barked.

Kylan shot David a pleading look. David considered arguing, but given that he was so pissed he could barely breathe and Mary was on the verge of a meltdown, there was a good chance things were gonna be said that Kylan shouldn't hear.

"Go on." David jerked his chin toward the house. "You need to start packing anyway."

Kylan scowled but did as he was told. The instant the door banged shut behind him, Mary turned on her heel.

"Over here," she ordered, and stomped across the yard to put the tipi between them and the house. The wind plucked at her hair, whipping it into a crown of spikes as she spun around to face David. "I knew it! I knew if I let you get too close, you'd find a way to get to him."

He took another step, looming over her so she had to tip her head back to glare up at him. "Congratulations. You've been looking for an excuse to blame me since the minute I showed up. Now you've got one."

"Oh, please." She shook the contract at him. "You just scammed a teenager, and you're still trying to pretend you're the man in the white hat?"

"I'm not pretending anything." He jabbed himself in the chest with one thumb. "*I've* been up front all along."

Her eyebrows met in a scornful peak. "Uh-huh. Like the way you didn't bother to run any of this by me before asking Kylan to head off across the country with you?"

"He's eighteen years old. I thought he should be asked first. Unlike you and your attorney, who didn't even include him in the conversation."

"We were speaking on Kylan's behalf," she said stiffly.

"Because you didn't want him to know what kind of bullshit you were pulling, or you don't believe he has the mental capacity to think for himself?"

She sucked in an audible breath, let it out on a hiss. "How dare you say that about him?"

"How dare you treat him that way?" David shot back. "You talk a great game, Mary, but when push comes to shove, you rob him of the chance to make his own choices, keep him wrapped up so tight he can't take a leak without your permission. And then you accuse *me* of disrespecting him?"

Her mouth dropped open, and for a moment, she was incapable of speech, but she didn't back off, not even an inch. And he wanted her to back off—was willing to say damn near anything to push her away—for reasons he didn't understand or care to examine.

Spots of hot color flared in Mary's cheeks, her eyes glittering. "Kylan has been with me for *five years*. You spend two days with him, and you think you know what he needs?"

"Yeah. I do." And he managed to sound like he meant it.

"What about that?" She waved a hand at the tipi. "If you think I'm such a horrible person, what the hell was that last night?"

That was perfect.

No. He couldn't say that. Couldn't think it. Not now. "Maybe I should ask you the same question. What was that, Mary? One more way to soften me up, squeeze the reward money out of me? How far were you willing to go?"

Her head jerked back as if she'd been slapped. The words left a taste like charcoal in David's mouth, the ashes of the flame that had flickered between them. He wanted to reach out. Wipe that look from her face. But it was too late. For both of them.

She squared her shoulders and curled her lip into a

sneer that matched the acid dripping from her words. "I don't even know you. And you expect me to put Kylan in your hands and trust that you'll do right by him?"

Trust. What a fragile, elusive thing. He'd thought he'd earned Mary's, but it was only an act. "If you don't know what kind of man I am by now, you never will."

On this point, he didn't have to fake his conviction. As far as he was concerned, he'd proven everything that needed proving, take it or leave it. She stared up at him for a long, tense moment, her face so pale, her eyes so bleak, his hands itched to reach out to her, to soothe the pain he was inflicting even as a deeper, darker part of him smiled in grim satisfaction.

You see? Didn't I try to tell you to stay away?

Yes. He'd let desire squelch that little voice, but he was listening now. Best that he'd seen the real Mary before he'd touched her, held her again. One more night might have pushed him past the tipping point. Into what, he refused to consider.

She spun away, took five steps, and stopped, spine rigid. Her voice was a flat monotone. "I'll discuss this with Kylan."

"You do that. And tell him I'm leaving at nine tomorrow morning, with or without him."

She gave a curt nod and finally, *finally*, strode away, out of reach. He wheeled around and stomped back to his rig, around to the rear door of the trailer. His hand was on the latch when he stopped himself.

What was he thinking? He didn't have to unload here. It was over. He'd won. He didn't have to leave Muddy behind ever again. He thumped a fist on the door in what should've been triumph and then headed for the pickup, almost losing a leg when the wind slammed the door behind him. Geezus. He thought it blew hard on the Colorado plains.

He reached for the ignition and nearly jumped out of his skin when something moved in the back seat. He jerked around, heart scrabbling up into his throat. "What the hell?"

"Shhh!" Kylan crouched behind the passenger seat, finger pressed to his lips. "Just go, before she figures out I'm not in my room."

"Why aren't you?"

"I want to come with you tonight," Kylan said with pleading, puppy-dog eyes. "Otherwise, she'll talk me out of going."

Oh hell. The kid was right. And, yeah, Kylan needed to learn to stand his ground, but this was no battle for a rookie. David huffed out an exasperated breath. "You can't just run off. You'll scare her half to death."

Kylan gave him a wobbly smile. "It's okay. I left a note."

Chapter 29

CONSIDERING THE QUALITY OF KYLAN'S PREVIOUS NOTE, David made him type up a text message and insisted on reading it before the kid hit Send.

> I'm spending the night with David. I really, really want to go with him. Please don't be so mad at me. Love you. Kylan.

Then, just to be double-sure no one could accuse him of stealing the kid, David copied Mary's number into his phone and sent a text of his own. Kylan insisted on coming with me tonight. I'll bring him back in the morning.

He kept one eye in the rearview mirror, expecting to see her pickup roaring up on them, but there was no sign of pursuit. They were unloading the horses at the Stampede Grounds when Kylan's phone beeped.

Mary's response was a single letter. K.

David got nothing, which was the best he could expect, but she wouldn't give up that easily, would she? Obviously, Kylan didn't think so. His head jerked up like he'd been hit with a cattle prod every time a vehicle came toward the fairgrounds from the west, but none of them was Mary's pickup.

If it was any other woman, David would have assumed she was just angry, refusing to speak to them until she cooled down. Since it was Mary, he was afraid she was plotting a counterattack. Hopefully, she hadn't kept any souvenirs from her trip to Afghanistan. Like a grenade launcher. Or a flamethrower.

He gathered up three bags of laundry, the hard knot of anger in his gut dissolving into what felt like a nest of worms slithering and squirming as he imagined Mary out there at her house. Alone. Wounded. By words that he'd said. What had come over him? Yeah, he had good reason to be mad, but how could he have been so cruel? As if he was trying to prove he was every kind of asshole she'd imagined he could be.

He slung the laundry bags into the back of the pickup and Kylan directed him to the laundromat, clear on the other end of town in a log building across the road from the community college, which made David think of Mary all over again. Had she thought of him, those kisses they'd shared, while she sat through her seminar there all day? Had she made plans for how they'd spend this last night together?

If so, they were both fools.

The laundromat was blessedly empty. Everybody else must be smart enough to stay in out of the howling wind. Then again, if these people hunkered down every time the wind blew, they'd never get out of the house.

Kylan helped haul the bags in and dump them on a table for sorting. Then he hunched over his phone in the corner while David separated the pile into colors and whites. As David fed quarters into the last washing machine, Starr's car whipped into the parking lot. Kylan jumped up and went to meet her outside. Probably not a good sign that David could hear her screeching over the sound of water gushing into four different washing machines. She did a lot of arm waving and chest poking. Kylan responded with shrugs and slouches and headshakes, but he didn't appear to be backing down.

Good for him.

Finally, Starr ran out of steam. She asked Kylan a question. He nodded. She asked something else. He shook his head. She turned to scowl through the window at David. He stared back, not even pretending he hadn't been watching.

Starr blinked first. She looked back at Kylan, asking another question. He shook his head. David clearly read her lips. *Please?* Kylan shook his head again, more adamantly. She pushed her mouth into a pout. Kylan leaned in, kissed her, and then backed away, turning to scurry into the laundromat. Starr stared after him until the glass door thumped shut. Then she shot David a death glare, slammed into her car, and drove away.

David raised his eyebrows at Kylan.

"She doesn't want me to go," Kylan said.

"I figured," David said. "What did you tell her?"

Kylan fidgeted with the chrome coin tray on the nearest washing machine. "I said she should be happy I was getting a chance to do something cool, instead of holding me back. That's when she got really pissed."

Sounds familiar. David cleared his throat. "Did she dump you?"

"Not yet."

"You think she might?"

Kylan jerked a shoulder. "Dunno. Maybe."

"That would suck."

"I guess."

David paused in the midst of screwing the top onto the bottle of laundry detergent. "You aren't sure?"

Kylan gave it more thought than David expected. "Starr's cool. I like her a lot. But she's all serious about us, and we're just kids, ya know?"

Eighteen. The same age David and Emily were the first time they talked about getting married. Just kids playing at grown-up love. And look how that had turned out.

"Yeah," David said. "I know."

After what happened with Emily, he had sworn he wouldn't settle for less than unqualified faith and support. Mary was about as trusting as a feral cat in a barn full of stray dogs. The two of them together were a disaster in the making. She had to know it as well as he did.

But why hadn't she come after Kylan, dammit?

Kylan rattled the coin tray, his eyes and mouth both turned downward. "What if Mary's so mad she never wants me back?"

Panic welled, nearly closing David's throat. Could they really have made her mad enough to give Kylan the boot? An image popped into his head...Mary, fierce and defiant on the shore of the lake at Two Medicine when he asked what came after Kylan's graduation.

"Never happen."

Kylan didn't look so sure. "How do you know?"

"She said so." David could see her, plain as day, framed by the lake and mountains, vibrating with the intensity of her conviction. "She told me no matter where you go or how old you get, you'll always be hers, and anybody who wants a piece of her will just have to deal with it."

Kylan's gaze jumped up, hope lighting his eyes. "Really? She said that?"

"Word for word." Or close enough. David braced a hip against the washing machine, the swish and thump of the agitator vibrating his bones, filling his lungs with what was supposed to be mountain-fresh scent.

The soap company's marketing team had obviously never experienced the real thing.

David had, and a whole lot more. The past three days had been crammed so full of authentic experiences his mind could barely sort the good from the bad. Huckleberry pie. The bear. The oily black smoke from burning tires he could still taste at the back of his tongue. And Mary, warm and willing in his arms.

"Do you want a piece of her?" Kylan asked.

David started, caught dead to rights. "Excuse me?"

"Not that kind." Kylan made a disgusted face. "But you like her, right? I mean, besides her butt. I know you like that. I seen you checking it out."

Embarrassment heated David's face and turned his words to adolescent stutters. "Well, yeah. I like her okay, I guess."

"You aren't sure?" Kylan asked, echoing David's earlier question.

"Yes, I'm sure. But—"

"'Cause she likes you," Kylan cut in. "I can tell. She don't make out with just anybody."

"Doesn't," David corrected, scowling. "And we weren't making out."

Kylan rubbed a hand over his still-smooth jaw. "Dude. You left a mark. You wanna sneak around necking with girls, you gotta shave first."

Shit. Now David was blushing outright. "What's your point?"

"I'm just wonderin'… You like her, she likes you…"

"Not anymore."

"Because of me." Kylan slumped, plunking both elbows on his washing machine and staring morosely at his hands. "I'm always messin' things up for her."

"It's not you. We fought about other things."

"Like what?"

"She lied to me about Muddy being yours. And she's so damn suspicious, always ready to believe the worst when all I've done from the start is try to make the best of this mess." *Crap.* What was supposed to be righteous anger sounded a whole lot like whining instead.

"It wasn't much of a lie," Kylan said. "I would've done whatever Yolanda wanted. She scares the shit outta me. And Mary doesn't have much reason to trust guys. Most of 'em are just lookin' to get laid."

"Well, I'm not." He could see Kylan was gonna ask what he was after, so he held up a hand for silence. "Look, Kylan, it wouldn't work, okay? I'm on the road all the time. I never know from one week to the next if I'll have two dollars in my pocket. And there are always women hanging around at the rodeos, angling for any cowboy they can catch. If Mary can't trust me when I'm standing in front of her, how's she gonna feel when she hasn't laid eyes on me for a month?"

"You could try it and find out," Kylan said stubbornly.

David shook his head. "I gave six years of my life to a woman who bailed when I needed her the most. I can't do that again."

"You think Mary's gonna cave the first time things get

a little rough?" Kylan snorted in derision. "In case you didn't notice, letting go ain't exactly her strong point."

Okay, the kid had him there. Mary didn't know the meaning of quit. But still… "That's the point. She's got…issues."

"Who don't?" Kylan's expression included David in that crowd.

David grabbed his bottle of laundry soap and stuffed it into one of the bags. "It's not gonna happen, so just drop it, okay?"

"Fine." Kylan sauntered over, plopped down in one of the plastic chairs, and stared at David.

"What?" David demanded.

"I was just thinkin', this is a first." Kylan gave him an irritating little smirk. "For once, I'm not the one running away."

Chapter 30

As punishment for being a wise ass, David made Kylan battle the wind to walk down the road and grab food from the Town Pump. He came back with enough fried chicken and potato wedges to feed an army, or two men who'd been roping all afternoon. He'd also tossed in two big bags of chips, a box of vanilla wafers, and supersize Cokes.

Kylan tore into the food like a starving wolf cub. David managed to snatch a drumstick from the bag without losing any fingers, but his stomach was so twisted with guilt and worry that he could barely swallow. He picked up his phone, put it down, picked it up again. If he called Mary, would she answer? *Could* she answer? What if he'd upset her so bad she'd had another flashback? Or a blinding headache? Someone should be there to look out for her.

Galen. Of course. Why hadn't he thought of it sooner? David found the number in his contacts and hit Send before he could chicken out. He sat through five rings before the generic computer voice told him to leave a message. He hung up, at a loss what to say.

"You sure you don't want some more?" Kylan asked, eyeing the last piece of chicken. Geezus. David was gonna have to shoe a couple of extra horses a week just to feed the kid.

"Go ahead." Desperate for a distraction from his

reeling thoughts and growing nausea, he pulled out a beat-up copy of Louis L'Amour's *Last of the Breed*.

Kylan eyed the cover, curious. "Is that about an Indian guy?"

"Yep. You'd like it. Best ending ever written. You can read it while we're on the road."

Kylan scrunched his nose. "I don't like to read."

Didn't like, or struggled? David hiked a shoulder. "We'll rent the audiobook. Give us something to do besides bitch at each other."

Kylan finished stuffing his face and commenced playing some kind of game on his phone, thumbs flying. David transferred loads from washers to dryers and then settled back to read, skipping to his favorite scenes in the book. The words couldn't hold his attention, distracted as he was by the doubts screaming inside his head. What if Mary was right? What if he couldn't handle Kylan? How did he know he had the patience, or the understanding, or the skills?

What if he lost Kylan the way he'd lost Muddy?

As his anxiety spiraled, the air in the laundromat condensed, too warm, too thick to drag into his lungs. Sweat beaded on the back of his neck. David dropped the book into his lap and leaned forward, the movement abrupt enough to get Kylan's attention.

"If we're gonna do this, you've gotta promise me something," David said.

Kylan's eyes went wary under his crooked cap brim. "Uh, sure."

"No matter what happens—if you're mad, or tired, or homesick, or whatever—you stick with me. If you feel like you're gonna explode, fine. Yell, stomp, take

a swing at me if you have to, but you don't run away. I
need you to swear it. Can you do that?"

The question hung between them, like an echo that
went out and bounced back, the layers of meaning sepa-
rating. Not just can you promise, but can you *do* that?
Control your emotions, your impulses?

Kylan did him the honor of thinking it over. Then he
nodded. "I can. Promise."

"Okay." David leaned back, able to take a deep breath
again. "Thanks."

"Whatever," Kylan said, and went back to his game.

When they got back to the rodeo grounds, Kylan
checked the horses and refilled water buckets, linger-
ing to scratch all of Frosty's favorite spots while David
packed away his clean clothes, leaving a drawer and part
of the closet empty.

He handed Kylan extra blankets and a pillow. "I'm
gonna go fuel up the pickup so we don't have to do it in
the morning."

"'Kay," Kylan said.

David scooted out the door while the kid was preoc-
cupied with figuring out how to fold the table down into
a bed. He did intend to fill the fuel tank, but he made a
detour first. Hopefully, Kylan wouldn't notice that he
turned the wrong direction leaving the fairgrounds.

David slowed when he got close enough to see
Mary's place. It wasn't stalking if he was checking to
be sure she was all right, was it? Though how he'd be
able tell from half a mile away was beyond him. Didn't
matter. He had to try.

He turned off the highway and parked on a grassy approach that led to a pasture gate, blinded by the sun as it settled into a sharp vee between two craggy peaks. The mountains compressed the round ball into a wedge, then a pinpoint beam, and then it blinked out.

In the rapidly purpling dusk, David had a clear view of Mary's yard. He blew out a relieved breath when he spotted Galen's black flatbed parked in the driveway next to Mary's pickup. Thank God. She wasn't alone. The house was dark, but light glowed from the barn door and smoke curled lazily from the top of the tipi.

The wanting hit hard, slamming into David like an avalanche, leaving his body bruised and aching. He should be there with her. Holding her. Her head on his shoulder and her body curled against his as they planned the month he'd spend with Kylan. Could it have happened if he hadn't been so furious?

And so scared.

Oh shit. David grabbed hold of the steering wheel, his heart beating in huge, lunging gulps, like a panicked horse bolting through the brush. Dear God. What had he done?

It wasn't supposed to happen this way again. He'd sworn he'd take better care, ease into a relationship one cautious step at a time. But here he was, over his head before he even knew he'd taken the plunge. In three short days, Mary had weaseled through all of his defenses with her vulnerable eyes and warrior's soul. And now he was at her mercy.

Assuming she had any to offer. After the things he'd said, the way he'd said them, how could she forgive him? What could he possibly say to persuade her?

Panic blanked his mind, erasing all the words. He sucked in air, ordered his lungs to relax, drawing on every ounce of his competitive discipline, the mantras he used to clear his racing thoughts when the chips were down and a championship was on the line.

Relax. Take your time. Focus on the now.

Now being the hours until nine o'clock tomorrow morning. He had plenty of them. Not much chance he'd sleep. His hands shook as he put the pickup in reverse, eased onto the road, and swung around toward town. As he hit fourth gear, his phone buzzed with an incoming text, and he jerked so hard the pickup swerved. He straightened it out and then took a quick look at the phone.

Galen.

David whipped over to the shoulder of the road to stop and read the message. I see you.

He punched in his reply, his big thumbs clumsy on the keys. Is she okay?

She's been better.

David cringed, tapped his response one fumbling letter at a time. Tell her she's not a horrible person. I might be though.

The pause was so long, David's muscles started to twitch with anxiety. Finally, his phone beeped again. Yeah. You've been better too. Maybe tomorrow'll be better for both of you.

While David squinted at the words, trying to guess whether they were encouragement or reprimand, the phone buzzed again. I hung your coat on Frosty's stall. Don't forget it in the morning.

He looked over his shoulder, saw the barn light blink

out. A shadow ambled across the yard toward the tipi. Conversation over.

David stared at the evening star, low and bright as an incoming jetliner. He imagined those old geezers up there on their porch, sipping whiskey straight from the bottle while they contemplated the mess they'd landed him in. And laughed their asses off.

He drove back to the fairgrounds, parked beside his trailer, and didn't remember until he was stepping inside that he'd forgotten to fuel up the pickup. Oh well. Chances were he'd be up plenty early in the morning.

At the sound of the door clicking shut, Kylan lifted his head from the pillow, blinking sleepily. "Was Galen and Cissy there?"

So much for fooling the kid. "Yeah. Guess I should've known Mary would call them."

"That's what she does."

"How'd you know I went to check on her?"

Kylan yawned, rolled over, and burrowed into his pillow. "That's what you do."

David hesitated, torn between asking for help and keeping his feelings safely under wrap. "So, um, how's Mary at holding a grudge?"

"Better than you are at roping."

In other words, a pro. David blew out a defeated breath. "That's what I was afraid of."

⌇⌇⌇

By seven thirty the next morning, David had jogged, stretched, and then driven down to the Town Pump to fuel up with diesel, coffee, and sausage-and-egg biscuits.

He'd also cleaned out the back of the horse trailer, filled the water tanks, showered, shaved, and ironed all of his shirts.

When he started dusting the cupboards, Kylan tossed his phone aside with an exaggerated sigh. "What are we waitin' for?"

David lifted a coffee mug and swiped a paper towel over the shelf. "I told Mary I'd pick you up at nine."

"Uh…in case you haven't noticed? I'm already here."

"Well, yeah, but…"

"What? You're afraid we might wake her?"

Of course not. If David knew Mary at all, she hadn't slept any more than he had. So why was he stalling? Because facing Mary scared the crap out of him. And until she told him otherwise, he still had hope.

"Fine," he said, slamming the cupboard. "Load up. Let's go."

Kylan was a lot less nonchalant when they pulled onto the highway. He fidgeted in his seat, flipping his phone over and over in his hands as they covered the short distance to Mary's place. Then he sucked in a breath. "Oh shit."

David looked where Kylan was looking and seconded the sentiment. Galen's pickup was still parked next to Mary's. JoJo's police car was parked right behind it. David's foot came off the accelerator, and they slowed abruptly. Why hadn't it occurred to him that Mary might take legal action to block their departure? All she had to do was contest the validity of the contract Kylan had signed. Claim undue influence, or whatever it was called. *Geezus*. The woman really did not know how to give up. While David was racking his brain for a way to get back in her good graces and drowning in guilt for being so mean, she was assembling the troops.

If he had a lick of sense, he'd be furious.

"What're you smilin' about?" Kylan demanded.

"Mary." David tried and failed to rub the grin off his face. "She's a piece of work."

"She's fixin' to kick your ass," Kylan said.

Yeah. That too.

When they turned into the driveway, all four of the people sitting on the deck stood—Mary, Galen, JoJo, and a woman who must be Cissy. David considered circling around and driving right back out onto the highway, but it wasn't like he could outrun a cop car, so he pulled up by the house and killed the engine.

While David and Kylan got out of the pickup, the quartet filed down from the deck, JoJo first, then Galen, and then the two women, side-by-side. David did a double take. Knowing Galen, hearing Mary's stories, he'd mentally painted Cissy as wise and maternal, well-padded from the birth of four children. A warm, comfortable woman.

Cissy Dutray was not soft. And other than the arm she had looped around Mary's waist, she didn't look particularly maternal. Her streaky dark hair was clipped into short, straight layers, framing a face that could've been in the movies, with the high cheekbones and dramatic, arched eyebrows of Hollywood's version of an Indian princess. Her jeans were slung low on narrow hips, her legs long enough to make snug denim look good. Even at this hour, she was fully accessorized with silver jewelry that matched both her belt and the glint in her eye that said, "Go ahead. Try to screw with me or mine."

Not a chance. David held up, letting Kylan move ahead of him toward the posse. The kid shot a panicked look over his shoulder.

"Got your back."

"Chickenshit," Kylan muttered.

They lined up like a small regiment, Galen and JoJo peeling off to station themselves at either side of the sidewalk, flanking Mary and Cissy. David tried to read their faces, but JoJo had his tough cop scowl on and Galen, as usual, wasn't giving anything away. If they were trying to put the fear of God in David, it was a waste of time. Mary had the corner on that market.

His first good look at her was a punch in the gut. She looked...great. A little tired maybe, but she'd taken the time to fix her hair and do her makeup. Her turquoise hoodie made her eyes glow greener than usual, and it was unzipped just far enough to show a snug white tank top. David went a little dizzy wondering if she wore anything underneath.

He could stare all he wanted. Her attention was focused entirely on Kylan.

She stepped away from the others to meet the kid, but instead of the determination David had expected, her expression was soft, hesitant. Cissy kept a supportive hand on her shoulder. He could see why. Mary seemed to sway in the breeze, featherlight, as if she'd lost that iron will.

David's heart clenched. He'd done that. Made her feel like less when she was so much more than he'd ever been.

"You okay?" Kylan asked her.

"Yeah." She reached up, smoothed back a chunk of hair that stuck straight out over his ear. "I'm sorry, Kylan."

His shoulders slumped. "Does that mean I can't go?"

"It's not for me to say." She pressed her palm over his heart, her eyes shimmering. "You're all grown up. I don't know how I missed it. Or when I crossed the line from looking out for you to trying to live your life."

Kylan put his hand over hers. "It wasn't that bad."

"Yes, it was. I had no right making your decisions for you."

Kylan shrugged. "I dunno. I make some pretty stupid ones."

She gave a shaky laugh. "Don't we all? But no matter the reasons, what I was doing with Muddy was wrong. Thank you for setting me straight."

"Whatever." He tilted his head, eyeing her like he suspected there was a catch. "You aren't even mad 'cause I signed that paper without asking you first?"

She scrunched up her face. "I really want to be, but then I'd be a total hypocrite since Cissy reminded me that when I was your age, I enlisted in the army without telling her and Galen."

"Seriously?" Kylan asked.

"Seriously," Cissy said, narrowing her eyes. "I wanted to kill her, but I was too damn worried someone was gonna beat me to it."

Mary gave a sheepish shrug. "I guess running off to a few rodeos is pretty mild by comparison. So, no, I'm not gonna try to stop you. I'm not even gonna call and text five times a day to check on you. But I do expect to hear from you at least a couple times a week, so I know where you are."

Kylan scooped her into a bear hug, hoisting her off her feet. "You're the best. Don't let nobody tell you different."

David had to swallow hard as she hugged Kylan back. When he set her down, she pushed him out to arm's length, wrinkling her nose. "I'm not letting you go smelling like that. You need a shower. I washed all your clothes, and Cissy ironed your shirts. Don't forget, you've got to pack everything you need for nationals since you won't be coming home first."

Kylan nudged her shoulder with his fist. "Din't take you long to start bossin' me again."

"Smart ass." She swatted his arm and gave him a shove. "Go on. You've got a long drive today."

Kylan didn't budge. "If you wasn't gonna try to stop us, how come JoJo's here?"

"Just wanted to say good luck at nationals. And behave while you're gone." JoJo fired a warning scowl at David. "I don't wanna have to drive halfway across the country to bail you out of trouble."

But he would. They all would. They might not be the kind of family you saw in picture books, the kind David had grown up with, but they were solid.

JoJo hooked his thumb in his belt. "If you don't need me, I'll get back to work."

"Maybe you'll get lucky and find someone who needs shootin'," Galen said. "I hear tourists are in season."

Cissy snorted a laugh. JoJo ignored both of them and sauntered to his car. They all watched him bump and sway down the driveway, then Mary brushed her hands together and turned toward the house, having yet to acknowledge David's existence.

"Well, we'd better get cracking," she said.

"Wait." Kylan grabbed her arm. "David needs to talk to you."

Mary froze for a beat. Then she slowly turned around, and all of a sudden everybody was looking at David. His mind blanked, and he couldn't recall a single word of any of the dozen or so speeches he'd memorized in the cold night hours.

"I, uh…" He shot a desperate look at Kylan, who jacked up his eyebrows as if to say *well?*

Cissy had pretty much the same expression on her face, except a lot less encouraging. Galen folded his arms and waited, content to be an onlooker.

Mary fixed her gaze on a point about a foot below David's chin. "I thought we pretty much covered everything yesterday."

"Uh, not really. Could we, um…" David jerked a thumb toward the driveway and stepped back a couple of paces, indicating he'd like some privacy. Nobody took the hint, including Mary, who remained rooted in place.

Kylan gave her a gentle push. "Go talk to him, else I'll have to put up with his moping all day."

"Please," David added.

Mary looked at Cissy, who considered and then nodded. "Might as well clear the air."

David backed up until his butt bumped against the front of Galen's pickup. Mary followed, dragging her feet and focusing her eyes anywhere but on his face. She stopped three paces away, staring so hard at his left shirt pocket that David checked to make sure he hadn't dribbled coffee on it.

"I have to apologize…" he began.

"No, you don't," Mary cut in. "You were right. I was wrong. Enough said."

"But we need to—"

"Don't worry. I won't interfere between you and Kylan."

David took a breath, tried again. "You and I… I wanted to tell you—"

"No explanation necessary." She settled her gaze on his left elbow. "Ships passing in the night, et cetera, et cetera. So we can just forget—"

"Would you mind if I pick my own words?" David burst out in frustration.

Mary's cheeks flushed, and her gaze dropped to the toes of David's boots. "Sorry. I have a bad habit of—"

"Telling other people what they think," David said, giving her a dose of her own medicine. "I noticed. But since I was awake most of the night practicing this speech, I'd like to go ahead and give it."

"Okay. Shoot." Mary shoved her hands into the pockets of her hoodie, pulling it tight across her chest and making his mind skitter off track for a second.

"Thank you." Except now the words seemed to be turned sideways, and he was having trouble forcing them out. He cleared his throat and tried harder, starting with the easy part. "I was really mad yesterday, and I said things I shouldn't have. I'm sorry."

She opened her mouth, but he held up a hand and she closed it again.

"You know how you freaked out the first time I took Kylan to Rusty's? Well, this is like that." He dragged in air, wishing she'd look at him but sort of glad she didn't because he might lose his nerve. "Turns out I have a few hot buttons of my own, and you punched them all. I was looking for an excuse to put space between us. You gave it to me. But there's no excuse for the things I said."

Her eyes slowly came up to meet his, as sharp and wary as a fox fearing a trap. He wanted to press his lips to her forehead, smooth away the crease there, but he hadn't earned that right yet.

"I didn't want to get involved," he said. "I didn't even want a date. But there you were, and I couldn't stay away."

"You're leaving now," she said stiffly. "Problem solved."

The words stabbed into him, sharp little arrows of indifference that left him bleeding. He lowered his voice another notch to disguise the pain. "I've given you plenty of reason to hate the sight of me. But Kylan and I...we're friends. I hope we stay friends. And that means I'm gonna be coming back here now and then, and you and I will see each other, and I'll probably act like an idiot, so you should at least know why."

She gave her head a quick, confused shake. "I have no idea what you're trying to say."

"I'm saying you matter to me. You're under my skin." He held out his hands, palms up, as if she could see the ache, the need. "I'm saying I've only known you three days, and already I can't have a thought without wanting to share it with you."

The cold resolve in her eyes wavered, then hardened. She waved a hand toward the tipi, the spot where he'd said all those horrible things. "But yesterday—"

"I said things that were flat-out wrong, and I knew it."

He gestured toward the tipi, as she had. "What happened between us last night had nothing to do with Kylan or Muddy or anything but you and me. I wasn't ready for you to get so close so fast. I panicked. Just a stupid, scared idiot who thought it would be easier to hurt you and push you away than to take the chance of being a fool again."

He risked reaching out, across the gulf that separated them, to touch her cheek. She went utterly still beneath his hand. He cleared away the tightness in his throat, his heart doing that lunge-and-gulp thing again. "You have to understand, Mary... I don't seem to know how to fall in love slow and easy. For me, it's like stepping off a cliff. All or nothing. No safety net."

She stared at him for a full count of five, quivering as if her body was straining to run. Toward him or away? Then hot color swept into her face. She slapped his hand away, stamping her foot. "Why are you saying this stuff?"

"Uh...because it's true?"

"Bull!" She rolled her eyes, irritated. "I don't know if this is some bizarre way of trying to smooth things over because of Kylan, or if you have an overdeveloped sense of guilt, but this is too damn much."

"It's not guilt!"

"Then what is it?" she demanded.

He threw up his hands, let them fall. "Insanity, apparently. You drive me crazy in every sense of the word, and I'd rather be crazy with you than without. I'm trying to ask you to give me another chance."

He sucked in air, out of breath, out of words. He'd given her all he had, and she didn't want any part of it. He couldn't stand there, letting her watch while his chest caved in, leaving another gaping hole. He jerked his gaze away, to where Galen, Cissy, and Kylan stood close together, shamelessly eavesdropping. David ducked his head and pushed away from the pickup. "I understand. You'd have to be crazy to trust me again. I'll go catch the horses and get ready to load up."

"Stop!"

He stopped, startled by Mary's command.

She held up her hands, shaking her head as if her ears were ringing. "Just…stop. I need a minute here, okay?"

"Okay," David said, willing to stand like a statue for the next eight hours if it meant he still had a prayer.

She tipped her head back and closed her eyes, dragging in a lungful of air. "You wanna talk about making somebody crazy? One minute, you're pulling me in. The next, you're pushing me away. And now this." She opened her eyes to glare at him. "How the hell am I supposed to know what's real?"

David hooked his thumbs in the front pockets of his jeans and hunched his shoulders, guilty as charged. "I'm not asking for much. Just let me call you. Pick up the phone when you see it's my number and talk to me. Maybe we can figure this out together."

"How do I know you're not just playing games?"

He met her gaze, held it, projecting every ounce of sincerity he possessed. "Do I seem like a guy who likes games?"

She stared at him for a beat, glanced over her shoulder and then back again, her brows crimping. "You and Kylan are…friends?"

"Why not? He's a pretty cool kid."

She huffed out a laugh. "I've always thought so. But most people—"

"I'm not most people."

She studied his face, her eyes softening, warming with something that made his heart gulp in a whole different way. "Yeah. I noticed."

"So…" He toed the dirt and tested a smile on her. "Will you talk to me, Mary? Please?"

The corners of her mouth curled up, and his heart bounded again. "Yeah. I can do that."

Relief almost buckled his knees. They stood there, smiling at each other, the day suddenly brighter and warmer despite the damn wind. David glanced at their trio of observers. "If we didn't have an audience, I'd kiss you right now."

Mary rolled her eyes. "Geez, Dudley. You are such a dork."

Then she stepped close and looped her arms around his neck to pull him down in to a kiss. He gathered her up and kissed her back until his blood boiled and his head spun.

Galen cleared his throat.

Kylan groaned. "Oh, *gross*."

David ignored both of them. He'd been praying all night for this kiss, and by damn, he was gonna make it a good one.

Chapter 31

THE SENSE OF DÉJÀ VU WAS SO STRONG IT MADE DAVID'S head spin. Once again, he stood behind the bucking chutes in Cody, Wyoming, television lights glaring in his eyes and a woman holding a microphone in front of his face. Except Laura had dark hair, not blond, and since she was happily married to the current world-champion steer wrestler, there wasn't much chance she'd be hitting on David.

She smiled up at him. "Thanks for taking the time to chat with us, David. I know you've got reporters beating down your door to hear Muddy's story. What's it like having him back?"

"It's…incredible." David grinned, still awed by the 180-degree turn his life had taken.

"No doubt. This thing has gone viral. You're all over the internet, you've been interviewed by *Sports Illustrated* and national news outlets, and now I hear you've been approached by one of the late-night talk shows."

"It's pretty wild." Not that he had any intention of flying off to California, but it was amazing to even be asked.

"Well, the story has everything, right? Drama, human interest." Laura's eyes sparked with mischief. "Even romance?"

David felt his face going hot, but his grin widened. "Yeah. All that."

And while David fumbled and flustered at all the attention, Kylan took it in stride, like it was no more than his due. David had watched in amazement as the kid skated through interview after interview, unfazed. Open, honest, funny as hell, up to and including his issues with fetal alcohol syndrome.

"Are you sure you wanted to talk about that?" David had asked after the first time Kylan mentioned it.

Kylan had shrugged. "Maybe it'll help if people see a guy like me being something besides a pain in the ass."

Just like that, the kid would pop up and say something that made David have to clear his throat and change the subject. "Since when are you not a pain? You don't have to tell every single reporter about Muddy throwing me down out at Rusty's place."

"But they get such a kick out of it."

"I only did it to make you feel better."

Kylan had given him a wide, cheesy grin. "It worked."

David had cuffed him on the shoulder but laughed. He would've been thrilled if Kylan could do all the interviews, including this one in Cody. Behind the bucking chutes, metal rang on metal as gates slammed, with the usual semicontrolled chaos of bulls snorting and riders slapping themselves around to get pumped up as if their bodies didn't take enough abuse out in the arena. Must be a roughstock thing.

"Obviously, Muddy is still as good as when he disappeared," Laura said to David. "Seems like every rodeo, the two of you get a little better."

"We're getting our rhythm back," David agreed. "I haven't been drawing the best calves, but we've won money anyway because Muddy can make a marginal calf better."

"And how does he feel about all this attention?"

David laughed. "He figures if all these people are gonna be hanging around, they should at least bring grain."

She laughed, too, because she knew Muddy. "Well, I'll let you go. I'm sure you've got places to be."

"Yeah. I'm up in Greeley tomorrow." He flashed a sheepish smile. "Plus, we want to get out of town before the fireworks."

Laura laughed again and then put out her hand to shake his. "Congratulations, David, and best of luck. You deserve it."

"Thank you." He hustled away, not to escape, but because he'd left Kylan looking after Muddy and they were all starving. They'd slid into Cody with only minutes to spare, making the run down from morning slack at the Livingston rodeo where he and Muddy were sitting second when they left. Add a third place finish here in Cody, and it made for a damn good day.

He found Kylan where he'd left him, but instead of Muddy, the kid was holding on to a palomino while the current world leader in the barrel racing stripped splint boots off its back legs. She straightened, strapped the boots onto her saddle, and then retrieved the reins, planting a kiss on Kylan's cheek. "Thanks, sugar. See you in Greeley."

David waited until she was a few paces away before he said, "A little old for you, don't you think?"

"She thinks I'm cute," Kylan said matter-of-factly. "Sort of like a puppy."

David snorted. "She should try feeding you. More like a Saint Bernard."

Kylan pulled Muddy's reins loose from the fence rail. As they turned to leave, Muddy reached out and tried to nip another horse on the butt. Kylan jerked on the reins. "Don't be a butthead."

Muddy gave a mighty shove with his nose, knocking Kylan sideways.

David couldn't help but laugh. If Muddy had any traumatic memories of his last visit to Cody, he hid them well. He was his obnoxious, glorious self, mane to tail. Kylan scowled at him and started toward the trailer. David slung the strap of his rope can over his shoulder and followed.

As usual, the tail of Kylan's shirt had come loose, and despite all of David's efforts, the brim of his cowboy hat stuck up higher on one side than the other. Honest to God, there was just something about the shape of the kid's head. There was no spiffing him up. Between Kylan's shambles and David's tendency to look like a back-alley thug on the lam from the law, they'd probably scared the crap out of a few late-night truck-stop clerks in the past ten days as they raced across five states to hit thirteen rodeos.

"Speaking of feeding me…I s'pose we can't eat until after you talk to Mary," Kylan grumbled.

"I'll keep it short."

"Yeah, sure." Kylan gave a long-suffering sigh. "You guys are pathetic."

Yep, they were. David had spent more hours on the phone in the last two-and-a-half weeks than in the four years previous all totaled. He and Mary talked about everything, large and small, from world peace to how to persuade Kylan to cut his hair so it didn't do the scarecrow thing. They hadn't found a workable solution for either.

It should have felt familiar, lying awake in the dark, the phone propped on his pillow with the sounds of yet another carnival roaring nearby, but everything with Mary was different. More real. More immediate. David's conversations with Emily had been woven through with dreams and schemes, always looking forward to the future, a bright and shiny someday. He and Mary were fellow warriors who'd survived their separate battles and learned the value of living for now.

"Be nice to get to your place tomorrow night," Kylan said. "Me and Frosty need to rope some calves."

"You'll get all you want for four days."

Not that they'd been lacking, except for these past few days, while David had hauled hard and fast to as many of the Cowboy Christmas rodeos as he could. Thanks to Muddy's sudden fame, people lined up to offer them places to stay and to rope everywhere they went. With the extra practice, Frosty's tolerance, and David's coaching, Kylan had improved by leaps and bounds. He might never be a threat on the pro level, but with hard work and the right horse, he could do okay at the amateur and All-Indian rodeos.

One thing about Kylan, he was used to having to work for what he wanted.

Several of those same kind souls had also volunteered horses for Kylan to practice his shoeing skills on. The kid had already learned enough to be able to trim a horse on his own, as long as it had reasonably normal feet. By the time Kylan went home, he'd be ready to start doing some work for Galen and some of the other ranchers.

Of course, that depended on when exactly Kylan did go home.

"How'd you talk Starr into changing her mind about coming to nationals?" David asked.

"I told her she had to quit worrying so much about what other girls are puttin' on my Facebook page, 'cause you and I aren't those kind of guys." Kylan steered Muddy around a pair of rodeo queens and through the gate to contestant parking. Then he smirked at David. "Bet you won't mind seeing Mary, either."

Mind? Hah. David had tried his damnedest to persuade her to come down early, but she had more curriculum-planning meetings, plus next week was the big Indian Days celebration in Browning, and she'd volunteered to help with the kids' rodeo and that pie auction. "I can't wait."

"That's good," Kylan said, as they skirted one last trailer to get to David's rig. "'Cause she's standin' right there."

David's head jerked around, and his heart leapt like a rabbit scared up out of the brush. *Holy crap.* Mary stood beside his pickup, sparkling like sunshine in a white sleeveless blouse and skinny jeans with rhinestones on the pockets, her hair ruffled by the breeze. She lifted a hand in greeting, her smile a little uncertain.

David dropped his rope can with a *thunk*, took four long strides, and scooped her up. The kiss was even better than what he'd relived a million times since he'd left her. Sweeter and deeper for every minute of conversation they'd shared in the meantime. When he finally came up for air, she gave a breathless laugh and twined her arms around his neck.

"I guess this means you're happy to see me."

"You think?" He spun her around in a circle, spooking Muddy, who glared at them in annoyance. "I can't believe you're here. It must be a ten-hour drive."

"Nine," Mary corrected.

David glanced around, looking for her pickup. "How'd you get here?"

"Galen and Cissy. They're still over at the arena, watching the bull riding. Galen said if he was gonna come this far for a rodeo, he intended to see the whole damn thing."

David set her on her feet, tracing a thumb over the softness beneath her jaw, feeling the *kerthump* of her pulse. "You saw me rope?"

"Yes." Her smile lit up every last shadowy corner of his soul. "You were awesome. Both of you," she added, with a smile for Muddy, too.

He rolled his eyes and yanked at the reins.

"Yeah, yeah," Kylan said, leading him on back to tie up beside Frosty.

David looked from Mary to Kylan. "How long have you known about this?"

"A couple days," Kylan said.

"And you never once let on?"

Kylan tossed him a triumphant smile as he slid Muddy's bridle off and replaced it with a halter. "Pretty sly, huh?"

"I made him swear secrecy," Mary added. "I wanted to surprise you."

"Well, you got the job done. But we've only got a few hours before we have to leave for Greeley."

And those hours weren't near enough. Kylan would have to go eat with his aunt and uncle, so David could have Mary all to himself.

Mary tucked her chin, slanting a look at him from under her lashes. "Um, yeah, about that... I thought maybe I could ride along. If you don't mind."

"Mind?" David all but shouted. "Why would I?"

"You're going home to the ranch tomorrow." Uncertainty flickered in her eyes again. "I don't want to butt in."

David set his hands on her shoulders to give her a slight shake. "Don't be dumb. My family can't wait to meet you. And I can't wait to introduce you."

"Are you sure?"

"Very. Except for my sister. You stay away from her."

Mary blinked, frowning. "Don't you like her?"

"She's okay, as sisters go, but if the two of you ever gang up on me, I'm toast." David tapped a finger on the end of Mary's nose, his grin impossible to squelch. "You said you couldn't get away."

Mary smiled. "My schedule got rearranged, thanks to my friends. Cissy took over my stuff during Indian Days, and Hilary insisted on filling in for me on the curriculum committee."

"I knew I liked them." And he was beginning to think he'd won Cissy over, too, though he wouldn't take her approval for granted any time in the next, say, ten years.

David's phone rang. He pulled it from the clip on his belt, saw his dad's number, and took a moment to appreciate being able to answer with a smile on his face. "Hey, Dad. Checking up on me?"

"Of course. You know how your mother worries

when you're racin' from one rodeo to the next, especially in the holiday traffic."

"We made it fine. Sittin' second at Livingston, third here in Cody. How's it going down there?"

"*Well*, I'm afraid I have bad news."

David's breath caught. "What?"

"You won't be able to rope when you get home." His dad broke into a gleeful chuckle. "It's pouring rain."

Chapter 32

TWO WEEKS LATER, DAVID STOOD AT THE ARENA FENCE IN Pueblo, Colorado, hands wrapped around the rail, knuckles white.

Mary nudged him with an elbow. "Take a breath before you pass out."

"I can't. I'm too nervous."

Which was why Kylan had banished him from anywhere near the roping box. "Geez, dude. Go take a chill pill. You're freaking me out."

At least it had stopped raining. A month earlier, David couldn't have imagined wishing for an end to the rain, but for the last ten days, the entire state of Colorado had been treated to daily afternoon deluges, line after line of thunderstorms that dumped inches of moisture onto the thirsty ground.

And onto the Pueblo arena, which now looked more like a mud-pocked lake. Short of roping in the midst of a downpour, the conditions couldn't get much worse. Frosty could handle it just fine, but Kylan—

"Next up, from the Big Sky State of Montana, Kylan Runningbird," the announcer declared. "You've all heard this young man's amazing story. He was fifteen-point-six seconds on his first calf, so he'll have to be really fast today to qualify for the short round."

David's heart clutched, the air balling up in his lungs as Kylan rode into the arena, looking calm as all get-out, damn him, as he adjusted his rope and piggin' string. David hadn't been this nervous when he'd roped that first calf on Muddy at Reno, with what felt like all the world watching.

Mary's hand came to rest on David's forearm, her fingers digging into his flesh as Frosty settled into the corner of the roping box.

"What was that about breathing?" David asked.

She curled her lip at him, her gaze locked on the roping box. Kylan nodded his head. Frosty splattered out of the box in hot pursuit of the calf, and every molecule of David's will went into wishing Kylan's loop onto the speckled longhorn.

The rope whistled through the air and settled snug around the calf's neck. Kylan stepped off, staggered through the mud, grabbed the calf, and wrestled it onto its side. His movements were a tad too deliberate as he strung the front leg, gathered the hinds, took one, two, three wraps and a hooey and threw up his hands, but he got the job done.

Air exploded from David's lungs, a blast of relief. He clapped so hard, his hands stung. Kylan looked over to where they were standing and gave a little fist pump, grinning from ear to ear.

"Fourteen-point-two seconds," the announcer said. "That gives Kylan a total of twenty-nine and eight on two, which won't be enough to get him to the short round, but let's give the Montana cowboy a big hand. I'm sure you'll all join me in wishing him the best of luck, whatever comes next."

Kylan tipped his hat to the roar of applause, then gingerly coiled his mud-caked rope and rode out of the arena.

Mary squeezed David's arm. "You done good, David. I've never seen Kylan look so confident."

"It's Frosty. The two of them really click."

"I wasn't just talking about in the arena, but you did good there, too." She angled him an inscrutable look. "I'm not getting him back until school starts, am I?"

David winced. He wasn't supposed to be the one to tell her. "Kylan didn't want to bring it up until after he was done roping here."

He was stunned when her eyes filled with tears. "It's not a done deal," he rushed to add. "And it doesn't have to be clear until school starts. I can bring him back sooner."

She shook her head, brushing at the tears with the side of her hand. "No. It's fine. Better than that. It's great. The two of you…" She sniffed, swiping again at a fresh well of tears. "It's wonderful seeing how you are together. And I swear, I'm trying really hard not to be jealous."

David cupped her face and kissed away the dampness on her cheeks. "Hey. He's still yours. Always will be. I could never take your place, and he wouldn't want me to try."

"I know. I'm just not used to having to share so much of him."

"That's not all he was planning to ask." David thumbed away a fresh tear. "We were hoping you'd stay, too, for another couple of weeks. That is, if you can stand being packed into the trailer with two stinky guys for that long."

Her mouth twitched at the corners. "Are you sure you want a girl tagging along, ruining all your fun?"

"We'll make an exception since you're a pretty good night driver."

"Gee, thanks." She swatted his arm and then tugged at his sleeve. "C'mon. Let's wade on over and find Kylan."

She set off, splashing through the mud with those quick, purposeful strides, forcing David to hustle to keep up. Her yellow rain slicker was made for someone six inches taller, and the tails dragged. With her baseball cap pulled low, she looked younger than most of the teenage contestants.

They caught up with Kylan behind the roping chutes, where he was scraping mud off his jeans. David's cousin, Adam, held Frosty, stroking the horse's neck and cooing into his ear. Adam's eyes lit up when he saw David and Mary. He adored Mary. Everyone in David's family adored Mary. The feeling seemed to be mutual. So much so that Mary had pulled David aside, her eyes troubled.

"This is a great place, David. Wonderful people. But you know I'm not planning to relocate?"

He'd looped his arms around her waist, pressed a kiss to her forehead. "You have a good place already. And lucky for me, my job is portable."

She'd kissed him then, so hard his brain hadn't unscrambled for hours.

She hurried ahead while his mind wandered, dodging through the mob of horses and kids to tackle-hug Kylan.

"Did you see them, Mary? Frosty did so good, and Kylan…" Adam made a circling motion with his hands. "He tied that calf so fast."

"He did great," David said, clapping Kylan on the shoulder. "Way to be solid."

"Thanks." Kylan glanced up toward the big covered grandstand where the bulk of his fan club remained warm and dry up under the roof—Galen, Cissy, a sizeable

Browning contingent, plus David's entire family. "Starr sent me a text. She said I ended up twenty-sixth."

"That's awesome." Mary gave him another fierce hug. "I am so proud of you."

Kylan squirmed, pulling free, but his chest puffed up. He'd exceeded the goal they'd set for the finals. David had a feeling Kylan would be pushing a lot of boundaries from now on. Not that David was kidding himself. He hadn't sauntered in and chased away all of Kylan's problems; they were just on an extended vacation. Eventually, Kylan would butt up against the frustration again. He'd try and he'd fail, but David hoped the successes he was building up would be a solid enough foundation for him to stay and fight. Believe that the good would come around again, the way it had for David.

David glanced at the rapidly clearing sky and sent up a prayer of thanks. Bless those crotchety old bastards for detouring him onto this trail, even if they'd knocked him down a few times on the way. David was convinced they'd had a plan all along, and he sure wasn't complaining about the results.

Frosty nuzzled Adam's chest, more than ready to be back at the barn. His belly and flanks were streaked with mud, his legs caked solid brown on white as if he'd been dipped in chocolate.

"Frosty wants his grain," Mary said.

"He earned it." Kylan looped an arm over the horse's neck and gave him a hug. Frosty didn't pin his ears or bare his teeth, unlike someone else they all knew.

"Me and Kylan are going to go clean him off and put him in his stall," Adam declared. "Then Kylan said I can come with him and Starr to get a hamburger."

He gazed at Kylan with childlike adoration, his dark hair and almond-shaped eyes the same color as David's, but his face smoother. Eternally young.

"I owe you somethin' for lettin' me use your horse," Kylan muttered with a mixture of pride and embarrassment. "Let's go. I'm starving."

As usual. The kid ate like a bear coming out of hibernation.

He and Adam headed for the barns, Frosty ambling between them while Adam talked a mile a minute and Kylan nodded along.

"Kylan is really good with him," David said.

Mary smiled. "He's never been anybody's hero before. He's enjoying himself."

The two of them stood for a moment, nowhere to go for a change, no rush to get there.

"Are your parents sticking around tonight?" she asked.

"Nope. The neighbor told Dad they got another three quarters of an inch of rain, so he can't wait to get home and check the gauge."

And to admire the fresh green of the pastures, the grass springing to joyful life with the long-awaited moisture. David knew it was foolish, but he felt as if the whole world had shifted. From the moment he'd finally found this place where he was supposed to be, everything that had been wrong had become right again, including the weather.

"Excellent," Mary said.

David blinked. "I thought you liked my parents."

"Love them," she said, and then gave him a smile that made his blood simmer. "I could use a little private time, if you know what I mean."

Oh yeah. David definitely knew. He'd spent a sizable percentage of the last two weeks contemplating ways to get rid of Kylan. Not permanently. Just a few hours. Long enough to see where those increasingly hot kisses of Mary's would lead if there was no one to interrupt them.

Traveling with her was driving him insane, in all the ways he'd expected. She was funny, unpredictable, occasionally maddening, and he wouldn't change a thing. Not even when she made him stop at the cemetery as they passed through Crow Agency so she could place flowers on Jinx Yellowhawk's grave.

"If he hadn't been such a complete waste of a human being, we never would have met," she declared by way of a eulogy.

Classic Mary, tough and soft, all twisted up in one fascinating package.

When David wasn't busy roping, he split his time between fantasizing about unwrapping her and debating how long he had to wait before he dared confess he was crazy in love with her. "We could go out to dinner while Kylan and Starr are at the dance."

She arched her eyebrows. "I'd rather ask if Kylan could stay at the motel with Galen and Cissy tonight."

David's heart expanded, squeezing the air clean out of his lungs. Him. Mary. Alone in his trailer for an entire night. "But…they'll all know."

"That we're having sex? Yep. They will." Her eyes sparkled with amusement and a touch of heat.

"That doesn't bother you?"

"Not as much as not having sex with you." She stepped closer, grabbing the lapels of his raincoat and stretching onto her tiptoes to narrow her eyes at him. "I love you to death, Dudley, and I respect your personal choices, but if you tell me we have to wait until we're married, I'm gonna have to hurt you."

He lost his air again, reeling from the *slam-bam* punch of hearing Mary say the words *I love you* and *married* in the same sentence. He gave her a hopeful smile. "Or maybe you could just…marry me?"

Her jaw dropped. Then she laughed, a peal of pure joy. "Eventually, yes. But not today. So…you wanna get naked or what?"

"Yes." He hauled her into his arms, planted a kiss on her lips. "Definitely, yes. In the worst way."

And now he knew exactly what that meant.

Acknowledgments

Given that my road to publication was nigh on end-less, uphill and against the wind, there is no way this book would have seen the light of day if not for dozens of people who've given me a hand up or a kick in the ass along the way. It's impossible to name them all, so I'm just going to throw this out there to all the writers in the Twitterverse who've propped me up and all the beta readers who've endured my early drafts without telling me to toss my laptop off the nearest mountain. I'd hug you all except you know I don't do that mushy crap.

Without Janet Reid this book wouldn't exist because the two year break after my son was born would have stretched on indefinitely if she hadn't said, "Hey you, time to write something new." And what I did write would have continued to be a hot mess without her unflinching feedback. And for trading me to the amazing Holly Root, who has continued to push me onward and upward.

Thanks to Crystal Posey because she is awesome in so many ways and accepted boxes of Coffee Crisps as payment in full for her amazing art and web work for far longer than she should have.

Cynthia D'Alba deserves all the credit for pushing and prodding me to make this into a full blown novel, then hooking me up with her wonderful, then Samhain editor, Heidi Moore.

And to Mary Altman and everyone at Sourcebooks Casablanca who decided to give this book a second chance and a new life, a big thank you from all the readers over the past couple of years who have wished for a mass market paperback version. Here you go, good friends!

To Nicholas Marco, who was the first publishing professional to tell me I didn't suck, and who bothered to check in from time to time over the years to see how things were coming along.

Special recognition to Karen Templeton. She was the first published author to speak to me online, which led to the rather astonishing discovery that she was a human being just like me and gave me the courage to think I might be able to make it, too. Over these many years she has taught me by her example what it truly means to be a professional. If I ever have the chance to meet her in person I expect to embarrass both of us. She has been warned.

A shout out to the "real" Muddy—a horse named Freeway—his owner Tod Slone, and the Durfey family. Their story brewed in the back of my head for over a decade before I finally came up with this highly fictionalized version of my own.

And last but certainly not least, to all of my Muddys, better known as Betsy and Scotty and Ember and the buckskin mare, aka Nicky, aka the hell bitch. If I survived all of you, this publishing gig should be a piece of cake.

Can't get enough Kari Lynn Dell?
Keep reading for a peek at the
first book in the Texas Rodeo series

RECKLESS *in* TEXAS

IT WAS LABOR DAY WEEKEND AND THE NIGHT WAS TAILOR-made for rodeo. Overhead the sky had darkened to blue velvet, and underfoot the West Texas dirt was groomed to perfection. Music pounded and the wooden bleachers were jammed with every live body within fifty miles, plus a decent number of tourists who'd been lured off the bleak stretch of Highway 20 between Odessa and El Paso by the promise of cold beer, hot barbecue, and a chance to get western.

Violet Jacobs maneuvered her horse, Cadillac, into position, mirroring her cousin on the opposite end of the bucking chutes. She and Cole both wore the Jacobs Livestock pickup rider uniform—a royal blue shirt to match stiff, padded royal-blue-and-white chaps to protect against the banging around and occasional kick that came with the job. Tension prickled through Violet's muscles as they waited for the next cowboy to nod his head.

She and Cole were supposed to be emergency backup during the bull riding, charging in only if the bullfighters—the so-called cowboy lifesavers—failed to get the rider and themselves out of danger. Trouble was, the odds of failure got higher every day. For a bullfighter, speed was key, and if Red got any slower they'd have to set out stakes to tell if he was moving. He'd worn out his last legs two weeks back. What he had left was held together with athletic tape, titanium braces, and sheer stubbornness. At some point, it wasn't going to be enough.

Violet's gaze swung to the younger of the pair of bullfighters. Hank vibrated like a bowstring as the bull rider took his wrap and used his free hand to pound his fist shut around the flat-braided rope. The kid was quicksilver to Red's molasses, as green as Red was wily. If he would just listen, work with Red instead of trying to do it all…

The gate swung wide and the bull blasted out with long, lunging jumps. Red lumbered after him like the Tin Man with rusty hinges. The bull dropped its head and swapped ends, blowing the rider's feet back, flipping the cowboy straight off over his horns. He landed in a pile right under the bull's nose. Hank jumped in from the right, Red from the left, and the two of them got tangled up. When Red stumbled, the Brahma caught his shoulder with one blunt horn and tossed him in the air like he weighed nothing.

Cole already had his rope up and swinging. Violet was three strides behind. The instant Red hit the ground, the bull was on top of him, grinding him into the dirt. When Hank scrambled to his partner's rescue, the bull slung its head and caught the kid under the chin with his other horn, laying him out straight as a poker.

Cole's loop sailed through the air, whipped around the bull's horns, and came tight. He took two quick wraps around the saddle horn with the tail of the rope and spurred his horse, Dozer, into a bounding lope. The big sorrel jerked the bull around and away before it could inflict any more damage. Violet rode in behind shouting, "Hyah! Hyah!" and slapping the bull's hip with her rope. He caught sight of the catch pen gate and stopped fighting to trot out of the arena toward feed and water. Violet wheeled Cadillac around, heart in her throat as she counted bodies. The breath rushed out of her lungs when she saw everyone was mostly upright.

The bull rider leaned over Hank, a hand on his shoulder as a medic knelt in the dirt next to him, attempting to stanch the blood dripping from his chin. A second medic supervised while two cowboys hoisted Red to his feet. He tried a ginger, limping step. Then another. By the third, Violet knew it would take a lot more than a can of oil and a roll of duct tape to fix the Tin Man this time.

─────

The Jacobs family gathered in the rodeo office after the show for an emergency staff meeting. The five of them filled the room—her father, Steve, was six-and-a-half feet of stereotypical Texas cowboy in a silver belly hat that matched his hair, and Cole, a younger, darker model cast from the same mold. Even Violet stood five ten in her socks, and none of them were what you'd call a beanpole. It was just as well she'd never set her heart on being the delicate, willowy type. She wasn't bred for it. Her five-year-old son, Beni, had tucked himself into the corner with his video game. Her mother, Iris, was a

Shetland pony in a herd of Clydesdales, but could bring them all to heel with a few well-chosen words in that certain tone of voice.

Now she shook her head, *tsking* sadly. "Did y'all see that knee? Looks like five pounds of walnuts stuffed into a two-pound bag."

"He won't be back this year," Violet said.

Her dad *hmphffed*, but no one argued. Even if Red wanted to try, they couldn't put him back out there for the three weeks that were left of the season. It wasn't safe for Red or for the cowboys he was supposed to protect. It was sad to lose one of the old campaigners, but he'd had a good, long run—clear back to the days when the guys who fought bulls were called rodeo clowns, wore face paint and baggy Wranglers, and were expected to tell jokes and put on comedy acts. Nowadays, bullfighters were all about the serious business of saving cowboys' necks. Leave the costumes and the standup comedy to the modern day clowns, pure entertainers who steered well clear of the bulls.

"Saves us havin' to tell Red it's time to hang up the cleats," Cole said, blunt as always. "Who we gonna get to replace him?"

Steve sighed, pulling off his hat to run a hand through his flattened hair. "Violet can make some calls. Maybe Donny can finish out the year."

Oh, come *on*. Donny was even older than Red, if slightly better preserved. Violet opened her mouth to argue, but her mother cut her off.

"It'll have to wait until morning." Iris began stacking paperwork and filing it in plastic boxes. "Y'all go get your stock put up. We've got a date for drinks with the committee president."

And Violet had a date with her smartphone. Fate and Red's bad knees had handed her an opportunity to breathe fresh life into Jacobs Livestock. She just had to persuade the rest of the family to go along.

Once the stock was settled for the night, Violet herded Beni to their trailer and got them both showered and into pajamas. She tucked him into his bunk with a stuffed penguin under one arm—a souvenir from a trip to the Calgary Zoo with his dad earlier in the summer.

"Can I call Daddy?" he asked.

She kissed his downy-soft forehead. Lord, he was a beautiful child—not that she could take any credit. The jet-black hair and tawny skin, eyes as dark as bittersweet chocolate…that was all his daddy. "Not tonight, bub. The time is two hours different in Washington, so he's not done riding yet."

"Oh. Yeah." Beni heaved a sigh that was equal parts yawn. "He's still coming home next week, right?"

"He'll meet us at the rodeo on Sunday."

He'd promised, and while Violet wouldn't recommend getting knocked up on a one-night stand, at least she'd had the sense to get drunk and stupid with a really good man. He would not let his son down, especially after he'd been on the road for almost a month in the Pacific Northwest at a run of rich fall rodeos. The rodeos that mattered.

She heaved a sigh of her own. Of course her rodeos mattered—to the small towns, the local folks, they were a chance to hoot and holler and shake off their troubles for a night. The contestants might be mostly weekend cowboys with jobs that kept them close to home, but they left just as big a piece of their heart in the arena as any of the top-level pros. Still, the yearning spiraled through Violet like barbed wire, coiling around her heart and digging in. It cut deep, that yearning. Nights like this were worst of all, in the quiet after the rodeo, when there was nothing left to do but think. Imagine.

At legendary rodeos like Ellensburg, Puyallup, and Lewiston, the best cowboys in North America were going head to head, world championships on the line. Meanwhile, Violet had successfully wrapped up the forty-third annual Puckett County Homesteader Days. Jacobs Livestock had been part of twenty-nine of them. If her dad had his way, they'd continue until the rodeo arena crumbled into the powder-dry West Texas dirt, her mother and Cole trailing contentedly along behind.

How could Violet be the only one who wanted more?

"Night, Mommy." Beni rolled over, tucked the penguin under his chin, and was instantly asleep.

Violet tugged the blanket up to his shoulders, then pulled shut the curtain that separated his bunk from the rest of the trailer. Finally time for dinner. She slicked her dark hair behind her ears, the damp ends brushing her shoulders as she built a sandwich of sliced ham on one of her mother's fat homemade rolls, a dollop of coleslaw on the plate alongside it. Before settling in at the table, she turned the radio on low. The singer's throaty twang vibrated clear down to her heartstrings, reminding her that the only man in her life had yet to hit kindergarten, but it muted the *tick-tick-tick* of another rodeo season winding down with Violet in the exact same place.

She prodded her coleslaw with a fork, brooding.

Red had been operating on pure guts for weeks, so she'd made a point of researching every card-carrying professional bullfighter in their price range. Was her prime candidate still available? She opened the Internet browser on her phone and clicked a link to a Facebook page. *Shorty Edwards. Gunnison, Colorado*. His status hadn't changed since the last time she checked. *Good news! Doc says I can get back to work. Any of you out there needing a bullfighter for fall rodeos, give me a call*.

Shorty was exactly what they needed. Young enough to be the bullfighter of their future, but experienced enough to knock Hank into line. Good luck persuading her dad to bring in a complete stranger, though—and not even a Texan, Lord save her. She might as well suggest they hire the devil himself. Violet drummed agitated fingers on the table, staring at Shorty's action photo. Jacobs Livestock needed new blood, an infusion of energy. Fans and committees loved a good bullfighter.

Her dad *had* said she should make some calls. As business manager for Jacobs Livestock, she would write up the contract and sign the paycheck, so why not get a jump on the process? She could discuss it with her parents before making a commitment.

Her heart commenced a low bass beat that echoed in her ears as she dialed his number. He answered. Her voice squeaked when she introduced herself, and she had to clear her throat before explaining their situation.

"Three rodeos?" he asked. "Guaranteed?"

"Uh…yeah."

"And you can give me a firm commitment right now?"

"I…uh…"

"I've got an offer in Nevada for one rodeo. If you can give me three, I'll come to Texas, but I promised them an answer by morning."

Violet's mouth was so dry her lips stuck to her teeth. She'd never hired anyone without her dad's approval. But it wasn't permanent. Just three rodeos. Sort of like a test-drive. If Shorty turned out to be a lemon, they could just send him back.

"Well?"

"Three rodeos, guaranteed," she blurted.

"Great. Sign me up."

She ironed out the details then hung up the phone, folded her arms on the table, and buried her face in them. When the first wave of panic subsided, she sat up, pressing her palms on the table when her head spun. *Chill, Violet.* She was twenty-eight years old and her dad was always saying the best way to get more responsibility was to show she could handle it. They had a problem. She'd solved it. Once the rest of them saw Shorty in action, they'd have to admit she'd made the right choice.

Because you have such an excellent track record when it comes to picking men...

Violet slapped that demon back into its hidey-hole. This was different. This was business. She was good at business. As long as Shorty Edwards was exactly as advertised, she was golden.

Chapter 2

THE LAST BRAHMA TO BUCK AT THE PUYALLUP, Washington, rodeo was a huge red brindle named Cyberbully. Three jumps out of the chute he launched his rider into the clear blue sky. The cowboy thumped into the dirt like a hundred-and-forty-pound sack of mud and stayed there, motionless, while the bull whipped around, looking to add injury to insult.

Joe Cassidy stepped between them and tapped Cyberbully's fat nose. "Hey, Cy. This way."

The bull took the bait. Joe hauled ass, circling away from the fallen cowboy with the Brahma a scant inch behind. The big son of a bitch was fast. Caught out in the middle of the arena, Joe couldn't outrun him, so he opted to let Cy give him a boost. With a slight hesitation and a perfectly timed hop, he momentarily took a seat between the bull's stubby horns. Startled, Cy threw up his head and Joe pushed off. As he was thrown free, he saw a flash of neon yellow—his partner sprinting in from the opposite direction. "C'mere, Cy, you ugly bastard!"

The bull hesitated, then went after Wyatt. Joe landed on his feet and spun around to see Wyatt vault up and onto the fence next to the exit gate with a stride to spare. The bull feinted at him, then trotted out.

"Ladies and gentlemen, give a hand to our bullfighters, Joe Cassidy and Wyatt Darrington!" the rodeo announcer shouted. "That's why these two are the best team in professional rodeo."

The air vibrated, fans whistling and stomping their appreciation as Joe jogged over to check on the cowboy, who had rolled into a seated position.

"You okay, Rowdy?" Joe asked, extending a hand to help him up.

"Yep. Thanks, guys." Rowdy swiped at the dirt on his chaps and strolled to the chutes, unscathed and unfazed.

Wyatt folded his arms, glaring. "We should let the bulls have the ones that are too dumb to get up and run."

Joe snorted. That'd be the day. Wyatt was hard-wired to save the world—even the parts that didn't want saving.

"That wraps up our rodeo for this year, folks!" the announcer declared. "If you have a hankering for more top-of-the-line professional rodeo action, come on out to Pendleton, Oregon, next week for the world-famous Roundup…"

One more rodeo, then six weeks off. Seven days from now, after Pendleton, he was headed home. Fall was Joe's favorite time of year in the high desert of eastern Oregon, weaning this year's crop of colts and calves under the clear, crisp sky.

He twisted around, checking the spot where the bull had tagged his ribs. Not even a flesh wound thanks to his Kevlar vest, but the big bastard had ripped a hole in his long-sleeved jersey. "Damn. That's the third one this month."

Wyatt took off his cowboy hat and wiped sweat from his forehead with a shirtsleeve. "You're gettin' old and slow, pardner."

"Five years less old and slow than you."

"Yeah, but I take better care of myself."

"Says the guy with five shiny new screws in his ankle." Joe nodded toward Wyatt's right leg, supported by a rigid plastic Aircast. "How's it feel?"

"Like they drove the bottom two screws in with a hammer." Wyatt rotated the ankle, wincing. "Still works, though, so they must've got 'em in good and tight."

Joe rubbed the sting from the elbow Cyberbully had smacked with the top of his rock-hard skull. He ached from head to toe with the cumulative fatigue of six straight days of rodeo piled on top of all the other weeks and months of bruises and bodily insults. "What the hell is wrong with us?" he asked.

Wyatt started for the gate. "I'm in it for the women and free booze. Let's go make that stupid shit Rowdy buy us a beer."

"Just remember, you're driving," Joe said, yawning.

Wyatt sent him a sympathetic glance. "Long night, huh?"

"Yeah." Tension crawled up his back at the memory. Goddamn Lyle Browning. Someone should've castrated the bastard by now. His wife had plenty of reasons to cry, but why did she insist on using Joe's shoulder?

Wyatt shook his head. "I shouldn't have left you alone at the bar. You were already upset before the weepy woman."

"I wasn't upset." The tension slithered higher, toward the base of Joe's skull.

"Bullshit. Your old man lives fifteen miles from here and couldn't show up to watch you in action. That sucks."

"I'm thirty years old, not ten. It's not like he skipped

a little league game." But he'd missed plenty. Most of Joe's high school sports career, in fact.

But that was ancient history. Joe tipped off his cowboy hat, peeled the ruined jersey over his head, then balled it up and gave it a mighty heave. It landed three rows up, in the outstretched arms of a little girl in a pink cowboy hat, who squealed her excitement. Joe smiled and waved and kept moving. He wanted to be gone. Far, far away from Puyallup and any expectations he hadn't been able to stomp to death.

"I haven't seen Lyle's wife around today," Wyatt said.

"Probably still hugging the toilet."

Or maybe she'd finally smartened up and left. 'Bout time. Lyle Browning was a sniveling dog, dragging along on the coattails of his dad's successful rodeo company. They'd grown up in the same small town and Joe had started working summers on the Browning Ranch when he was fifteen, but he and Lyle had never been friends. Early on, Joe had had some sympathy. Had to suck for Lyle, his mom dying when he was so young, and his dad not exactly the nurturing type. At some point, though, a guy had to take responsibility for his own life.

As they stepped into the narrow alley behind the bucking chutes, a hand clamped on Joe's shoulder. "Hey, asshole. I need to talk to you."

The words were slurred, the voice a permanent whine. Joe turned and found himself face-to-face with the last person he wanted to see. He brushed off the hand. "Whaddaya want, Lyle?"

Lyle Browning tried to get in Joe's face, but came up short by a good six inches. Even at that distance, his breath was toxic. "You fucking prick. How long you been sneaking around, fucking my wife?"

"Don't be stupid."

Lyle rolled onto his toes, swaying. He smelled like he'd passed out in the bottom of a beer garden dumpster. Looked like it, too. "Everybody saw you leave the bar together, you son of a bitch, and she told me what happened when you got back to her room."

The *fuck* she did. But Joe could think of a dozen reasons Lyle's wife would want her husband to think she'd gone out and gotten a piece. At the very least, it'd sure teach him to screw around every chance he got. Lyle had mastered the art of trading on his daddy's name with the sleaziest of the buckle bunnies who hung around looking for a cowboy-shaped notch for their bedpost. Too bad for them, they got Lyle instead.

"See?" Lyle crowed. "You can't deny it."

Joe ground his teeth. Hell. He couldn't. Not without humiliating her all over again in front of the gathering crowd. "You're drunk. Crawl back into your hole and sleep it off. We'll talk later."

"We'll talk now!"

Joe put a hand on Lyle's chest, making enough space to take a breath without gagging. "Back off, Lyle."

"Don't push me, asshole!" Lyle reared back and took a wild swing.

His right fist plowed into Joe's stomach. Even if Lyle wasn't a weenie-armed drunk, it would've bounced off Joe's Kevlar vest. His left fist grazed Joe's chin, though, and that was too damn much. Joe popped him square in the mouth. Lyle squealed, arms flailing, then toppled straight over backward, his skull smacking the hard-packed dirt. He jerked a couple of times before his eyes rolled back and the lights went out.

Joe barely had time to think *oh shit* before Dick Browning's voice sliced through the crowd. "What the hell is going on here?"

A whole section of the onlookers peeled away to clear a path. Dick crouched over his son and gave him a not-very-gentle tap on the cheek. "Lyle! You okay?"

Lyle moaned, his head lolling off to one side. Dick jumped up and spun around to face Joe. Where Lyle was scrawny, Dick was wiry, tough as a rawhide whip. He was only a hairbreadth taller than his son, but somehow, when Dick decided to get in your face, he made it work.

Joe took a step back and put up his hands. "He took a swing at me."

"What did you expect? You mess with a man's wife—"

Like Lyle was any kind of man, but Joe didn't dare say so. Sweat beaded on his forehead, part heat, part panic, as his gaze bounced off Dick's and around the curious crowd. This was not the time or place to set Dick straight. "Can we talk about this later, in private?"

"You disrespect my family, assault my son—there is no later," Dick snapped. "Consider yourself unemployed. And don't bother showing up at Pendleton, either."

Joe flinched, the words a verbal slap. "That's crazy. You know I wouldn't—"

"Then why would she say so?"

Joe opened his mouth, then clamped it shut. God*damn*it.

Wyatt yanked him backward and slid into the space between Joe and Dick, smooth as butter. "If that piece of shit you call a son could keep his dick in his pants, his wife wouldn't be out at the bar drinking herself into a coma."

"This is none of your business."

"If it's Joe's business, it's mine. We call that friendship—not that you'd know." Wyatt leaned in, got his eyes down on Dick's level. "Don't give me an excuse, Herod, or I'll lay you out in the dirt with your spawn."

Joe grabbed him, afraid Wyatt might actually punch the old man. "You can't—"

Wyatt yanked his arm out of Joe's grasp. "It'd be worth the bail money."

For a long, tense moment they remained locked eye to eye. Then Lyle groaned, rolled over, and puked. Dick jerked around, cursing. "Somebody give me a hand getting him over to my trailer."

Out of reflex, Joe took a step. Wyatt jabbed an elbow into his sternum. "Don't even *think* about it."

He hauled Joe away, around the back of the grandstand, over to the sports medicine trailer that also served as their locker room.

"Who is Herod?" Joe asked, unable to process the rest of the scene.

"The most evil fucking tyrant in the Bible, but only because Matthew never met Dick Browning." Wyatt yanked open the door to the trailer and dragged Joe up the steps.

Matthew. Herod. Christ. "Who says that shit?"

"I'm a preacher's kid," Wyatt said. "I get my gospel up when I'm pissed."

Preacher. Hah. Try *Lord High Bishop of Something or Other*. Wyatt's family learned their gospel at Yale Divinity. He read big fat history books for the fun of it. For two guys who had nothing in common, Joe and Wyatt had been a dream team from the first time they worked in the same arena, and hell on wheels outside those arenas. The mileage added up, though, and a thirty-year-old body didn't bounce back from hangovers the same way it used to. Joe sure didn't miss them, or waking up next to woman whose name was lost in his alcohol-numbed brain.

As they stepped into the trailer, one of the athletic trainers grabbed a gauze pad and slapped it on a split in Joe's knuckle. "You're dripping. Wipe it off, then I'll see if you need stitches."

Wyatt leaned against the counter and folded his arms. "What he needs is a rabies vaccination."

The trainer's head whipped around in alarm. "It's a dog bite?"

"No," Joe said.

"Close enough," Wyatt said. "He cut it on Lyle Browning's face."

The trainer smirked. "So, more like a rat. Better dissect Lyle's brain to see if he's rabid."

"Good luck finding one," Wyatt said. "But I volunteer to knock him over the head. And his little daddy, too."

"Not very Christian for a choir boy," Joe muttered.

Wyatt's grin was all teeth. "One of a long list of reasons the Big Guy and I are no longer on speaking terms."

Fifteen minutes later, the last of the cowboys had cleared out of the trailer and the trainers had gone to have a beer, leaving Joe and Wyatt stretched out on the padded treatment tables. Stripped down to a pair of black soccer shorts with his blond hair slicked back and a bottle of water dangling from long, manicured fingers,

Wyatt looked exactly like what he was—the product of generations-deep East Coast money. When asked how he'd ended up fighting bulls, he liked to say it was the best legal way to be sure his family never spoke to him again. The reporters thought he was joking.

Joe's knuckle was bandaged, but his whole hand throbbed in time with the pounding in his head. His initial shock had morphed into fury, churning like hot, black tar in his gut. He punched the pillow with his uninjured fist. "I *should* skip Pendleton. It'd serve Dick right."

"Don't be an idiot," Wyatt said. "Just because you're his chore boy on the ranch between rodeos doesn't mean Dick has shit to say about when and where you fight bulls."

Joe scowled, but couldn't argue. The mega-rodeos they worked were too much for any one stock contractor to handle. Cheyenne lasted two weeks. Denver had sixteen performances. Rodeos that big hired a main contractor to gather up at least a dozen others, each bringing only their best bulls and horses. The rodeo committee also hired the bullfighters. Down in the bush leagues, you worked for the contractor. At the elite level, they were freelancers. Joe and Wyatt were the most sought-after bullfighters in the country, stars in their own right, which meant they could pick and choose from the most prestigious rodeos.

It irritated Wyatt to no end that Joe chose to stick mostly to the rodeos where Dick Browning had been hired to provide bucking stock, and continued to work on Dick's ranch for what was chump change compared to his bullfighter pay. Wyatt blamed misplaced loyalty.

And yeah, Dick had given him his start, but Joe had paid that debt a long time ago. The ties that bound him were buried deep in the hills and valleys of the High Lonesome Ranch. He loved that land like nothing else except the stock that ran on it.

How could Wyatt understand? He wasn't a cowboy.

He cocked his head, his gaze sharpening. "You're really pissed."

"Wouldn't you be?" Joe shot back.

"Hell yeah, but I would've throat-punched both of them ten years ago. This isn't the first time Dick has blown up in your face. It isn't even the first time he fired you."

"I deserved it most of those other times." When Joe was a showboating twenty-year-old with more guts than common sense. The anger boiled up again. "I'm not a brain-dead kid anymore."

"So tell him to go fuck himself."

Joe shook his head and Wyatt hissed in frustration. "Geezus, Joe. What's it going to take?"

Joe couldn't imagine. The High Lonesome had been the center of his world for too long. Solid ground when his home life was anything but. Dick's great-grandfather had veered south off the Oregon Trail to homestead there. He had given the ranch its name because the rugged miles of sagebrush desert were high in altitude, lonesome in the extreme, and spectacular in a wild, almost savage way that possessed a man's soul. Joe could cut off a limb easier than he could walk away.

"You were right before." Wyatt adjusted the ice pack on his ankle, then reached for his phone. "If Dick wants to shoot off his mouth, slander you in front of half of pro rodeo, you should call his bluff. Let him explain to the committee in Pendleton why you're not there."

Joe bolted upright. "I can't leave the Roundup short a bullfighter."

"You won't." Wyatt's fingers danced over his touch screen before he lifted it to his ear, holding up a palm for silence when Joe tried to speak. "Hey, Shorty! This is Wyatt. I heard you're looking to pick up a rodeo or two before the season ends. How does Pendleton sound?"

Joe opened his mouth, but Wyatt shushed him again.

"Yes, really. Would I joke about something that big?" A pause, then Wyatt grinned. "Oh yeah. I forgot. That was a good one. But I paid you back for the airfare, and I'm serious this time. Joe wants out. You want in?" Another pause, and a frown. "Where, and how much?" Wyatt listened, then grimaced. He covered the phone with his hand and said to Joe, "Shorty Edwards can come to Pendleton in your place, on one condition."

"What condition?" By which Joe meant to say, *Are you fucking crazy?*

"How do you feel about Texas?" Wyatt asked. When Joe only gaped at him, he shrugged and said into the phone. "Guess that means yes. See you in Pendleton, Shorty."

He hung up and tossed the phone aside.

Joe stared at him, horrified. "You did not just do that."

"Bet your ass I did." Suddenly every line of Wyatt's body was as sharply etched as the ice in his blue eyes. "I will do whatever it takes to pry you away from that son of a bitch."

"Dick's not that bad." But there was no conviction in Joe's voice. He was tired and hurting and every time he replayed Dick's words, heard the contempt in his voice, his chest burned with humiliation and fury. How could he stroll into Pendleton and pretend it was all good?

"If you stay, you'll end up just like him—a shriveled up, rancid piece of coyote bait."

Joe stared at the ceiling, sick of arguing. Sick of it all. Silence reigned for a few moments. Then Wyatt sighed, and the pity in his voice cut deeper than Dick's lashing tongue.

"Have some pride, Joe. Go to Texas. Get a little perspective." Wyatt flashed a knife-edged smile. "At least give humanity a chance before you sign over your soul to the devil."

Chapter 3

A HARD BUMP AND THE SCREECH OF RUBBER ON tarmac nudged Joe out of the closest thing to sleep he'd had in the past thirty-six hours. He rubbed the blur from his vision as the plane taxied to the terminal. *"Welcome to Dallas-Fort Worth, where the local time is 1:33 p.m. and the temperature is ninety-seven degrees. Please remain in your seats…"*

Make me. Joe was on his feet before the plane came to a complete stop, shaking the kinks out of legs that had been crammed into coach way too long. Every decent flight out of Sea-Tac had been overbooked, forcing him to hop a commuter flight to Spokane, suffer through a five-hour layover, a four-and-a-half hour flight, then spend what was left of the night and most of the morning in the Minneapolis airport. But by damn, he was on the ground in Dallas on schedule. Jacobs Livestock was expecting a bullfighter to show up by five o'clock this afternoon and they'd get one. They just weren't expecting Joe.

"Easier to ask forgiveness than beg for permission," Wyatt had insisted. "Besides, what are they gonna do, complain you're too good for them?"

Joe wasn't inclined to care if feathers got ruffled. Jacobs was getting double their money's worth, and with every mile, every hour that took him farther from where he was supposed to be, at Pendleton, the needle on his give-a-shit meter dropped another notch. If the point was to punish Dick, why did Joe feel like he'd been sent down to the minor leagues for bad behavior?

He grabbed his battered gear bag from the overhead bin—the luggage handlers could misroute his clothes to China, but they weren't touching his bread and butter—and vibrated in place while he waited for the aisle to clear. An eternity later, he broke free of the shuffling herd. His twitching muscles whimpered with relief when he was able to lengthen his stride, weaving past roller bags and shuffling Bluetooth zombies, down the terminal to the nearest restroom. He took a leak, then sighed wearily at his reflection as he washed his hands and splashed water on his face. Shaving and laundry had fallen by the wayside while he'd scrambled to make last-minute travel arrangements, by turns too pissed off at Dick and assaulted by second thoughts to care how he looked. Besides, the three-day stubble was a nice match for the dark circles under his bloodshot eyes.

Violet Jacobs would just have to take him as he was, scruff and all. In thirty years, only three women had earned the right to tell Joe to clean up his act. Roxy had been his partner in crime, his staunchest supporter and a near-constant exasperation since the day she gave birth to him. Helen, the cook at the High Lonesome, had been trying to put some meat on his bones since he first showed up there as a gangly teenager, and LouEllen at The Mane had been cutting his hair just as long. She had a knack for trimming it so no one but Wyatt noticed. Joe just looked less like he should have an electric guitar slung over his shoulder than a bagful of knee braces and body armor. Unfortunately, she'd been out of town last

month when he'd passed through between rodeo runs.
No one else touched Joe's hair, regardless of how much
Dick bitched.

He ran damp fingers through the straggly mess and
called it good. Then he tapped a text into his phone.
Arrived gate E-16. Have to grab my bag.

The reply bounced right back. Come straight out the
door nearest baggage claim. I've got the yellow car.

Wyatt had arranged this ride from the airport to the
first rodeo—four hours west of Dallas—and Joe had
been forbidden to offer to pay for gas. Whether Wyatt
had called in a personal or professional favor Lord
only knew, and Joe hadn't bothered to ask. He snagged
his duffel off the carousel, walked out the door, and
stopped dead at the sight of the car parked directly
across the street, its owner contributing to the traffic
congestion in the loading zone as she lounged against
the hood, her long, bare legs crossed at the ankles.
Oh yeah. Wyatt definitely had personal business with
this one. Joe blew out a breath that was half laugh and
headed for the car.

He might not make a great first impression, but he
was damn sure going to make an entrance.

Violet swiped away a trickle of sweat that oozed down
her temple and glared at the last stinking water tank
left to be cleaned. Emphasis on the *stink*. Whoever
used these stock pens last had left water in the tanks to
ferment into foul green soup. Violet's father and Cole
drained and upended all of them, propping them on their
sides against the fences for Violet and Beni to attack

with a hose and a scrub brush while her mother brought up the rear with a bucket of bleach water.

Violet smelled like the Swamp Thing after a hard day, probably looked worse, and their new bullfighter was due to pull in any time now. Not that she had to impress him, but she was nervous enough about bringing a stranger on board that she'd feel better if she at least combed her hair and put on a clean, dry shirt. She scowled at the green-black slime coating the bottom of the tank, steeling herself to move in, when a flash of canary yellow caught her eye. A Corvette turned into the rodeo grounds and crept along the dusty gravel driveway, its engine grumbling in disdain. Violet's heartbeat kicked up. Could this be Shorty? She wouldn't put it past a bullfighter to go for the flash, even if it would be hell to keep the dirt off all that gleaming paint and chrome.

The car stopped and idled for a moment as if the occupants were inspecting their surroundings—a bare dirt parking lot, the old wooden grandstand, a ramshackle hut that functioned as a rodeo office…and Violet. She was tempted to dive for cover behind the tank until the car passed, but the doors opened instead. The driver emerged first and Violet's jaw dropped. *Wow*. Give this woman pom-poms and a pair of miniscule white shorts and she could stroll right onto the sidelines of the next Dallas Cowboys game. Her cloud of brilliant red curls seemed impervious to the humidity, and her elegant nose wrinkled as she surveyed the stock pens. She made a face and what sounded like a joke as a man climbed out of the passenger seat. He responded with a tight smile.

Definitely not their bullfighter. Shorty was, well,

shorter, compact, and dark. Violet judged this guy to be close to six feet, long, lean, and as potentially hazardous as the car he stood beside. His shrewd gaze cataloged every rusty nail and weathered board of the aging rodeo grounds, snagging for a moment on Violet, and then moving on as if she were just part of the scenery. The intensity of that gaze contrasted oddly with his shaggy brown hair, bleached to gold at the tips, and the wrinkled T-shirt that hung loose on broad shoulders. When he turned to reach into the backseat of the car, she wouldn't have been surprised to see him pull out a skateboard instead of a pair of road-weary duffel bags. Who—

"Hey, Mommy!"

A blast of water hit the stock tank and ricocheted, drenching her in slime. She shrieked, whipped around, and a second blast caught her square in the face. Beni cackled in delight as Violet choked and sputtered. She made a lunge for the hose, skidded, slipped, and landed flat on her butt in the middle of a rapidly growing puddle. Beni giggled louder and doused her again as she wallowed around, trying to get her feet under her.

"Beni!" she heard her mother say. "Give Grandma that—"

Then a shriek as Beni hit the trigger on the hose nozzle.

"Benjamin. Steven. Sanchez. You stop that right now!" Violet made another grab for him.

Beni ducked and dodged, howling like a hyena with the nozzle gripped in both hands, using the powerful spray to fend her off. Suddenly, the water stopped. Beni shook the nozzle and squeezed the trigger. Nothing happened. His eyes went wide and his mouth made an *uh-oh* shape. He dropped the hose and ran, diving under the fence and tearing past the skater dude, who stood with one hand on the lever of the water hydrant. Violet glanced over at the car then back at the hydrant, at least thirty yards away. He'd covered the distance in the space of a few heartbeats.

So he didn't just *look* fast.

She started to wipe the water from her face before she realized her hands were coated in rancid mud, which she had now smeared across both cheeks. Awesome. She brushed the drips from her eyebrows with one forearm then squelched across the pen to where the stranger stood outside the fence.

"Can I help you?" she asked.

His eyebrows rose. "Looks like it's the other way around to me."

He wasn't from around here. No sign of a Texas drawl in those lazily amused words. His gaze took a stroll from her bedraggled hair, down the front of her sopping-wet denim shirt, and over her mucked-up jeans and boots before returning to her grubby face. Her cheeks heated under the scrutiny.

"Thanks for that." She spared a dark glance for where Beni had disappeared around the end of the bucking chutes, seeking temporary asylum with Cole or his grandpa. "My son and I will be having a chat later. Are you looking for someone?"

"You, I assume."

Violet blinked. "Me?"

"You hired a bullfighter." He spread his hands, inviting inspection. What she saw didn't inspire confidence. His T-shirt was worn through at the collar and the Mint Bar logo was so faded and cracked she could barely read the *Hangovers Installed and Serviced* tag-line. His jeans were, if possible, even more decrepit, and his face was rough with at least a few days' worth of stubble.

"You aren't Shorty," Violet said, confused.

"No kidding. I was…" He stopped, a muscle in his jaw working as if chewing off the end of an unappetizing explanation. "Shorty got an opportunity to work Pendleton. I'm taking his place."

Her gut went alternately cold then hot as she absorbed the implications. No way. This could *not* be happening. The one time she stuck her neck out, acted unilaterally to hire an unknown, and he had left them flat. Her father was going to be furious. Come to think of it, so was she.

"He doesn't bother to call, give us a heads-up, nothing? Just sends"—her voice climbed an octave and she chopped a hand toward him, flicking mud onto the *B* of Mint Bar—"whoever? And I'm supposed to just accept it, assume you're good enough to turn loose in our arena?"

His chin snapped up and his deep-set eyes narrowed. "I'm better than anything that's ever set foot in one of your arenas, sweetheart. But if you want me to leave—"

Violet drew a breath to tell him yes, and provide detailed directions to exactly where he could go, when a small, damp hand closed around her arm, the grip like iron.

"Violet." Her mother's voice was soft, the tone unmistakable. *Mind your manners, young lady.* She extended her other hand to the imposter. "I don't believe I've had the pleasure. I'm Iris Jacobs."

As he accepted the handshake, he angled a smile

at Violet that glinted with a grim sort of triumph. "Joe Cassidy."

Oh. Oh dear God, *no*. She hadn't just… She couldn't have failed to recognize… But of course it was him. So obviously him that she wanted to head-slap herself. Beni had an autographed poster of Joe Cassidy and Wyatt Darrington *on his bedroom wall,* for pity's sake. Violet swore silently, closed her eyes, and prayed the puddle she was standing in would swallow her whole.

Chapter 4

JOE CASSIDY WAS GOING TO BE TROUBLE. VIOLET JUST hadn't figured out what kind yet. Fifteen minutes on Facebook and she'd learned why he was in Texas. Rumors were flying fast and hard about the blowup between Joe and Dick Browning, starting with Joe leaving the bar with Dick's daughter-in-law, and ending with Joe punching Dick's son.

Drinking, fighting, and adultery. Yep, her dad was real impressed with her decision-making skills. And now, to top it all off, their starstruck rodeo announcer had given Joe a wireless microphone, so instead of lounging around behind the chutes until the bull riding—the final event on the program—he was in the arena, schmoozing the fans. Violet tried not to glance over to where he leaned against the fence chatting with a trio of autograph seekers. Female, of course. They flashed a lot of tanned skin, white teeth, and big hair as they shoved their rodeo programs through the fence. He said something that made them giggle.

Violet felt her lip curl. Lord, the man put her teeth on edge, and not just because she'd made a complete fool of herself. He strutted around like he was God's gift to rodeo, radiating energy like those big static electricity balls at the science museum. When one of the buckle bunnies put a hand on his arm, Violet was surprised the girl's bleached hair didn't stand on end. Violet was not surprised to see the blonde scribble on the corner of her rodeo program, tear it off, and tuck it into Joe's hand.

"You're in for a real treat today, folks. Our next bareback rider is a fan favorite…especially with the single ladies," the rodeo announcer declared in a voice that was the equivalent of an exaggerated wink. "Delon Sanchez is a seven-time National Finals Rodeo qualifier, currently number one in the world standings!"

The crowd clapped enthusiastically, enjoying the exceptionally nice view as Delon leaned over the horse. His sleeve was rolled up to the elbow, exposing the muscle that bulged in his forearm. Little wonder his grip on the stiff leather handhold was nearly impossible to break. Riata Rose wasn't nearly as awestruck. The mare slumped against the side of chute, sulking, as he worked his hand into the rigging, the squeak of rosin and leather audible. The chute crew massaged her mane and shoved on her hip as Delon lowered himself onto the horse's back, but Rose wouldn't budge.

Into the lull, the announcer's voice boomed. "Hey, Joe, did you know Violet here is the only female pickup man in Texas?"

Oh hell. Not that again.

"Shouldn't it be pickup *girl*?" Joe made it sound indecent, like she plied her trade on street corners.

The announcer grinned down at her from the crow's nest, oblivious. "Well, now, I'm not sure. Do you prefer pickup girl, Violet?"

She gave an exaggerated shrug, but couldn't stop the sidelong scowl she fired at Joe. He answered with a mocking smile. She snapped her focus back to the chute, but Riata Rose was in a mood and had no intention of cooperating until she felt damn good and ready. The mare sank onto her haunches. Delon shook his head and climbed off. In that position, the mare could flip onto her back in an instant and crush him.

While the crew tried to persuade Riata to play nice, Joe moved down the fence to an older couple, their knobby knees sunburned pink below baggy walking shorts. He held out the clip-on microphone so the woman's strong German accent could be heard over the loudspeakers.

"What do you do? You don't look like a cowboy."

A valid question. If it weren't for his white straw cowboy hat, he could have been mistaken for a soccer player, lean and edgy as a feral cat, in silky black shorts and a long-sleeved red jersey plastered with sponsor logos. His shaggy hair might be a fashion statement or just neglect, but either way it added to his general air of *too cool for you*.

"I'm a bullfighter," he said.

"You fight the bulls? With the sword?" The woman made a stabbing motion, enthusiastic enough to make Joe step back.

"No, ma'am. I just jump in after the ride ends and distract the bull long enough for the cowboy to get away."

"Oh." The woman looked disappointed. "Why don't you ride?"

"Have you seen the horns on those things?" Joe gave an exaggerated shudder. "You couldn't pay me to get on one."

Laughter rippled through the audience, for which Violet was reluctantly grateful. Joe was doing a good job of filling dead air, the same way he chatted with the cluster of fans that waylaid him every day after the bull riding. He'd also gone along with the impromptu autograph session the committee had included in their pancake breakfast. Three days in, even her dad couldn't complain about Joe's behavior.

Joe caught Violet's glance—okay, maybe it was more like a frown—and his eyes narrowed. He held her gaze as he leaned closer to the German woman, his voice dropping to a purr. "I might consider climbing on a bucking horse if it meant Violet would pick me up."

The crowd laughed and cheered in approval. Violet glared at Joe, kicking Cadillac up a few steps and angling the horse to turn her back on Joe. Big mistake.

"Hey, Vi?" he called out. "In case you're wondering…those chaps make your butt look just fine."

Her face went hot as a pancake griddle as every eye in place tracked straight to the back of her saddle. She slapped her hand against her thigh as if to encourage Riata Rose, hoping no one but Joe noticed her middle finger was extended. Three more horses to buck, then she could ride out of the arena, march up to the announcer's stand and crank the dials on the sound system until the feedback fried Joe's ears. And honest to God, if he made a crack about her not being any shrinking violet, she and Cadillac would run him down on the way.

One of the crew rattled the sliding gate at the front of the chute as if to open it and let Riata move forward. She fell for the fake, straightening. Delon slid into position and nodded his head. The chute gate swung wide and the mare blew straight in the air, all four hooves off the ground. The instant she touched down, she launched again, even higher.

Delon matched her, lick for lick, the loose rowels of his spurs singing as his knees jerked up and back, every stroke precise. Shoulders square, no wild flopping or bouncing, rock solid in the midst of a storm, while the silvery fringe on his chaps whipped around him. Violet kicked her horse into a lope to circle around in front of Riata Rose. The mare followed her lead, bucking in a tight loop in front of the chutes, clear to the eight-second buzzer.

On cue, Rose flattened out into a bounding lope. Cole closed in one side, Violet on the other. As she thundered up alongside, Delon yanked his hand from the rigging and grabbed Violet around the waist. The mare's shoulder slammed into Violet's leg, but the contact was routine, absorbed by her shin guard. She clamped her knees hard against the saddle as she veered left to pull Delon clear, then reined her horse to a stop. He dropped on his feet only a few yards from the bucking chute where he'd started.

"Ladies and gentlemen, let's hear it for Delon Sanchez!" the announcer hollered. "If he keeps riding like that, this will be the year he brings a gold buckle home to Texas!"

Delon tipped his hat to acknowledge the cheers, then held up a fist. Violet bumped hers against it. He smiled up at her, out of breath and breathtaking with those sparkling brown eyes and chiseled cheekbones. His smile made her heart sigh a little, because it was the same one she saw on her son's face every single day.

"And the judges say...eighty-two points!" the announcer boomed. "There's your new leader, folks!"

Riata Rose flung her head up, prancing around the

arena like a total prima donna, then ducked out the catch pen gate. Delon saluted the crowd then reached back and down to unbuckle the leg straps on his chaps as he stood beside Violet's horse.

"Soon as I get my gear packed up, I'm gonna grab Beni from your mom and hit the road."

"His backpack and suitcase are by the door in my camper."

"Thanks. Don't worry about picking up milk or anything—we'll grab some groceries on the way."

Thank the Lord above. They were all going home for the first time in three weeks. Tonight she'd dither as long as she wanted in a shower big enough that she didn't bang her elbows when she shampooed her hair. "I can't wait to sleep in a bed without wheels under it."

"I hear ya." Delon rolled his shoulders, then angled a look toward where Joe stood chatting with another fan, the microphone turned off. "Is he giving you a hard time?"

"Nothing I haven't heard before." Usually she could ignore it. Cowboys had been making her the butt of asinine jokes since she started picking up broncs as a teenager.

"Joe's not like most of the guys you know."

Yeah. She'd noticed. "We can handle him."

Delon aimed another narrow-eyed look at Joe. Then he slapped Violet's leather-clad knee. "We're outta here. I'll see y'all at the ranch."

About the Author

Kari Lynn Dell is a ranch-raised Montana cowgirl who attended her first rodeo at two weeks old and has existed in a state of horse-induced poverty ever since. She makes her home on the Blackfeet Reservation, where she lives in her parents' bunkhouse along with her husband, her son, and Max and Spike the Cowdogs. There's a tipi on her lawn, Glacier National Park on her doorstep, and Canada within spitting distance. Visit her at karilynndell.com.